THE
DISHARMONY
OF
SILENCE

A NOVEL BY

LINDA ROSEN

Black Rose Writing | Texas

First printing

This is a work of fiction. Names, characters, businesses, places, events, and incidents are either the products of the author's imagination or used in a fictitious manner. Any resemblance to actual persons, living or dead, or actual events is purely coincidental.

ISBN: 978-1-68433-430-8
PUBLISHED BY BLACK ROSE WRITING
www.blackrosewriting.com

Printed in the United States of America
Suggested Retail Price (SRP) $19.95

The Disharmony of Silence is printed in Calluna

*As a planet-friendly publisher, Black Rose Writing does its best to eliminate unnecessary waste to reduce paper usage and energy costs, while never compromising the reading experience. As a result, the final word count vs. page count may not meet common expectations.

"Your visions will become clear only when you can look into your own heart. Who looks outside, dreams; who looks inside, awakes." — C. G. Jung

THE

DISHARMONY

OF

SILENCE

CHAPTER 1

1915

"The Roths aren't coming." Yes, those were the words her mother had just said. Lena's heart sank. She lowered her head, hiding her watery eyes, then gripped the edge of the lace tablecloth and gave it a tug as if she, an eleven-year-old, could change things.

"So that's why we didn't put the leaves in the table," she said, looking across the mahogany dining room set to where her mother stood. "I don't understand. They always come for seder."

The early spring sun shone through the apartment window lending a sense of purity to the lace cloth. Ida straightened her side. "*Bubeleh*," she said, "I'm sorry. It's only the three of us tonight." She fiddled with her apron straps, adjusting and re-adjusting them.

"You know, Mama, I don't really care if Mrs. Roth comes. She's such a sourpuss, but what about Jack?" Silently, Lena hoped there was some way fifteen-year-old Jack could still come.

Ida furrowed her brow, although Lena detected a slight giggle in her mother's disapproval. Sure, her words were nasty, but no matter how close the two families were, Mama knew Mrs. Roth always looked like she'd just sucked on a lemon.

"No, honey. None of them will be here."

Lena sensed a deep sadness from her mother's flat voice and could not understand what would have happened to make the Roths so angry. The two families had been close friends back in the old country and when Karl arrived in New York in 1905, without his family, he became part of theirs. Lena wasn't quite two when she met the man she called Uncle Karl though she didn't remember that. What did stay in her mind was his bouncing her on his knee and singing *Oyfn Pripetchik*. His hands always smelled like freshly ironed sheets.

Lena watched her mother walk to the breakfront and open the leaded glass cabinet, then slowly pull three white dinner plates from her *Pesach* set. Ida looked at the plates in her hand and frowned. "Papa said they had an argument over cards and Uncle Karl refused to come." She put three soup dishes on top of the short pile, then shook her head and changed her tone. It was matter-of-fact rather than disappointed. "I called Rebecca–I mean Mrs. Roth; I know that's what she wants you to call her–and tried to convince her to let bygones be bygones. She wouldn't budge."

"What'd they argue about?" Lena said, hoping it wasn't serious and that maybe she could coerce her mother to call again. Lena wanted so much to sit next to Jack, to see his big brown eyes light up as they sang *Dayenu* together and all the other holiday songs. He made it so much fun.

"Papa didn't say. All I know is it had something to do with the pinochle game." Ida placed the dishes on the table. Keeping her eyes averted from her daughter's, she adjusted the bow on her collar and centered the brooch.

Lena picked at the lace on the edge of the cloth. "Maybe Jack and his sister can still come. I want to see her baby."

Ida sighed. "No, sweetheart. None of them will be with us. Though I am sure you'll see the baby soon. She'll bring her over one day when her mother doesn't know about it."

Ida spread her lightly freckled hands over the tablecloth, smoothing out the wrinkles the iron had missed. She fluffed the corners and placed a cut-crystal bowl to the side of the seder plate. Later, she would float rose petals in it. A touch of elegance among shank bones, roasted eggs, and bitter herbs.

Lena could tell her mother wanted to say something else. She watched her mother's mouth play with words, but nothing came out. Ida placed the forks and knives on either side of the china plates, adjusting and readjusting them, making perfectly straight lines of the shiny silver. "Come on, Mama, be honest. You always tell me no fibbing."

"Fine," Ida said and let out a long, slow breath. "Mrs. Roth and Uncle Karl are very angry right now. They've got a lot on their minds. So she said they wouldn't be in touch with us; that none of them would." Ida hesitated a moment and, again, Lena saw the sadness in her mother's eyes.

Ida turned and walked toward the kitchen. In a very low voice, as if convincing herself, she added, "Until they get things straightened out." The click-clack from the elevated train on the corner rattled the open window. A little louder, Ida called over her shoulder to Lena who remained steadfastly in the dining room looking at the three place settings. "Come on, let's check the pot roast."

Lena followed her mother into the kitchen. The scent of beef with carrots and potatoes simmering on the stove, suffused with savory herbs, perfumed the air. Her taste buds tingled as she schemed up ways to get to see Jack again. He always made her feel special and older, not like some little girl he had to put up with at holiday dinners. Plus, he made her laugh. If only he still lived across the river, it would have

3

been easier. She often went with her mother back to the stalls and shops on Orchard Street where the vendors hawked their wares. Now, though, the Roths lived in the Bronx and it was a major schlep to get there from Brooklyn-plus, she had no reason to be in that borough. Her mother would never let her go alone. And she'd never bump into him in the corner candy store where all the kids from her neighborhood hung out, like her friends did when they wanted to see a certain boy. There had to be some way. Maybe she could get her mother to suggest he come along with his sister when she brought the baby to visit. This fight between their parents, no matter how long it lasted, was not going to keep her from Jack.

CHAPTER 2

Ninety-five Years Later

I circled my thumb around the filigreed frame on my mother's cameo. Seated cross-legged on the bronze carpet in her bedroom, the musky hint of White Shoulders in the air, I gazed at the lady's face sculpted in ivory. She seemed so serene–not a feeling I could claim with Mom in the nursing home these past two months. I wanted to hold on to that serenity–the quiet, calm composure my mother used to have–so I put the brooch in the pile of jewelry to keep and sifted through more pins, bracelets, and earrings all stuffed in the leather jewelry box she'd had since I was a little girl. It was time to decide which pieces to keep, which to sell. My mother certainly wasn't going to wear them anymore. The last bout of pneumonia had stripped away every vestige of the mother I knew. The smiling woman with the cornflower-blue eyes who swam laps three times a week was gone. Someone with vacant eyes had taken her place–someone who spent her days seated in a wheelchair, in a housecoat zipped up by a nurse's aide, the odor of urine her perfume now. My eyes welled up, and I swallowed hard. That woman was not my mother, not the Mom in whose footsteps I wanted to follow.

A pair of silver earrings looked so delicate, I picked them up and played with the rhinestones dangling from the small hoop as they glistened in the sunlight streaming through the bedroom window. Even so, they weren't my taste, and I put them in the "for sale" pile along with the tennis bracelet Mom bought at the temple's Chanukah boutique a few years back. She had wanted me to have the delicate chain with the fake diamonds, though I was never a fan of knockoffs. If I'd had a daughter, I could have given it to her. But I didn't. No daughter, not even a son or a husband. And oh, how much easier all this would be now if I only had someone to share it with. Not only to share the responsibilities or to give me a break so I didn't feel the compulsion to visit my mother every day, but someone to cling to. I didn't even have Dad to wrap me in a blanket of love. He died ten years ago. There was no one to cry with, no one who would miss her like I do already. That would be family, and when Mom died, which I realized would be sooner rather than later, I wouldn't have any. A chill ran through my body every time that realization hit me. Everything seemed to spin out of control.

Antique jewelry had always called to me. Was it the unknown stories it held or the beauty of its metals and stones having survived travels across the ocean, across the years? With losing Mom, I needed something to hold on to. I picked up the cameo again and ran my index finger over the cool silver flower holding back a strand of hair that flowed over the woman's shoulder. This brooch was old enough for it to have been carved out of ivory, not out of shell like more recent cameos. My mother's aunt had given it to her when she was sixteen, claiming it was a family heirloom. That was almost seventy years ago. I wore it for my Sweet Sixteen party and that wasn't yesterday either. Forty-seven years ago, to be exact, though I remember it like it was yesterday. We stood in this same room and Mom pulled the cameo out of this same jewelry box. "It compliments your red hair," she'd said pointing to the soft brown tones surrounding the woman's profile. I asked Mom where she got the pin and when I learned it was from her aunt, always the curious one, I said "Why did she give it to you and not her daughter?" Mom tossed my question aside as if it had no more importance than those warning tags on mattresses, but I knew my mother and her aunt had a special relationship. She'd practically raised Mom. Her own mother had died when she was a baby and her father not long after.

My cell phone pinged. It was probably a text from Anita, my closest friend. She knew what I was doing today and had made me promise to meet her at the movies this afternoon. She didn't want me being all melancholy and morbid staying in Mom's house all day. In truth, as hard as it was to pull away, to even think of selling my childhood home, I had to thank Anita. Without her and the aerobics classes I teach three mornings a week, I'd be walking around unable to concentrate on anything, a hollowness in my chest, constantly focusing on the past when Mom was fun to be with. Her decline came so fast, I could barely grasp what was happening to her–to us.

I uncurled myself from the floor and took the phone from my pocketbook. Anita always got right to the point. "How long you been at it?" I checked my watch and texted back. "Three hours." Her instant reply was succinct. "Enough! Starbucks. Half hour." Jeez, she was insistent. The movie didn't start 'til four o'clock and on a Thursday afternoon the theater would not be crowded. I could stay here, work another hour and still make it in time, skip the coffee; but no, Anita figured I didn't have to finish today. Sure, the closing was set for six weeks from now–she knew that–yet I still had to get the estate sale done and have enough time to either donate or toss whatever was left. So far, I'd only made a little dent. A book of poems my father gave my mother when they were first married was already in a box, waiting in the trunk of my car, and Mom's bone china tea cups and saucers that my parents bought on their twenty-fifth anniversary trip to Europe were bubble-wrapped, also packed up for the journey to my condo. My stomach roiled when I thought of all the rest I had to decide on: what to sell, what to keep, what to throw out.

The phone pinged again. It was Anita. "Don't even think of not coming," she wrote. "You need a break."

"Oh hell, it's just stuff," I told myself and shoved the iPhone back in my bag and slung the strap over my shoulder. Ever since I'd realized I had to sell my mother's house to afford the nursing home since Medicare only covered ninety days and they were almost up, I kept telling myself the same thing. "It's just stuff. Get rid of it." But no! It wasn't just stuff. It was an entire life–everything Mom and Dad had accumulated in their fifty-one years of marriage that was left in closets and drawers, on shelves, and in the basement. Who would want any of it? I didn't have room in my condo for another thing, yet it was so hard to throw out her books and records, even the 78s stashed away downstairs–the ones no one could play anymore. I stood looking around the room, at the photos on the dusty dresser next to the perfume bottles and at the blue brocade chaise lounge across the room, its cushion indented from years of Dad stretched out on it reading his mysteries. I blinked back tears and flicked off the light, leaving the jewelry box with all its faux gems on the floor, then walked out into the hall heading to the front door. I stopped short and shook my head hard, called myself an idiot. I wasn't thinking straight. My mind was so jumbled with everything happening so fast: Mom's quick decline, selling her house, and, most of all, not knowing how I would cope after she died. I'd be an orphan. It didn't matter that I was sixty-three. I never realized before how much I needed a family. It was always something I took for granted. I walked back into the bedroom and slipped the cameo into my pocketbook.

***

The barista pressed the plastic top on the cardboard mug and handed me my tea. The aroma of Earl Grey seeped from the steaming cup. I walked over to sit with Anita, already drinking her grande mocha latte.

"So, did you accomplish a lot today?" she asked.

I shrugged. "Not as much as I should have." I took a sip of the comforting blend. "It's not easy going through everything, all those memories."

"Want me to come with you? I can help."

I choked up from her offer, but shook my head. "Not yet." I certainly could have used someone's help, just not Anita's. She'd run through the house tossing out everything just to get the job done. I needed to do it my own way, as always.

"So, show me what you took from the house." Anita placed her latte on the table and scooted forward. I took the cameo from my bag and handed it to her. "Nice," she said. "I have a really old cameo pin too. It was my mother's. They were quite common once, but I don't see anyone wearing them now." I shrugged. I didn't care if they were popular or not, I just liked it. "It looks old," she said and held it up to the light. "You can tell if it's worth something if there aren't any chips in it, or cracks." Anita turned the brooch around staring through the caramel colored background. "Cameos are the only type of jewelry I know of that's worth more if they don't show their age."

"How do you know that?"

"I checked into it one time, when I thought of selling mine. You should find out what it's worth." With wide-open eyes, I shook my head in disbelief. "Okay," she said. "So you don't want to sell it. Let's check it out, anyway. I've never seen one with a silver flower in the woman's hair." Anita took out her cell phone and tapped the Google icon.

"What are you doing?"

"I'm getting images of cameos. See if it's a common one." Her finger slid down the screen. "How old is it?"

I told Anita it was a family heirloom that *my* mother got on her sixteenth birthday. "So, I have no idea how old it is. It's been in the family for years."

"Was it her mother's?"

"No. Her aunt—her father's sister—gave it to her."

"Well, maybe it *was* her mother's. That aunt would have been *her* sister-in-law, wouldn't she?"

I thought about that for a second. "Yeah, but why would she have a piece of her sister-in-law's jewelry?"

"Well, anyhow," Anita said, "whoever owned it would be a lot older than eighty-five. That's how old your mother is, right?" I nodded. "And the person is probably dead." I lifted a shoulder, agreeing. "Then let's look at cameos from the early twentieth century, maybe even late nineteenth." She scrolled through more website offerings. "Here, look at these pictures." She handed me the phone. I scrolled through a few pages. "Do you see any with a silver flower?" she asked. I shook my head no. There were all kinds of cameos framed in gold or silver, some narrow, some broad, some plain, others ornate like mine.

"There aren't any with the woman's hair pulled back," I said. "A few have it swept up on her head, and there are some with the woman wearing a necklace, an actual chain with a tiny diamond pendant."

Anita pulled the phone from my hand. "But none exactly like yours, right? So, it's probably worth some money."

I sat back and stared at my friend in disbelief. She took a deep breath. The whir from the latte machine carried through the café.

"Okay. I get it," she said, giving me a gentle, sorrowful smile. Her voice was as sweet and soft as warm chocolate pudding, quieter than the excited tone from a moment ago. Anita was one woman who could shoot her mouth off, not realizing she was hurting my feelings, and in the next second, be as compassionate as a grandma to a crying toddler. We'd met over forty years ago, in 1970, on my first day of teaching. She danced at my wedding and then carried me through my divorce from that piece of scum, Alan, who should have a scarlet L for liar branded on his chest with a hot iron. He didn't rate embroidery stitched on a shirt like Hester Prynne. And Anita supported me during my twelve-year affair with Stan when my own mother did not. That was hard for me to deal with, even though I didn't see myself as the other woman as Mom called me. Stan's wife was in a nursing home. If he didn't think he was cheating, why should I?

I looked at Anita as she studied the cameos on her phone and thought about what she had said when she invited Mom and me to seder shortly after Dad died. "You're like family, Carolyn, and you shouldn't be alone on a holiday. Neither should your mother." Even though her words filled me with warmth, the one that stuck out was "like." Yes, we were close, closer than some siblings I know of. But, we weren't blood. And it's blood that binds you to family–the kind of family you can really count on. At least I believed so.

Anita took a sip of her latte and reached over to touch my hand. "It doesn't matter if the pin is worth a thousand dollars or two dollars; it's your Mom's. I know. You're not only losing your mother. By selling her home—your childhood home—you feel like you're losing your history and it hurts." With my index finger, I swiped away the wetness under my eyes. "And those things you've taken—the cups and saucers and bracelets and pins—they're your physical connection to your mom. You're right, Car. You should hold onto them."

I released my hand from under hers and picked up my cup of tea. My hands hugged the paper mug. The scent of bergamot was soothing–almost as much as my friend's heartfelt words.

After the movie and a slice of pizza and salad, I said goodnight to Anita and headed home. I poured myself a glass of wine and opened my laptop. Even though I had no intention of selling the brooch, Anita had gotten my curiosity up. Who originally owned my mother's cameo? I assured myself it couldn't have been her mother's. It had to have been someone in her father's family or why would her aunt have had it? Plus, I wanted to know if it was rare. I was sure it wasn't worth much. Mom hadn't come from money. Her grandpa Karl was a presser, whatever that was. As a little girl, I always pictured him standing over a steaming hot iron pressing shirt sleeves and collars. And her grandmother didn't work; she barely spoke English and whatever words she did manage were mixed up with Yiddish. As for her mother's family, Mom didn't know anything–just that they came from Russia and her mother was born in New York shortly after they arrived. That side of the family was a mystery. It always intrigued me. As far as I aware, there was no one around to shed any light. I'd always wanted to do our genealogy, but teaching took up all my energy with all the testing and reports I had to do in addition to actually educating kids. Now, with Mom declining, I felt a real urgency to get it done. Wouldn't it be something if I found a living relative from her mother's side of the family, a cousin we knew nothing about? I'm sure she'd love that, having had no connection with them at all. Plus, it grieved me to admit, I wasn't going to have Mom forever, and when she's gone I'd be the last of that family line. My chest was heavy with sadness just thinking about it. And without any relatives to connect with from any side of Mom's or Dad's families, basically I'd be alone and that left me with a longing so intense it hurt.

CHAPTER 3

I slipped the iPod onto the docking station, pressed the On button, and turned up the volume. "Okay, let's get started," I called out over the din of conversation. The women dispersed to their spots on the floor. It always amazed me how like a magnet those spots were. If one moved a tiny bit to the left, she was discombobulated, totally out of sorts; and another absolutely had to stand on the right directly under the window, even if it meant pushing someone out of the way.

"Take a deep breath and let your belly expand," I said. They all followed my movements as I raised my arms overhead, inhaled through my nose, and exhaled from my mouth. I always started an exercise class with a deep cleansing breath. "It helps to center yourself," I explained, "to focus and clear your mind." And I certainly needed that.

Through grapevines, hopscotches, hustles, and rocking horses the endorphins climbed, and I thought I forgot about Mom. My focus was on the women who came to my fitness class at 9:30 every Monday, Wednesday, and Friday morning. This was their hour and it was my job to give them a safe, effective workout. I loved every minute of it.

A half hour into class we segued into strength training. I grabbed the towel from my bag and wiped the sweat from the back of my neck while the women got their weights from the closet.

To the steady, pulsing beat of Billy Joel's piano, we pressed a hand-held weight overhead. I explained about safe and effective exercises as Billy sang about his uptown girl and added pliés, bringing in lower-body strength at the same time. Thoughts of Mom crept back in. She had absolutely no lower-body strength at all. I should have worked with her months ago when I noticed she was losing it, though she wouldn't have listened anyway. Doggie paddling across the Y's pool was all she wanted to do, and I was glad she was doing something.

I tried to push Mom out of my mind and concentrate on my women. "Remember, press your buttocks back," I called as the song changed to "Penny Lane." "Just don't go down too far. Picture a dirty toilet." They laughed. "Hey," I said, "There's no way you're gonna sit on it, right?" As much as I was focused on the class, my mother would not leave my head. I wished I'd taught her this exercise; then maybe she'd be able to get off the toilet by herself. But she wasn't even able to walk to the toilet, much less get up from it.

Most of the women in my class were over seventy, some even over eighty. I was one of the youngest, and besides unwanted flab, we all had a little arthritis. Some had knee pain or back issues, but independence was the goal for every one of us. The ability to get off a chair by ourselves at ninety–not to mention the toilet–was what we wanted, so we did squats.

Independence. Damn! I thought Mom would be independent for many more years, though pneumonia had other plans for her.

I looked over at my favorite blonde holding three-pound weights and doing bicep curls with her dirty toilet exercise. She recently celebrated her eighty-fifth, same age as my mother. Damn.

Frustration blew from my lips. I shook it away and reeled myself back in.

"Did you ever stop at one of the bathrooms on the thruway?" I asked, keeping the mood up. A debate began over which roads had the worst restrooms. I let the chatter go on for a bit, then rallied them back with chest pulls while standing with their legs crossed to throw off their balance a little. It was good for the core.

Balance. A great word. And I had absolutely none of it in my life at the moment. Damn it, that had to change.

CHAPTER 4

Sweaty and still in my workout clothes, I packed up the iPod, slipped on my sweatshirt, and drove to Maple Valley, my mother's new abode. What a difference from her blue-shingled split-level house that always smelled of fresh flowers, not stale urine.

It was much better visiting Mom in the morning. Grace, the nurse's aide in charge of her, had explained sundowning to me one afternoon when I was practically in tears. I didn't understand why my mother was so argumentative. "Is it just with me?" I'd asked. "Or is she always like that? She never was before."

"Oh no, honey," Grace said. We were standing in front of the nurses' station just outside Mom's room. "Some patients get more anxious when the sun goes down. Like Sarah, they upset easily, get restless and confused." Another nurse behind the desk chimed in. "It's called sundowning. Usually happens with Alzheimer's patients." Grace must have seen the fear in my face. She placed a comforting hand on my shoulder and said, "Don't worry. It's common in older patients like Sarah. It doesn't only have to be with Alzheimer's."

Grace was a godsend. She always made me feel better. So to make things easier on myself, I visited early in the day, and on this particular morning, I found my mother in her wheelchair, in her room, staring at the television, though I didn't think she was actually watching. There wasn't even a flinch when I turned it off. I pulled over the green vinyl chair and sat facing her.

"Hi, Mom, how're you feeling today?"

Her face pinched. I knew that look. It said, how do you think I feel? And I wasn't going to take the bait. Why argue or try to pump her up saying she looked good? Instead, I got to the question that had been eating at me ever since Anita posed it.

"Mom, you know the cameo brooch you used to wear? Do you have any idea how old it is or whose it was?"

She shrugged.

I moved to the edge of the chair and leaned in. "You never wondered or asked your aunt? Could it have been your mother's, or her mother's?"

She gave me a blank stare, as if she had no idea what I was talking about. I knew better. If Mom wasn't so tired and depressed, she would have answered. Now, it took too much energy to even try. "I looked up cameos online," I said, as if we were in a normal conversation, like we used to have. "I didn't see any like yours." Again she shrugged, as if she didn't care. But I cared. My search last night took me to websites with lots of pictures of all kinds of cameos, some with the woman's profile facing right, some left. Those to the right, like Mom's, were more common, and when I checked on eBay, I saw all kinds of prices, and none were exorbitant. The most expensive was going for three hundred dollars, with many way under that. "From the catch on the back, I know your brooch is an antique." She lifted her brows as if saying no kidding. "Yeah, I know, but how old is it? The website said if the pin on the back is a plain clasp, where it loops under a C-shaped piece of metal with nothing rolling over to lock it in, it's antique."

Her eyebrows squished together. "So?"

Right. So what? We already knew the brooch was old. I had one more option. "Would Nan know whose it was?" Nan was Mom's older cousin, her aunt's daughter, and the only person alive who might possibly know, if her memory was intact. She was ninety-five, living in Riverdale at a facility for independent seniors.

Mom stared at me, her expression as blank as the television suspended from the ceiling, then her mouth curved into a tiny smile and she repeated the name, "Nan." There seemed to be a wisp of melancholy in her voice. Was she remembering days long gone when she and Nan were young, living in the same building in the Bronx, or was she just sad? She shook her head from side to side so I asked again if she thought Nan would be able to shed some light on the cameo's original owner. All I got back was an empty expression, the same nonplussed affect she'd taken on since coming to Maple Valley.

Since I wasn't about to discover anything more, what was the sense in pursuing the conversation? I suggested we go out to the lobby. The recreation director was playing her guitar. Mom shook her head. "Well, there's going to be a concert soon in the all-purpose room. Let's go." Again, she gave that negative shake, and the sun wasn't even going down yet. Every muscle in my body clenched. Dealing with my former students with all their adolescent angst was so much easier than dealing with my mother now.

Grace walked in just then, her usual cheery self. "How are we doing today, Sarah?" she asked, her voice like a sweet southern song. Grace was the best; she could make Mom smile, even if it only lifted her lower lip a bit, not her eyes. I sighed and she placed a warm, friendly hand on my shoulder. "Ooh," she said. "You're so tight you're gonna bust." She massaged that meaty spot between the neck and shoulder then leaned over and said, "Take a day off, Carolyn. Mom will be fine for one day. You need it." I sure did though I was my mother's only visitor and she looked forward to seeing me every day. Even with her being ornery, I knew I brought a little joy into her bleak days. She'd told me I was her safety net. Mom didn't seem to respond to Grace's suggestion, so I replied, "I might just do that." I felt guilty merely thinking of it.

CHAPTER 5

The next day, instead of taking it off as Grace had suggested, I went back to Mom's house. I unlocked the back door, so I didn't have to fiddle with the lockbox from the realty company on the front, and stepped into the kitchen. My parents had redone the cabinets back in the late eighties, putting in the fashion of the times–white wood with butcher block trim. The new owners would probably rip it all out first thing, along with the counter top that matched, and that would be fine. But anything not nailed down was mine to decide on. I headed straight to Mom's bedroom.

Having already taken the jewelry I wanted, I picked up the rest from the floor where I'd left it the other day and put it back in the jewelry box for the estate sale. Next, I tackled her closet.

I pulled out skirts and dresses with abandon and dropped them on the floor. My hand stopped midstream as I reached for Mom's cornflower-blue suit, the one she bought a few years ago on one of our shopping trips to the city. It was in such good condition and much too nice to drop in those clothing bins at the recycling center. I pushed it aside, saving it for a consignment shop, which I promised myself I'd get to one day. It was difficult making decisions on all of her things, so I tried to work as if I were a robot. No emotion, just clean it out. I didn't have the time to delve into memories with every piece I touched as I had been doing, which was making progress very slow, although I did have to be careful not to leave anything by accident. The people I'd hired to run the estate sale told me they'd sell whatever was left, even a lone pickle fork.

An hour later with skirts, dresses, shoes, and bags stuffed in boxes, I walked into the living room. My heart ached looking at the painting of the Victorian lady in the peach dress hanging over the fireplace. What was I going to do with her? I loved that portrait, but there was nowhere to hang it in my condo. She wouldn't fit with the black-and-white photographs that filled the walls, some taken by me, some by Stan. Yet I couldn't leave her. The lady in the dining room arranging fruit in a cut-crystal bowl was part of the family. It would be like disowning my sister, or maybe my grandmother. When I was a young girl I used to confide in her, even cry to her, as I would have if I'd had a warm, cuddly grandma. I remembered the time in high school when the boy I'd hoped would ask me to the senior prom invited my best friend. Home alone, I sat on the living room floor crying my eyes out, looking up at her as if she could hear me. And when I was younger, I'd complained to her whenever Dad made me practice piano. I sat on the bench in front of the piano telling her how much I hated playing "Für Elise," as if she was able to do something about it.

I stood in front of the fireplace looking up at my lady. Just like Mom's cameo, her expression was serene. She seemed so tranquil with the sunlight streaming through the window behind her. And then my mouth fell open. Pinned to the top of her ecru bodice was a cameo brooch. I stepped closer for a better look. With her up on the wall, I couldn't see the small details clearly.

I ran into the kitchen, grabbed the step ladder from the pantry closet, and dragged it to the fireplace. Never a fan of heights, I took a deep breath, climbed up, and lifted the large rectangular frame off its hooks. It was heavier than I thought, and I held tight to it as I made my way back down.

I placed the painting on the floor and knelt down for a closer look. I was right. The cameos were exactly the same, even the little silver flower behind her ear. How come I'd never noticed that before? Why would I, though? She's hung on the wall all my life. I guess I took her for granted. Besides, until yesterday, I hadn't thought about the cameo since probably my sixteenth birthday. Mom rarely wore it. So who was this woman and who was the artist and why did she have the same exact brooch as my mother? If I'd seen it all over the internet, I wouldn't have been so shocked, but this was the only image with the silver flower holding back a strand of hair.

Afraid to touch the canvas, fearing I'd rip it, I bent over and kept my hands planted on the floor as I peered in looking for a signature. I searched the corners. Nothing. Sometimes artists sign the back of their canvases, so I turned it over. There in the right-hand corner I found it. Kate Hemple. In black paint. Funny how all these years I never knew the artist's name.

Leaving the painting on the floor, I went back to the kitchen and grabbed my phone from my bag. Google was my friend again. I searched for Kate Hemple. I began with the first suggestion and immediately realized it couldn't be the artist I was looking for. This Kate would only be around thirty, a newscaster on an NBC Midwest affiliate. I searched two more listings before finding someone I thought might be my Kate. An artist living in Los Angeles. The link took me to an art gallery's website with images of several landscapes painted by Mrs. Hemple. The work didn't look like my portrait, although the artist's age would be right. They had her listed as born in 1926 with no date of death. I did the calculations. She would have been young, in her mid-twenties probably, when she painted my Victorian lady. So what? It's possible. Mrs. Hemple seemed to be a prolific painter, had many works on display at the Robert Everett Gallery, and she'd be around eighty-three–maybe eighty-four–still working. Lucky her. Mom was eighty-five and dying.

There was a link on the right side of the gallery's website for YouTube videos. I checked my watch. No time to look now. I had to get to Maple Valley and pick up a grilled cheese sandwich first. I'd promised Mom I'd bring her favorite sandwich from T&R, the luncheonette on North Avenue, and I didn't have much time.

Paper bag in hand, I hurried down the corridor to Mom's room. "Carolyn," Grace called out from behind the nurses' station. "I thought you were going to take the day off."

I held the bag up and let her know I was just bringing lunch. "Tomorrow," I said. As she had suggested, I was going to take the day off from visiting, sleep late, and then go to the Botanical Gardens with Anita and enjoy a beautiful afternoon with lunch on Arthur Avenue. I could almost taste the homemade *pasta al vongole* made with fresh, plump clams, and lots of garlic. I knew if I didn't take some time off and relax a little, I could get sick. Then I'd be no help to Mom.

My mother was sitting in her wheelchair again at the side of her bed. I brought the tray table to her and presented the grilled cheese as if it were pheasant under glass from a fancy New York eatery. I even draped the napkin on her lap, hoping she'd find my act entertaining. She didn't. She just picked up her lunch and looked at the yellow cheese melted between two crusty pieces of seeded rye bread. I sat on the edge of her bed and watched her bite into the sandwich. "Have you ever heard of Kate Hemple?" I asked.

With a full mouth of squishy bread and cheese, Mom shook her head no.

"She's the artist who painted the portrait you have hanging in your living room."

The little lift of her shoulder told me she didn't care.

"And did you know the lady in that painting is wearing the exact same cameo brooch as yours?"

Mom's face scrunched up in disgust, and she pulled a chewed-up piece of sandwich from her mouth. "This is awful," she said. "Where did you get it?"

My back stiffened. I couldn't deal with her attitude. Frustration mixed with anger deep inside me, with utter sadness tossed in. She was always so disgruntled, more like her crabby grandmother Rebecca—the woman she swore she'd never be like—rather than the lovely woman she used to be. With a clenched jaw, I told her the sandwich was from T&R. Mom's pickled face remained. I told myself not to get aggravated and had to force myself to relax, though to be honest, that was difficult. I tried again asking if she'd ever noticed the cameo. "Enough about paintings and cameos, Carolyn. It was a pretty painting, that's all." With a disgusted toss of her hand, she dismissed the entire subject.

I hated my mother being so cantankerous, and I was sure if she was aware of what she was doing, she wouldn't like herself this way either. This wasn't the life she wanted to lead, and she was probably very frustrated, which made me feel totally inept. There was nothing I could do to help other than visit her. I'd tried taking Mom to arts and crafts class here, even though she was never one for cutting and pasting, so that idea ended. Concerts in the recreation room satisfied for a short period, though after a little while, she'd get antsy and want to go back to her room. That's why I needed to find some concrete information about the artist. I was positive it would perk her up and we'd have something to talk about, to focus on. The woman my mother used to be would have been intrigued by the similarity of the brooches; she always loved a mystery and deep in my bones, I felt the painting had a connection to my mother's brooch.

I couldn't sit there any longer. Every muscle twitched with anticipation. I gave Mom a quick kiss goodbye and hurried home to watch that YouTube video on the gallery's website.

CHAPTER 6

I opened the window, letting in the cool evening breeze, then sat at my desk and flipped open the laptop. While the computer booted up, I gazed out the corner window to the Hudson River with the Tappan Zee Bridge to the left, its lights glistening on the water. Then I slid the mouse over Google's colorful icon and typed in two words: Kate Hemple.

I clicked on the website for the Robert Everett Gallery in Santa Monica, California, the one I'd looked at before. Now I had time and a clear mind to sit back and watch the interview on YouTube.

Mrs. Hemple sat straight and tall in a broad-backed armchair covered in red leather. She was a slender, older woman with silver hair dressed in black slacks and a simple pink V-neck sweater. Across from her sat the interviewer from the *Los Angeles Times*, in a matching chair. Several landscape paintings hung on the wall behind them, which made me believe they were seated somewhere in the gallery. Listening to the questions, I learned she'd been painting since she was a little girl. "My first professional work was in my twenties, when I painted portraits of society women," she said. "I came to landscapes several years later." Okay, I thought, this must be my Kate Hemple and my lady must have been one of those society women. I wondered who. I was doing the arithmetic with the interviewer's voice a muffled sound in the background. Kate would have been twenty-two in 1948, when I was born, and my parents bought the painting in 1953 when we moved to New Rochelle. A breath caught in my throat when I heard her next answer. "Yes, I did do a painting of a family member. Once. It was of my grandmother. I had her standing in her dining room, next to the table. She was arranging fruit in one of her own crystal bowls." With wide-open eyes, I stared at her image on the video. I barely breathed as I reiterated her word. Grandmother.

Questions exploded in my head. Like popcorn in a hot pan, they jumped from one to the next. I had to speak to the artist and find out if the cameo was in fact her grandmother's and why she had the exact same brooch as my mother. I doubted the gallery would give me her phone number, so how was I going to meet her? If she was having a show, I'd go and speak to her, even if I had to fly cross-country. Unfortunately, there wasn't any announcement of one. I replayed the video to make sure I'd heard everything correctly, and as she was describing what her grandmother was doing in the painting, my decision was made. After all, if my lady was Kate Hemple's grandmother, she was obviously the person who should have the painting. I would return it to her. Then I would ask her directly.

I checked my watch. Nine o'clock. With the three-hour time difference, I might be able to reach someone at the gallery. I reached for the phone and dialed. Two rings . . . three . . . I listened to the trilling sound on the other end of the line. Finally, a man's voice answered.

In my most professional-sounding tone, I introduced myself, then explained why I was calling. Mr. Everett sounded a bit confused. "You mean to tell me you have a painting signed by Kate Hemple and you'd like to give it back to her?"

Maybe I wasn't very clear. After all, I hadn't given much thought to this idea before my slightly arthritic index finger punched the numbers into the phone. All I knew was I had to meet Kate Hemple. I told Mr. Everett how long my family had had the painting and that I cherished it. I explained about selling my mother's house and not having any family who was able to take the painting and give it a proper home. "I thought if I found the artist, I would return it to her rather than letting it go in an estate sale to some stranger." I didn't mention the cameo. I hoped my offer would be the vehicle to bring me to Kate. Otherwise, I didn't know what I'd do. "I don't mean to insult anyone," I said when he didn't comment. "Mrs. Hemple's work is beautiful. Please, Mr. Everett, would you ask her if she'd be interested in having it back?" Then I offered to personally bring the painting to Los Angeles and said something that probably sounded corny, but I meant it. "Meeting Mrs. Hemple would be like meeting my lady's mother."

A moment after hanging up with Mr. Everett, Anita called to confirm our trip to the garden. I was so excited with my decision, I blurted out my game plan. Her emphatic opinion practically shook the phone wires strung across town.

"That's just nuts, Carolyn," she shrieked. My jaw stiffened as I listened to her rant. "Why would an artist want her work back? She sold it, jeez, how many years ago?"

Keeping my tone in check, I answered, "Almost sixty." I clutched the receiver tightly, convinced this was my decision to make. Mine alone.

"Are you kidding? She probably doesn't even remember painting that canvas. How old is this woman?"

"I told you, about eighty-four. Anyway, if she agrees, I'm going to LA to return it."

Anita was my best friend, but sometimes she drove me crazy. When my mind was made up, she was not about to change it.

CHAPTER 7

No matter what the season, the rock garden was my favorite spot in the New York Botanical Gardens. It always amazed me I was actually in the Bronx. It's like an oasis. Lavender alpine flowers nestled in rocks and crevices, pink hellebores, yellow daffodils–a kaleidoscope of colors on a rocky hillside. A perfect place to relax, it's like being in some mountainous region in a far-away country, not one of the five boroughs of New York City. I followed the gravel path around the pond to a sparkling waterfall, squatted, and brought the camera to my eye. To blur the background and focus on the water, I adjusted the aperture to 2.8. Stan had taught me the technique the first time we went on a photo shoot together. A little farther along the path, I lay on the gravel with my Nikon pointed up and fiddled with the settings.

"What the hell are you doing?" Anita said, coming up behind me. "You're gonna get all dirty."

"Getting a better perspective." Keeping the lens focused on the flowers, I explained that Stan had told me to get a more interesting shot, it's better to be higher or lower than your intended image. Well, that got Anita going. At least twice a year since Stan's death she introduces the topic of me and men, yet for the twelve years he and I were together, she never bothered me about available men. She understood I was happy. I had always known Stan wouldn't divorce his wife and I was okay with that. He was honest about it and honesty was the most important part of a relationship, in my opinion. He even told his wife about us. Whether she remembered or not, who knew? I highly doubted it. Most of the time, he'd told me, she didn't even know he was her husband. She had early onset Alzheimer's, and I couldn't imagine anything worse. I helped him, as much as possible, always reminding him to buy her birthday presents, sometimes even picking up a bouquet for him to bring her, and never complaining when he had to cancel our plans if the nursing home called with an issue he had to address. I only wished his sons could have accepted me, but I didn't push that either. I just never figured he'd die before her. A massive heart attack snatched him from me five years ago. My eyes welled up remembering sitting in the back row at his funeral, his kids refusing to let me up front where they sat with their mother. They shouldn't have brought her. She was fidgeting, constantly looking around, having no idea where she was or what was going on. But I didn't say a word.

"It's time you met someone," Anita said. She peered down at me from her five-foot-seven-inch frame, and I kept my eyes focused on the camera so she wouldn't see my tears. "Do you really want to be alone the rest of your life?" She brought up Jdate and Match.com. I got up, wiped my eyes, and meandered around the pond with her following close behind. She offered to help me write my profile. "And we'll take a great picture of you."

"Anita, stop. Please. I'm not interested." There was no way I'd ever consider Match.com or any online dating service. I'd never trust those guys. Alan's lies had left a deep scar that was never going to fade. With Stan, it was different.

We'd started out as friends, just two people in a photography class having coffee together once in a while. It was easy to trust him, but meeting someone online . . . no way. Maybe for the twenty-somethings it was easier. Men my age, though, were bound to have secrets, and I couldn't deal with that again.

Anita followed me as I climbed the hill overlooking the rock garden. The cherry trees were abundant with pink buds, new life about to bloom. I needed something new in my life too–something to burst open like these buds and lighten up my life like the sweet-scented flowers would for the tree. I snapped a bunch of pictures while Anita kept talking about my profile for the online dating services.

"Physically fit woman who likes photography looking for a man . . ."

"Enough!" I sounded like a teacher yelling at an unruly class. "I don't want to talk about this. I can't think about meeting men. My mother takes up all my energy."

"I know, Car. I'm sorry. I just hope one day you'll meet someone. No one should be alone."

Those words hit hard. Again, I thought of family and how I'd be alone, without one. It hurt so much.

From the rock garden, Anita and I meandered along the paved and dirt paths passing rose colored azaleas. The spring flowers perfumed the air. At the Snuff Mill, I stood on the banks of the bubbling Bronx River and clicked off shots of the old building on the hill above me. I walked up the slope for a better view of the structure. A sign told me that in the eighteenth century, before all this land became a botanical garden, the mill was used for tobacco manufacturing. The simple words eighteenth century brought back my mother's cameo and its being a family heirloom. Just then my phone rang. As if he'd read my mind, Mr. Everett was on the line. "Mrs. Hemple would like a photo of the painting," he said.

"Please take one on your phone and email it to me." There weren't any pleasantries, just the command. I assured him I would do so the moment I got home. All jittery, glad he'd called back first thing in the morning and that the artist hadn't blown me off–which, honestly, I had been afraid of– I fumbled trying to put the phone back in my pocket.

"What's wrong with you?" Anita asked. I told her what Mr. Everett had said and her response was like a punch in the gut. "She doesn't trust you–doesn't believe the painting is hers."

"It is, though. She'll see it and then she'll want it."

"You're sure about that?"

"Yes," I said with definitive surety. Yet was I really? Did my wanting her to want the painting make me so positive?

Anita furrowed her brow. "Why is this so important to you, Car? You're all aflutter, like someone in a Jane Austen novel. I've never seen you like this."

I told her about wanting to find a living relative, not only for me but for my mother. "Mom never knew anything about her mother's family. When she was old enough to ask, her grandmother—the nasty one who raised her—said they were all dead."

"So you want to find someone from her maternal side to make your mother happy." Anita didn't sound convinced this was a smart idea. That didn't matter to me. "And you're so sure this artist is your family?"

"More hopeful than sure. I am certain there's a connection to the cameos, and the woman in the painting holds it. You said yourself it isn't a common brooch. We couldn't find another like it online."

"So you're figuring maybe the lady in the painting owned it first–that the artist's grandmother is related to you somehow and the family heirloom was hers?" I told Anita I did. From the skeptical look on her face I knew she wasn't on track with me, then her brow softened and her eyes opened wider. "Could be," she said. "Remember Bill's story?"

Several years ago, Anita's husband went to play golf while they were on vacation in Florida. Because he was alone, the club found him three other men to play with. The foursome was heading to the first hole when Bill introduced himself to the guys. He said his full name, Bill Nacht. One of the men asked him how he spelled his last name and then asked where he grew up. It all seemed strange to Bill, according to the way Anita had told me the story one afternoon in the teacher's lounge, especially when the guy asked Bill his parents' names. It turned out, after further discussion, the man in the golf cart was Bill's half-brother. A brother he never knew existed. And when I heard the story, I thought it was strange, too, though fascinating. I couldn't imagine my family having a secret like that.

Anita dipped her head. Again, she looked like she wasn't so sure, and I didn't care. I was. "You know, Car," she said with her brows raised high, as if her wide-open eyes would knock some sense into me. "This Kate Hemple might have just used her artistic ability and created the cameo, painted it on the dress. It might not have been her grandmother's."

My hopes sank as fast as a balloon stuck by a sharp knife. One minute I was elated, convinced I'd found something or someone I could tell Mom about, and then in just a few words, it all crumbled. I felt so dejected. Still, I was going to Los Angeles to give Kate Hemple her painting and ask about the cameo. This had to be done in person. On the phone, she might toss the whole conversation aside and hang up. No, I had to meet Mrs. Hemple. No matter what Anita said, I was sure there was a connection, and I had to find out what.

The rest of the afternoon I tried hard to sound casual, not to show Anita that I was twitching to get home and take the picture. She had tried to talk me out of flying all the way cross-country, pointing out that it could be for nothing, but I was adamant and didn't want to discuss it any further. The sooner I sent the photo to Robert Everett, the sooner I'd hear back. Then I'd call Grace to tell her I'd be going away for a few days. As long as my mother remained stable, I'd go in two weeks. If it wasn't for the fact that the prices of flights were exorbitant if made immediately, I'd fly out the next day.

It was late afternoon when I finally got back home. I went right to my bedroom where the painting was nestled under my bed, still wrapped in Mom's blue sheet. I bent down and pulled it out congratulating myself on the job I'd done taping the sides. Nothing had come apart. I unwrapped my lady and set her up against the side of my bed. I would have preferred to hang the portrait on a wall for Mrs. Hemple to see her in a proper place, but there weren't any free spots large enough. My bedroom, as well as my living room, was filled with photographs, most of them my own. And bookcases or windows filled the other walls. I knelt down and focused the cell-phone camera on the portrait. My red comforter made a perfect background. Three clicks later I was satisfied and emailed the shot.

I threw my clothes in the hamper, stepped into a hot shower, and lathered my hair with shampoo. Its citrus scent had me imagining big, juicy California oranges.

CHAPTER 8

Eighty-seven years earlier

The plush velvet bedroom slippers were the perfect choice. Lena ran her fingers over the metallic beads dotting the toes. She would never place her own size six feet in such a fancy pair, but her manager wanted a holiday look, a display of things a wealthy woman would wear on Christmas morning while her husband beamed with pride as she opened his store-wrapped gifts. Lena placed the pair on the glass-topped counter next to the pink slippers with the slender heels and fur trim. She stepped back and examined her display.

"Which ones do you wear?" The voice came from the men's furnishings department across the aisle. Lena shot a look over her shoulder. The smiling eyes of the good looking young man in a three-piece suit met hers. "I'm sorry," he said. "I didn't mean to startle you."

"Oh, no. That's all right." She turned to face him. His angular face with the prominent cheekbones and his auburn hair that swept back, exposing thick eyebrows, appealed to her. "Have you worked here long?" she asked. "I don't remember seeing you before." There was something familiar, though. Something she couldn't quite grasp.

"I've been with Abraham & Strauss about a year now, though selling ties and cufflinks is new for me." The well-dressed, well-proportioned gentleman made his way across the wide, carpeted aisle. The way his feet turned out caught her attention. She squinted, trying to dig up where she'd seen that stride before. He came closer and her hands flew to her chest. Her breath hitched.

"Jack? Jack Roth? Is that you?"

The young man stopped midway and looked directly at her. Lena realized he had no idea who she was. She let him wonder for another moment. He took a few more steps and she laughed.

"Jack. It's me, Lena Pearl." Then a thought crept in. She stepped back and bit her lower lip. Would he stay or would he turn and walk away? Their families hadn't spoken since the night of the pinochle game. No matter how many times her mother tried to get together to reconcile, Mrs. Roth had refused.

The young man's mouth hung open. His eyes scanned her curvaceous frame. "Lena? When did you grow up?"

The bell signaling the start of the day clanged while words tumbled out of Jack's mouth. "I can't believe it's you. Have lunch with me. We've got to catch up." He hurried back to his own department before the customers streamed in, walking sideways, his eyes never leaving her face. "What's it been? Ten years?"

"Eight," Lena answered. "March will be nine." She slipped behind her wood-framed, glass-enclosed counter. "And, yes, I'd love to have lunch. The Automat at one?"

All morning long, Lena bounced on her toes while helping customers. Her co-workers complained of her constant humming. The flutter in her chest–the same one she felt as a pre-teen every time she saw Jack–returned.

Seated across the table on red-plastic-covered chrome chairs, Lena and Jack became reacquainted. They laughed over past events, especially the seders when Lena's father used to lead them in song as they dipped their fingers in wine for each of the ten plagues.

"You never failed to spill your whole glass." Lena said.

"Yeah, but it was only grape juice. No fun!" he answered. "Your father and mine–with the real stuff–had no problem downing four of them."

"About fathers," Lena said. "Are you going to tell your parents we met and had lunch together?"

Jack drew back from the table. He had been leaning in, close to Lena. Her question made him stop.

"Your parents might not be too happy to find out," Lena said. "I'm going to tell mine, though. I'm sure my mother will be happy."

"Well . . . yes. I think I will tell them," Jack said. He slapped his hand on the white table. "I love my mother, but I've got to live my own life." He caught Lena's uplifted brow. "What?"

"They might not be too pleased about us getting to know each other." Lena was trying to be diplomatic, which was very difficult in this situation. "If you remember, it was your parents who refused to see mine. My mother tried calling a few times, and yours always said the friendship was over and hung up before my mother could say anything else."

"Yes, my mother is tough." Jack sighed and raised his shoulders a bit, then dropped them hard and scrunched his eyes together, like he was contemplating something. Lena waited. Finally, he laid it out, "I think my mother was envious of your parents."

"Why? What would she . . ." Lena's palms opened. She had no idea what Jack was getting at.

"It's just my own thinking," he said, pressing a palm forward. "Your parents had a nice apartment–two bedrooms–and we were cramped in a tiny, one-bedroom place with my uncle's family."

"But you got out of there."

Jack nodded. "Yes, though my father always struggled and yours . . ." He gave her an apologetic look. "If it wasn't for your father and his butcher shop, I'm not sure we would have had meat on the table back then."

Lena understood how difficult that must have been and how difficult it must have been for Jack to admit it. "They were so close," she said. "It's such a shame they never reconciled. We were like a family–the only one my parents had here."

Jack shook his head from side to side. "You're right. But when my mother makes up her mind–about anything–no one can change it. Not even my father." He leaned back against his chair. "On second thought, maybe I won't say anything about us yet."

"No. You should tell them." Lena's tone was definitive, without a hint of question in it, though she was worried about Rebecca's reaction. And she would have liked to ask Jack what he meant by the word "yet."

On the way back to the store, Jack extended an invitation to his friend's New Year's Eve party. "It's on Twenty-Third Street, 405 West Twenty-Third. Bring a friend if you want. There'll be lots of people."

"But I don't know your friend."

Jack flipped his gloved hand in the air. "That doesn't matter. Half the people there probably won't know Izzy. It starts at eight, but come anytime you want. Well, after eight I mean."

Over the next few days, Lena tried to come up with a way to invite one of her girlfriends to the party rather than

Moe. That way, she could be with Jack. Though what if Jack had a girlfriend? He'd never said this was a date; he merely said she should come and bring a friend. In fact, he'd repeated the invitation every time she saw him at work, and he always told her she should bring a friend. Moe was more than a friend though. At least he thought so, and he'd certainly be expecting to spend New Year's Eve with her. They had spent the last three New Year's Eves together, and each time Lena had avoided adding a ring to her left hand. She wasn't ready to be married, even though several of her friends were. Between college and working, where would she find time to prepare dinner every night for a husband? Though Jack . . . well, that was different. She found herself smiling at everything whenever he was around.

***

The letter above the doorbell read "H." "This is it," Lena said. A stack of books held the door open while the pungent smell of cigarette smoke filled the air. They stepped inside.

Moe took her coat and made his way to the bedroom where everyone had tossed their outerwear. Lena stood at the edge of the living room and glanced around. Gin seemed to be flowing like water. Everyone held a glass filled with the clear liquid. She'd never been to a party like this before. She'd heard they existed, although not in her crowd. Uneasy, she wondered if Jack's friend made the gin in his bathtub, like so many others at the time, or if he had connections. And she wondered where Jack was. She'd heard the police weren't interested in arresting anyone and that the governor opposed Prohibition so she wasn't worried about that, but where was Jack?

A jazzy tune from the Victrola on the floor in the corner filled the room. Her shoulders shook to the music. She felt giggly and wanted to join those girls dancing. They were doing that new one—the Charleston. Lena had tried it in her bedroom in front of the mirror, though she'd never done it in public. She and her friends danced to music from the radio–Bessie Smith and Eddie Cantor–nothing as lively as this. It looked like fun. Then that old cringing sensation started to creep in–the one she used to feel when she was younger and stood on the sidelines hoping a boy would ask her to dance. Refusing to accept that adolescent angst, she tossed it out and made her way to the bar. At least that way she looked like she was part of the gang, part of the party. As she crossed the room, she looked for Jack. He was nowhere in sight.

A tall, bulky piece of furniture covered in red leather looked like an actual bar. Lena had never seen one in an apartment before. Several bottles of gin stood alongside bottles of soda water next to a glass bowl filled with lemons and limes, all the ingredients needed to make those new cocktails, gin rickey and bee's knees. Lena had never tasted either. The jug of red wine was more to her liking. A dark-haired guy with deep-blue eyes stood behind the bar pouring drinks. He spritzed seltzer in a glass filled halfway with gin and looked up at Lena.

"What would you like, sweetheart? I don't believe I've ever seen you before."

"Oh, I'm Lena. Jack Roth invited me."

A voice came from behind her. "Give this little lady a glass of wine, Izzy." Lena smiled and relaxed to the warm feel of Jack's hands on her shoulders. "She and I have waited years to share one."

Lena twisted her head back. "I sure hope it's not Manischewitz."

Jack gave her shoulders a squeeze and came around to her left side. "I'm so glad you came."

Before Lena could respond, Moe walked up, stood on her right side, and slipped his arm around her.

"What are you getting?" Moe asked. Lena wiggled to release herself from his grasp. She smiled at him and merely said "wine" then looked back at Jack and took the glass from his hand.

"Thanks." She looked into Jack's confused eyes. A smile spread across her cheeks, and she stood a little taller as she introduced the two young men. "Jack, this is my friend Moe." She extended an upturned palm toward him. "And Moe," she said, extending her other palm to her long lost friend, "this is Jack. He's the guy I told you about who invited us here."

Jack peered at Moe. "So you *did* bring a friend. Good, good. I told you to." He thrust his hand in front of Lena, across her body, to shake Moe's. "Glad to meet you."

Realizing Jack did not have a date with him–that he had expected her to bring a female friend–Lena's heart crumbled. Oh, why hadn't he been clear about it? But if he had been, she thought, how would she have gotten out of bringing Moe? Anyway, she was kind of enjoying the banter between the men. Her head shot back and forth, as if watching a tennis match, as each one seemed to claim her. She sucked in her cheeks to avoid the smile that wanted to fill her face.

"In all the years I've known Lena, she never mentioned you until last week," Moe said, releasing his hand from Jack's grasp.

"Oh, I've known Lena practically all my life." Jack sounded as if their being together was a common occurrence. "We just lost touch for a little while."

"Funny how she's never mentioned you."

Lena wasn't sure if she should puff her feathers or crawl into herself like a turtle. The exchange carried on for a bit with both men trying to sound pleasant, each speaking as if she were an object passed down through generations, a beloved family heirloom. Then Jack excused himself. "I've got to make the rounds," he said. "I promised Izzy I'd make sure everyone's glass was filled." He ended with wishing Lena a Happy New Year. "In case I don't see you when the clock strikes twelve," he kissed her lightly on the lips. "Wish your parents a Happy New Year for me."

Lena savored his tobacco-flavored kiss. She lingered on the taste for a moment. So, she thought, it's okay if my parents know I've seen you. What about yours? Will you ever tell them?

***

The early morning chatter among the saleswomen was the music Lena enjoyed. She placed the last bedroom slipper on top of the counter and glanced at her watch. In five minutes, customers would pour through the doors. She knelt down behind the counter and opened her handbag, pulled out an envelope, and told her coworker she'd be back in a second.

"Happy Birthday, Jack," she called as she crossed the aisle.

Jack was standing behind the men's furnishings counter examining collar pins. He looked up and smiled. "You remembered." Lena placed a birthday card on top of the counter. A little package wrapped up in wax paper and tied with a bow was perched on top.

"Well, I remember odd things from my childhood." She gave a slight shrug. She hoped she didn't appear too forward.

"And yours is sometime in September, right?" Jack placed the box of collar pins next to the leather-buttoned suspenders completing the display of accessories for the well-dressed man, then picked up the wax paper package.

He untied the bow. "I remember coming to your apartment. I guess every year we celebrated . . ."

"Not every year, Jack. You missed the last eight."

"Yes." His chin dropped down. "We've let too much time go by. I'm sorry about that. I wish I could have changed things, but . . ."

"It wasn't up to us, Jack. We were children. We did what our parents wanted."

"Well, I'll never forget those birthday cakes anyway. Your mother was the best baker." He lifted a cinnamon rugelach from the wrapping and his eyes lit up. "My favorite," he said, inhaling the earthy scent of the cinnamon-topped, buttery, flaky, crescent-shaped pastry. "I guess she's still at it."

Lena felt warm all over knowing she had chosen the right recipe. "She is," she said, "though I made those."

"You did?" Jack's eyes widened, impressed. "So, how about joining me for a cup of coffee later? I'll share my rugelach with you." Lena loved the glimmer in his eye.

Sharing a pastry on their coffee break on Monday had led to dinner on Tuesday and again on this Friday. They walked to the restaurant beneath a full moon and chose the booth tucked in a corner. Their favorite.

"Tell me about Moe," Jack said, leaving the menu the waiter had just brought flat on the table. "Are you keeping company?"

Lena was glad he'd asked. She'd been trying to figure out a way to let him know, hoping it was important information, though composed her face as if it weren't. "No, we're not serious." She lifted a shoulder a bit. "We've known each other a long time, but we're not engaged–not even promising to become engaged." She played with the corner of the paper menu feeling a little guilty knowing Moe thought differently.

"So it's okay you're out with me tonight?"

She nodded and enjoyed the dance his irises performed.

"Good," he said. "Because I'd like tonight to be the start of many more." Jack took her hand in his and looked directly in her eyes. "How does that sound?"

It sounded perfect. Lena had been dreaming of this ever since she was a little girl although she never thought it would actually happen. She wanted to cup Jack's cheeks in her hands and draw his face to hers, then give him a long, lingering kiss. Instead, she answered, "I'd like that."

"Little Lena," Jack said, and brought her hand to his lips. She could barely believe he was kissing her fingers. "Did you ever think when you were six and I was ten that we'd be sitting like this someday?"

Lena smiled. If he only knew. The quiet din of the other diners' voices was the best music she'd heard in years. It was time to make a clean break with Moe. They couldn't keep seeing each other when he wanted more than friendship, even if he said he'd wait. Moe was positive one day Lena would realize she loved him and "not like a brother," as he often said, and Lena was sure she wouldn't, especially now. Plus, her mother would be thrilled. She always loved Jack, ever since he was a little boy in Russia, though she wasn't so sure how Jack's mother felt about her. She imagined she'd find out soon enough. Jack would have to tell them about her, if they were going to be keeping company.

Over the next four weeks, Lena and Jack had lunch together and took their coffee breaks at the same time, but college classes interfered with their getting together in the evenings. On the weekends, as long as they weren't scheduled to work at night, they went out. Lena's favorite times were when they went dancing in the city. At the end of the evening, Jack accompanied her on the subway back to Brooklyn, then took the long ride to his home in the Bronx.

They both still lived with their parents as was the custom with her single friends. It was rare when Lena and Jack had the same weekday off to spend together, so when they learned that they were both free on Valentine's Day, Lena wondered if her manager was in cahoots with Jack's. They had tried to keep their relationship a secret at work, but Lena's coworkers knew they were an item. Because Jack's parents still had no idea, he didn't want the information getting all over the store even though no one there knew his family. If the Roths ever did find out secondhand, they surely wouldn't be pleased, and Lena didn't want to add any more fuel to their feud with her parents. She wished Jack would tell them about her already. She longed for the Roths and Pearls to make amends.

***

Jack kneeled down and grasped the laces on Lena's ice skates, a copy of the brown skates eleven-year-old Sonja Henie had worn in the Winter Olympics the previous month. "Too tight?" he asked.

"No, perfect." She watched his strong fingers tie the laces in a bow. Before he stood up he pressed a kiss on her knee.

Yes, it was all perfect, she thought. The knot, the bow, the day. Hand in hand, Jack and Lena skated around the pond in Central Park. There weren't many others on the ice that sunny, crisp Thursday afternoon. A few mothers were leading their young children around, a man in a heavy sweater and striped scarf skated fast, and a group of three women whose coats brushed the tops of their skates glided smoothly across the ice. Jack led Lena to the center of the rink. He took both her hands in his so they were facing each other. "Trust me?" he asked. Lena's brow rose all the way to her hairline. What was he going to do, she wondered? Or say? "Don't look so frightened, follow me. I won't let you go." Jack pushed off, taking her with him and spun her around.

"Stop!" she shouted, though her smile said "Go," and Jack picked up the pace. They twirled round and round laughing, then he grabbed her in a big hug. They teetered and Jack pressed his toe to the ice and held Lena tight.

"Don't worry," he said. "I'd never let you fall. I'd never let anything bad happen to you." He lifted her chin and kissed her sweetly on the lips. "Let's go somewhere more private," he said and took her hand. She glowed as they skated off the ice to an empty bench alongside the rink where they'd left the picnic basket. "This isn't exactly private," he said looking at the people seated on nearby benches, and kissed her again–a deeper, longer kiss. As their lips parted he winked. "Now let's have some of that hot cocoa you brought." Lena poured. The sweet scent of rich chocolate perfumed the air between them. Jack lifted his metal cup, toasting her. "What a grand idea you had. This is delicious."

Lena looked up at him like a child caught in a fib. "Actually," she said. "It was my mother's idea. It's her thermos."

"Well, tell your mother I said thank you." Jack leaned over and gave her cheek a loving peck. "And not only for the thermos," he added, wiggling his brow.

Jack was perfect. He adored her and constantly told her so. Moe had never been as demonstrative, and Lena hadn't realized how much she wanted that. She was sorry to have hurt him, yet relieved she was no longer dishonest with herself and with him. Moe was sweet; they'd grown up together. But she never felt an electric jolt when he touched her, like she did with Jack, and she never got weak-kneed from a kiss either. Lena knew she couldn't spend the rest of her life married to someone who felt like a brother. With that break-up behind her, Lena's only agony was over Jack's telling his parents about the two of them. She was afraid her question might ruin their beautiful afternoon, but it had been eating at her and had to be voiced. She clasped Jack's empty hand in hers and swallowed hard. "Sweetheart," she said looking straight at him, "why haven't you told your parents about us? Please, hasn't enough time passed?"

Jack pulled his hand from her grasp. His eyes got cold. "Don't pressure me, Lena. I'll tell them when I'm ready."

Lena's chin trembled. She felt broken inside. She held back tears wondering how they could go on together if he never told his parents. Would she have the guts to give him an ultimatum? She didn't have it in her now to press him any further. She was too afraid.

CHAPTER 9

Eighty-six years later

It was one of those June-gloom kind of days in LA. I parked my car on Washington Boulevard and walked along the canals. I might have been in Venice, Italy, instead of Venice, California, except for the orange-and-purple birds of paradise flowers lining the walks and the little trees that looked like they had red bottle brushes attached to their branches. Two blocks down, I turned right onto Ivy Lane and walked up the winding path to the blue front door. Before I had a chance to knock or ring a bell, it opened.

"Hello, dear," said a tall, slender woman. "You must be Carolyn. I'm Kate." The lines on her face showed her age, yet her paint-stained jeans and cotton shirt with splotches of black, brown, and dark green made Kate look like a younger woman.

We stood at the door. She gave me the once-over, probably wondering if I was for real, not sure what sort of person would return a painting after so many years. I didn't have my nose pierced and my diamond studs were in my ears where they belonged. My navel was covered by a T-shirt and a pair of khaki capris, so I didn't look like a weirdo.

"Did you bring the painting?" She sounded like a little girl who was promised a treat and was afraid she wouldn't get it.

So that's why she was looking me up and down. "Yes, of course. I just wasn't sure how to get here or where to park, so I left it in my car."

"Oh." She sounded relieved.

"I'll go get it now." I turned to go and she stopped me. "No. It can wait. Let's get acquainted first. I'll make some tea."

Now that's a nice lady. She made me feel welcome. I was afraid she might treat this strictly like a business deal–hand over the painting and leave. We sat in her sun room, though without the sun, me on the chintz sofa, she opposite on the white wicker chair, her bare feet paint-speckled. The room looked out onto her garden and the paintings, hanging on the stucco walls, brought the flowers inside. The best view was behind me. Above the roof line and through the trees, I saw the Pacific Ocean.

"Mrs. Hemple," I started slowly though I wanted to blurt out my question about the cameo. "The lady in the painting . . ." She put up her hand. "Wait, dear. Let me get the tea. It's herbal. That's all I drink. Is that all right?"

"Yes. Thank you." I didn't want to start off on the wrong foot and tell her I preferred mine bold and black.

"Then we can relax and chat. Robert told me you said the portrait meant a great deal to you, and I want to hear all about it."

I heard her rustling around the kitchen, opening and closing cabinets and turning on the faucet. I took the time to admire her brightly painted room. There were pictures of little boys and young men on a round table covered with a lace cloth that looked like it had seen better days. A cut-crystal bowl filled with sea shells sat on another small table next to the wicker chair. It looked just like the bowl in my painting. I wondered if it was her grandmother's.

"Robert said you found me on Google," Mrs. Hemple said as she stepped back into the room with a floral tea pot on a hand-painted tray. She poured, holding one of those little silver things that catch the tea leaves over a bone china cup. I had to remember this really was 2010. When I had tea at home I dunked a bag in a mug, and Anita didn't even boil water–she used her Instant Hot. "My son-in-law works for Google," she added. "It's quite a world today; you can find anything you want with a few clicks."

I nodded then asked, mainly out of politeness, "Out here, or is he up north in Silicon Valley?"

"Neither. He's in Reston, Virginia–the Silicon Valley of the east, as he calls it. He moved there about a year after my daughter died. He couldn't stand living here anymore. He said he needed to start a new life. All I know is, it's far from Los Angeles."

"Oh, I'm so sorry. I didn't know." I wanted to bury myself under the chair, crawl away. How horrible to lose your daughter, I thought. It's bad enough watching my mother failing. I couldn't imagine what she'd be like if it were me instead. Children, no matter how old, are not supposed to die before their parents. My heart ached for her.

Mrs. Hemple hushed me with a wave of her hand. "Still," she said, breaking the uncomfortable silence, "I don't know what made you look for me, why you want to return my painting. Please, don't get me wrong. I really am happy to have the portrait."

I told her when my parents bought the painting and where it hung. "The lady in the dining room was part of my family," I explained. "When I was a little girl I talked to her, even when I got older. And there was one time I cried to her. I didn't want anyone to know why I was so sad, and she was a good listener." I giggled a little; I couldn't help it. "Something really intrigues me though. The woman in the painting is wearing a . . ."

"That woman is my grandmother."

"Yes, I know. I watched the YouTube video. The painting must be very special to you. Why did you sell it?"

"Oh, it was so long ago. Back in the fifties, before I moved out here, I was painting portraits of women. But you know that already." She let out a little laugh. "Robert insisted on posting that video. I've never been good at promoting myself. I'd rather stay in the background and just paint and let him do all the other work." She flipped her palm open, as if what she was saying was obvious. "He said we have to keep up with the times, therefore YouTube. Anyway, Grandma Ida was one of my models. I also had commissions from women uptown, although they were privately sold."

"Your grandmother was very pretty. Truly lovely. And she's wearing a cameo in the painting. Was it hers?"

"Oh my gosh," she said, bringing her hand to her chest. Her face turned away from me and she stared out the bay window. I let her have her moment of reflection. A few more seconds wouldn't matter if I'd finally have my answer.

"No," she said, looking at me again. "My grandmother said she had a cameo, but she'd lost it. This is incredible. I remember it like it was yesterday." Again, she looked off in the distance, nodding as if recapturing the moment.

***

Ida stood next to the mahogany dining room table resting her hand on the curved armchair. Kate stepped back from her to view the entire ensemble: dress, shoes, and jewelry. "No, Grandma," she said. "The pearls aren't right. Don't you have a brooch you could wear instead?"

Ida brought her hand to her throat. The softness of the ecru lace kissed her fingers. "I used to have a cameo. It would have been perfect."

"Used to?"

She nodded and gave her granddaughter a doleful look.

"Did you lose it?"

"I believe I did." Ida's voice was soft and faraway. She seemed to be contemplating the floral design on the dining room wall.

"How? What happened?" Kate assumed the cameo was very important to her grandmother from the sad timbre of her voice and the droop of her shoulders. "When did you lose it?"

Ida waved away the question. "Forget it, sweetheart. Just create one." She reached behind her neck and unclasped the double strand. "I'll take the pearls off and you paint whatever you want."

Just like when she was a little girl confused about something, Kate tilted her head and looked up at her grandmother with narrowed eyes. She wanted to know the story. This time Ida didn't respond. She simply removed the pearls and handed them to her granddaughter. With the jewelry dangling from her fingers, Kate walked to her easel wondering why Ida was being so secretive, then placed the jewelry on the easel's shelf. She adjusted the canvas and turned back. The sun streamed through the window casting a golden glow on the centerpiece, a cut-crystal bowl filled with fresh apples and pears.

"Beautiful," Kate said. "Grandma, move a little closer to the table. I want to make it like you're arranging the fruit."

Kate picked up her pencil. With simple, crude strokes she sketched the preliminary lines of what would evolve into an oil painting. Every time she looked up, she wondered about Ida's mournful eyes. It was obvious she didn't want to talk about the lost cameo. "What did your pin look like?" she asked anyway. "Describe it to me."

A soft smile crept up Ida's lightly freckled cheeks, though sadness veiled her eyes. "It was beautiful. Grandpa gave it to me when your mother was born. It was the first piece of jewelry he bought me in America."

Kate pulled back from the canvas and gazed at her grandmother's wistful expression. "You must have been so sad when you lost it." Her voice was soft and tender.

"Yes, honey. I was." Ida sighed and closed her eyes.

A moment passed; the air seemed heavier. Neither woman spoke though Kate watched every breath her grandmother took. She watched the rise and fall of her chest as it moved from quiet, gentle lifts to one large expansive breath, like the final punctuation mark on a declarative statement.

Ida opened her eyes. "Focus on the painting, sweetheart, and make sure you put a little silver flower on the cameo. Grandpa had the jeweler add that to make it special. Paint it behind the woman's ear, as if it's holding a strand of hair in place."

With each brush stroke, Kate grew more disturbed. It was obvious she'd upset her grandmother. Her stomach throbbed, telling her there was something more to this lost piece of jewelry. Obviously though, her unease would have to remain until Grandma was ready to explain. As Ida suggested, Kate focused on the painting and waited.

***

Mrs. Hemple's watery eyes left whatever she was looking at through the window and turned back to me. "My grandmother promised to tell me how she lost the cameo when I finished the painting. She said it was a big story and she didn't want my attention taken away from the work I was doing. From her reaction, I realized it was important and Grandma was right—just knowing I upset her took my mind off the work. I remember forcing myself to concentrate and not ask any more questions. You see, the little gallery in Greenwich Village where I sold my work was having a show and I had a deadline to meet."

"So did you ever learn how she lost the brooch?" Adrenaline rushed through my body.

"No, I didn't." Mrs. Hemple sounded so dejected and my heart sunk. "Grandma died shortly after. Unexpectedly." A heavy quiet filled the room. I sipped my tea. The dainty china top of the pot clinked as she lifted it and asked if I'd like a refill. As she poured, her eyes narrowed and caught mine. "Why are you so interested in the cameo?"

"Well . . . my mother had one just like it with the silver flower in the woman's hair."

She pulled her face away from mine, yet kept staring as she carefully placed the bone china pot on the coffee table. Then she shrugged and picked up her tea cup. "Lots of people had cameos. There were all kinds. Some had flowers on them, some little diamonds. Many had the same filigreed frame that Grandma's had."

"Yes. My mother's did. It was exactly the same as your grandmother's."

She pursed her lips and, for a moment, seemed to consider something, then shrugged again. "A coincidence," she said and took a sip of tea.

It didn't look like I'd get an answer to the case of the cameo, as Anita called it. Mrs. Hemple seemed to be steeped in some thought, probably how sorry she was not to have gotten the story—and to have lost her grandmother so suddenly. I didn't ask anymore about the cameo. Instead, I sat back and feigned relaxation. My eyes caught a framed piece of art across the room. I pointed to it. "Is that Ebbets Field?"

"Yes. It's a jigsaw puzzle. My husband did it with our grandsons."

I crossed the room for a closer look while Mrs. Hemple kept talking. "The Brooklyn Dodgers were his first love. It's very authentic. See the Abe Stark sign?"

I took in the jigged and jagged pieces glued together, and we talked a bit about baseball. "The grass always smelled so fresh," she said. "It was wonderful for us city dwellers." I sat down next to her, listening to her reminisce about going to games with her husband, and then she threw up her hands. "Enough about baseball. I'd like to know a little about your mother. After all, she was the one who bought my painting so many years ago and obviously liked it enough to keep it all these years."

"Oh, please, Mrs. Hemple," I said scooting to the edge of the couch. "It's not that I don't like the painting." In my teacher voice, I explained why I wanted to return it to her, leaving out my interest in the cameo. Obviously, we were done with that topic, to my chagrin.

"I understand. The canvas is too large for your home. That's fine. And please, call me Kate. Mrs. Hemple is way too formal for me." She smiled and added, "I told Robert to let you have another painting from my collection in exchange."

"Kate," I said. Using her first name seemed right. "I really do appreciate it, but that's not necessary."

"I insist. Call Robert and let him know when you'll be able to go to the gallery. You are staying a few days out here, aren't you?"

I nodded and thanked her again, repeating it wasn't my intention to exchange the painting for something else. She waved me off saying, "Now, tell me about your mother."

I told Kate my mother grew up in the Bronx. "Her grandmother raised her. Her own mother died when she was little."

"Like me. My grandmother raised me, except I grew up in Brooklyn." She lifted her shoulders. "I guess we have something in common."

Yes, I thought, we sure do. Not just a painting. We've both lost loved ones, though mine was Stan and not my child, though it still hurts. And I've lost my mom, in a sense. She may still be alive; however, she's not the mother I had, and that pain is so deep. Of course, there's also the cameo, and now this. How curious.

"Did you have any brothers or sisters?" I asked. "My mother was an only child. I am, too."

Kate shook her head. "Me, too. No siblings." She smiled at yet another similarity then perked up. "Carolyn, would you mind seeing some pictures of my grandparents? I'd like to share them with you since my grandmother was such a large part of your childhood too."

"Yes. I've practically lived my whole life with her hanging on the wall." We laughed and I told her I'd be glad to see the photos. I watched her push aside a few albums on the bookshelf and retrieve a big, old scrapbook. She hurried back looking much younger than the woman who met me at the door, like she could bounce up and down.

"My grandparents, Ida and Harry, came over in 1903," she said, as we sat next to each other turning pages in her well-worn album, the pictures faded with age. The sun streamed through the window, finally peaking through the clouds. "This one's my mother." She pointed to a black-and-white printed on something akin to yellowed cardboard. It was of a little girl in a white dress with anklet socks and Mary Janes standing next to her wicker doll carriage. "My grandmother gave the doll to me when I was around six and I remember carrying it everywhere."

"Where were your grandparents from?" I asked.

"Russia. Minsk to be more specific."

"My mother's grandparents also came from Russia. My mother always referred to it as Minsk Gabernia. Is that the same place?"

"It's possible. I really don't know much about the old country. A long time ago, I painted a picture for my grandmother of what their village looked like. She had a great way of evoking images with her words."

Images, paintings. "Oh, Kate, I'm sorry. I was so caught up in our conversation, I forgot about your painting. I'll go get it right now."

"Do you need help?"

"No, no. I'll bring the car around." I hurried out the door. Yes, I was giving Kate her painting. My lady was going home where she belonged, but I still did not know why the two cameos were exactly alike. Did her grandmother describe it to her, like she did with the village? Like a dog with a bone, the coincidence gnawed at me.

CHAPTER 10

I drove the car around the block, parked in her driveway, and opened the back hatch. Kate walked out and gave me a hand and together, walking sideways, careful not to stumble, we carried the portrait into the house.

"How did you ever get this on the plane?"

"I gate-checked it. I really wanted to bring it, even though it would have been easier to ship. And, honestly, I was curious about the cameos being the same."

"I'm sorry I couldn't help you with that, dear."

I was sorry, too. More than I would admit to her. We took the painting into her studio where Kate said we'd have more floor space to work. We laid it down on the linoleum stained with every color of the rainbow and then some. Kate got a hammer from the cabinet in the corner and we got busy. On her knees, she pulled the nails from the wooden frame that protected the canvas while I, squatting next to her, held it steady. Then together, we peeled off layers of bubble wrap as if we were disrobing my lady.

"Oh!" Kate squealed like a little girl the moment the entire painting was revealed. "It's exactly how I remember her." Kate sat back on her heels, her eyes taking in the entire canvas, then stopping at the cameo for a moment longer. I waited for her to say something about it, though all she said was, "It's really good. I wasn't sure what I'd think of it after all these years. My style and technique have changed so much, yet when Robert described the piece to me, I knew it was mine. I had to have it. You see, I had planned on painting another one of Grandma–one I didn't have to sell–but she died before I had the chance."

All I could do was smile. I figured it was okay to tell her more. I stood up hoping my knees wouldn't creak. I was stunned she sat on her heels so easily.

"Mom used to say I looked a little like the lady in the painting, though I think it was just the red hair."

"Yours is brighter, more coppery," Kate said as she got up from the floor. "Grandma Ida's hair was a deep red, almost auburn, like mine used to be." Again, her mind seemed to travel somewhere else for a moment. We stood next to each other staring down at the painting on the floor. "I'm so glad to have her back," she said, glancing at me then gazing back at the painting. "When Grandma died, a huge hole was scooped out of my heart. Her death was so unexpected. She had been in good shape, healthy I thought." Kate shook her head from side to side, very slowly. "Just like Beth, except Grandma's was an aneurism and Beth's . . ."

Kate brought her hand to her throat and swallowed hard. I knew that feeling of a lump in your throat when you talked about someone you'd lost, as if all the tears in the world were caught right there. I walked over to the sink, filled a glass with water, and brought it back to her.

"Beth's death was such a shock," she said after she took a sip. She placed the glass on the low wooden table that looked like a horizontal slab from a tree trunk and sat down on the faded sofa. "Beth was always a little overweight but healthy, or so I thought. She died of a heart attack almost two years ago. She called me that afternoon and asked me to bring her some Gatorade—said she'd been running to the bathroom all day between diarrhea and vomiting." She took a breath and lowered her head. Speaking into her lap, she quietly said, "I wanted to call the doctor but she said it would pass—that it was probably all the junk she'd eaten the day before at a barbecue."

She sniffed back tears. I sat down next to her and gently stroked her shoulder. A moment later, she lifted her head and shook it. I imagined she was shaking off very sad memories and maybe some guilt.

"Later that night, Ben, my younger grandson, called telling me his mother was in the hospital. He was there with his father and brother and said I didn't need to come. Needless to say, I couldn't sleep. I couldn't do anything. I wanted to drive over, but Ben was insistent saying there was nothing I could do and he'd call as soon as he knew something. Then, around ten, my bell rang. It was Jonathan, Beth's husband. He looked pale, pathetic, and somehow I knew before he even uttered a word." She took a deep breath and a sip of water. Staring off into the distance she formed the whispered words. "There's nothing worse than losing your child."

At first she sniffed back tears, then they poured like a waterfall. I held her hand, letting my thumb stroke gently over a dusting of faded freckles, and uttered a few benign words. "I know. It's hard." But words never helped.

"I'm sorry, dear," she said, retracting her hand from mine. "I didn't mean to dump all this on you. I don't usually talk about it."

"That's perfectly all right. You needed to." Although we had just met a little while before, I wasn't uncomfortable with her pouring her heart out. It seemed natural.

There was a moment when neither of us spoke and then, as if she was addressing the wall directly opposite us, she continued.

"At Shiva I overheard two of Beth's friends. They were both on the ambulance squad that night. One of them said, 'her sugar levels were so out of whack' and the other said, 'yeah, that happens with a heart attack.' I don't know if that's true and I never asked, but I do have a suspicion Beth had diabetes and never knew it. She was always thirsty and had suddenly lost a lot of weight." She shifted her body to face me and picked up the glass of water again. "Those are two signs of the disease, I learned too late. And if it goes undiagnosed, it can cause death." She sipped her water, then continued. "That's why I'm worried about my grandson. Ben's put on so much weight since his mother died, and I know obesity can lead to diabetes."

"You're right. I've had a few clients with the disease, and when their weight dropped, their insulin levels improved. Exercise is very important in controlling diabetes."

"Yes, I heard you were a fitness instructor."

"How?"

"A friend Googled you." She gave me an enigmatic smile. "After we learned you wanted to return my painting, she played detective. You're on Facebook and LinkedIn."

I laughed and told her I barely ever did anything on those sites, and, to myself, I thought it very interesting how we had both checked each other out on the internet. It was logical, I suppose, that she wouldn't have trusted me. I could have been some wacko. That's probably why she checked me out so thoroughly earlier at the door. "Kate," I said, wanting to ease her fears, "teenagers eat tons of fat and at strange hours, so it might not be anything. Have you talked to Ben?" Conversation was so easy with her, and she made me feel like she truly wanted my input.

Kate shook her head. "No. Maybe someday I will. I'm not sure how to broach the subject. I don't want to make him feel self-conscious." She sat back. Her shoulders relaxed. "One painting, and look at all it conjured up." Then she sat up straight and tall and her eyes brightened. "Let's talk about something more fun. So, earlier we decided that your mother's family and mine might have come from the same town." I nodded, pleased by her upbeat tone. "Wouldn't it be something if they were acquainted, or perhaps even good friends? Beth was planning on doing our genealogy, but . . ." Kate shrugged, this time a quick one, devoid of grief. "You see, my grandparents never really told me much. I knew my grandfather had four brothers; two had come to America, the others probably perished in a pogrom. My grandmother had a sister living in Illinois. I barely knew her. Except for the yearly holiday cards which hardly come anymore, I lost touch with whatever cousins I had." She patted her thighs. "You know how it is–one generation dies and those left forget the old ones that are still around."

That made me think of Nan and how I was definitely going to start my own genealogy search. I could do Kate's at the same time. Maybe I'd find out our families lived on the same street or came over on the same boat. "Since my mother became ill," I explained, "I've had this strong desire to find out about my ancestors–where they came from, what sort of work they did, what ship they came on–maybe even meet some relatives I never knew about. Mom knows nothing about her mother's family and I think... no, I'm sure she'd love to learn something. I don't know how much work it entails, but I'd be happy to look into your genealogy when I do mine."

With a negative shake of her head, Kate told me not to. "Beth was interested. I'm really not."

"Are you sure? What about your grandsons? One day they might want to know about their ancestors."

She tilted her head, obviously giving some thought to my suggestion. "No, I don't think so."

I prodded a bit more. I said it was for the boys, though really I was curious. I liked Kate and would love to have found out if our families were friends in the old country.

"I really am not at all interested. If someday the boys are curious, they can do their own research." Kate pointed to a picture on the wall. "That's Ben," she said. "He's the one who would be interested, but right now he's studying hard. I doubt he has any time." She stared at the boy with the expression that looked like he was up to something. "He's the one I'm worried about. He goes to Columbia, and I know what you mean–I have no idea what he eats in that fraternity house of his." She looked back at me. "Maybe that's why he's so heavy."

From photographs taken in the 1920s to grandsons, we segued to my plans for the rest of my stay in Los Angeles. Kate reminded me to go to the gallery and then walked me to the front door and we said our goodbyes. I was sorry there was no reason for me to see her again. I liked Kate and decided I would look into her genealogy anyway. Maybe our families did know each other. There were so many similarities, especially the cameo brooch. It still niggled at me. As if the pin itself had stuck me, I couldn't let go. Unfortunately, it seemed as if I'd come to the end of the road–the case of the cameo would remain an unsolved mystery–unless the genealogy turned up something interesting.

As the door closed behind me, the image of my lady came to me, as if she, herself, was saying goodbye. I was glad she was going to hang on Kate's wall. A warm sense of satisfaction enveloped me. I had made the right decision.

CHAPTER 11

The Pacific, with its sandy beach, was only a few blocks from Kate's neighborhood and, like the tide, I was pulled toward its shore. As I rounded the corner, a Starbucks stared at me. I walked inside and was bombarded by the bold scent of java. Passion fruit iced tea was my choice, and I sipped it heading to the beach. The sweet aroma from the refreshing beverage reminded me of my mother; it was her favorite. I so wanted to tell her about finding Kate and how she wanted me to have another painting from her collection, and that I really didn't want one. The mom she used to be, when she was healthy and active, even snarky sometimes, would tell me to be polite and appreciative. "Choose one," she'd say. "There must be something you'd like. You'll find a place for it, Carolyn. Be a little more flexible." But Mom now . . . she probably won't even care. I let out a huge sigh and continued walking down the street.

Bike rental shops, the ubiquitous T-shirt shops, and greasy hot dog and pizza stands lined Washington Boulevard like the boardwalk on the Jersey Shore. What a difference from Kate's quiet enclave. After three short blocks, the down-market atmosphere evaporated as the gentle waves of the ocean came into view with the silhouette of the majestic Santa Monica Mountains on the northern horizon. The beach was the widest I'd ever seen, with a wooden pier stretching far out into the deep blue water. I remembered it from *Falling Down,* a Michael Douglas movie I'd watched with Stan, cuddled up in front of the television. I shoved that memory out of my head, wanting to relax and drink in the tranquil scenery without any more disturbing thoughts, though I would have enjoyed the view so much more if he had been with me. It had been a glorious morning getting to know Kate, even with the tears and heartaches that visited us and the questions that it left. Stan would have loved digging into them.

Sandals in hand, I walked to the shore, shaking off the melancholia, and let the salty champagne bubbles tickle my feet. I took a few pictures of the seagulls hopping through the foam and then called Robert Everett to make an appointment for after lunch.

I drove the two miles to Santa Monica, grabbed a slice of pizza at Wolfgang Puck's on the Third Street mall–the sweetest sauce I'd ever tasted–then strolled a few blocks to the gallery. The paintings were lovely and, honestly, some would have looked well with my photographs since they were mostly of landscapes and architecture. The one of a royal blue front door with the exotic birds of paradise bookending it drew me in.

"That's part of a larger work," Robert Everett told me. "Kate and many artists plan out their larger pieces by working in sections. This one is her own front door."

I thought I'd recognized it. He showed me the finished work—a huge oil of the street complete with canals, pink bougainvillea, red bottle-brush plants, and doors in all shades of the rainbow. As much as I was enchanted, it was way too large for me.

"Since Kate insists, would it be all right for me to take the smaller one?" I asked. "Something about that door really speaks to me."

Mr. Everett wrapped up the unframed eight-by-ten, and I drove back to my hotel in the Marina. Kate lived only a few blocks away and since I didn't want to be a nuisance, I called instead of ringing her doorbell. She answered after several rings. "I hope I'm not bothering you," I said after announcing myself. "I know you planned on painting all afternoon."

"No, it's fine. Robert called to tell me you'd been to the gallery."

After thanking her, I told her which piece I'd taken. "Honestly, I wasn't expecting to go home with another painting, but I'm very happy with it. It'll look great on the narrow wall between my kitchen and dining room, so whenever I eat, I'll be thinking of you." Then I asked one more time if I could do her genealogy. Even though I was going to do it anyway, I'd rather she wanted me to. It would have been so much easier if I found something fascinating. Then I wouldn't have to admit I'd been sneaking around.

"No. Focus on your own journey, dear. I really am not interested. Please, don't bother."

"It's no bother, Kate. You said you knew nothing about your father's side of the family—that you'd never met anyone. Maybe I could find some information for you."

"No. Absolutely not. Why should I want to find them—or any of their descendants for that matter? Obviously, none of them wanted anything to do with me."

Wow. She was pissed, and I wondered why her father's family just wiped her out of their lives after he died. Jeez, she was a child. Wouldn't the grandparents have wanted to see her again? Even though I understood how she felt, I needed to find out if her parents actually came from the same town as my mother's. Deep down, I believed there had to be a connection and it all had to do with the cameo brooch. I reminded Kate of what she said about Ben being interested in genealogy. "He probably knew his mother was looking into the family history." I was treading on shaky ground mentioning Beth and felt kind of bad about it. But I really wanted her to agree to let me do the search.

Kate let out a huge sigh. She sure sounded frustrated with me. But when I had something I really wanted to do, I could be as persistent as a squirrel digging for nuts. This time, though, I had to give up or she'd hang up on me and never want to talk to me again. I liked her too much for that.

"Okay," I said. "I won't bother you about it anymore." Frustrated, I hung up the phone then grabbed my bathing suit, wiggled into it, and made my way to the hotel pool for a half hour of laps, as long as there weren't any kids in my way. I didn't need anything else annoying me.

Los Angeles in June is not the LA you see in the movies. It shifts from cloudy and overcast to sunny and bright then back to just plain gloomy all in the same day. After my swim, which helped clear my head, I closed the curtains, shutting out the bleak sky, and snuggled into my Marriott king-sized bed letting sleep medicate my jet lag and all the mixed emotions from the day. An hour later I emerged from a restful nap. With the late day sun peeking through the clouds, I lay in bed letting my mind play over the nice parts of the day and the pleasure I felt leaving the painting with Kate. As much as it meant to me, it meant so much more to her. Maybe it's the same feeling a surrogate mom has when she carries a baby for another woman and then, after the birth, hands over the newborn to the real parents. She knows she'll never see the baby again, yet there's a special connection she cannot break. And doesn't want to.

I threw off the covers, dressed, and headed to the Mexican restaurant a few blocks from the hotel. Its red door and turquoise windows were inviting. While waiting for my frozen margarita, I took out my iPhone and searched for websites to start on Kate's genealogy. I figured her marriage certificate would be a good place to begin. That would give me her maiden name and from there I'd look up her parents. I found a website and typed in Kate Hemple and New York in the box where it asked for city, assuming she was married there since that's where she lived at the time. After I tapped Search, it brought me to Archives.com, where I found out there were ninety-six records for the name Kate Hemple in the US and in order to view them I had to become a member. I didn't want to pay for that if I didn't have to. Another site sounded like a good possibility: www.publicrecordspy.com. That made me laugh; maybe I was a spy. That one also wanted me to pay. It was less than the previous so I typed in my credit card information and waited for the next step.

My frosty libation arrived with some guacamole and crispy homemade chips just as a list of names popped up. I scrolled through all, wishing the first names were also alphabetized. There were so many Hemples, some with an "le" and some with "el." I wondered if it would be easier to look via her maiden name then slapped my head. I didn't know that name. I scrolled through another twenty-five and then–there it was. Kate Roth Hemple. My stomach did flips. Roth? My mother's maiden name was also Roth. My heart beat fast. I downed the margarita and left. I needed to walk, to think.

As I headed back toward the hotel, I was so excited thinking Kate might be my cousin. I would tell Mom about her and maybe even introduce them. Kate was in great shape. She could fly to New York. I felt my cheeks spread into a huge smile thinking how I'd have a family, one that I could connect with. Nan was actually family, but at ninety-five she wasn't cooking holiday dinners and inviting me. I passed a food market and drug store, warmed by memories of holidays when my family gathered at our house and how, year after year, without fail, my great-grandmother Rebecca, with her wrinkled brow and puckered lips, complained that my mother's chicken soup was bland and we'd all shout, "Pass her the salt." It became a family joke. Just looking at salt shakers made us laugh, even for years after she died. I yearned for that warmth again. With Kate as my cousin, I would have that. She had grandsons. Ben was in New York. We'd get together. I'd invite him to dinner. College kids appreciated a home-cooked meal. Then, as I turned the corner onto Via Marina, my legs buckled. What if Kate wasn't a cousin but my aunt? She could be my mother's sister. I could barely breathe. They had the same last name and their families came from the same town in Russia. I sucked air, gulped breath into my lungs. I forced myself to calm down saying it couldn't be. Mom would have known she had a sister, even if they were brought up separately. But what if Mom didn't know? Oh God! Now I for sure had to do both Kate's and my genealogy. I needed answers.

CHAPTER 12

The next day, after tossing and turning all night and popping Tylenol to calm my nerves and wishing I had something stronger, I drove the few blocks to Kate's house. Knowing she painted in the morning, I arrived around one. I didn't want to annoy her and risk wrecking the bond we seemed to have formed yesterday. I needed that bond, if what I thought was true. I wondered if she would draw the same conclusions, and I still wasn't sure how I was going to tell her we might be related. I had thought about it all night. There was no way I wanted her to know I had looked up her marriage license. She had been adamant about my not doing her genealogy, and if she knew I had gone behind her back, she might not want to see me again, and I couldn't take that. If she really was my aunt, I needed to be embraced by her, included in her family, not kicked out. And, I realized, if I kept quiet about doing the research, I was not lying. I was simply omitting a fact. A lie was something you actually said aloud—a falsification of where you had been or what you had done—and I could never do that with the way I felt about liars. I had no use for them after what I had gone through with my ex-husband and his deception. It killed our marriage. Even now, every time I think about it, my body tenses. Every fiber of my being quivers in anger.

***

Walking between tall buildings in Manhattan in a March rainstorm was like traversing a wind tunnel. I hurried home from the subway, my trench coat soaked, holding tight to the umbrella, afraid it would fly off and impale the man in front of me. All I wanted to do was get in the apartment, rip off my wet pantyhose, and soak in a hot tub. Alan had night classes so I didn't have to make dinner. As usual, he had grabbed a sandwich at the deli, then headed down to NYU. I was so proud of my husband. We thought it was a stretch when he applied to the university's law school, and here he was, halfway through his second semester while holding down a full-time position as a bookseller at the Strand. Like many of my teacher friends, it was my salary that kept us afloat. It seemed to be the way of the times–wives taught and husbands attended law school. With a student deferment, the men were able to avoid the draft and would not have to fight in the jungles of Viet Nam. I certainly did not want Alan going off to war, especially one we had no business being in, and I didn't mind supporting him either. His earnings, which were not much, were targeted for his school loan. In a few years, with his law degree, he would make a lot more and we would be able to start a family. I wanted two children, maybe three, to fill my home with love.

Wrapped in my thick terry bathrobe, I sat in the big, old, comfy armchair and opened the day's mail. These must be his mid-term marks, I thought, when I read the return address on a business-sized envelope. I put it aside for Alan to open and then grabbed it back. I couldn't wait. He wouldn't mind. He said he had done very well on the exams. I took a quick glance. No grades were listed. The word "confirmation" stuck out. I read further, digesting every word of the letter that made me want to throw up. I started to sweat and needed to breathe. I blew out my cheeks over and over again. Alan had been lying to me. He was not in school. This formal document confirmed his resignation from all classes. Oh shit, I thought. Now he will be drafted and shipped out to the rice paddies. Why did he do this? Where was he going every night? I didn't have to wait long to find out. Just at that moment, the door opened and in he walked.

"Didn't expect me, did you?" he said and gave me a kiss. "Classes were canceled tonight."

I threw the letter at him. "Really?" He stepped back, stunned by my anger, and turned away. "Damn it! Explain this," I shouted.

Alan didn't need time to read the whole page. He slumped down on the couch and buried his head in his hands. "I couldn't hack it," he said. "I was afraid to tell you. You'd be so disappointed in me."

I looked up at the ceiling. It was impossible to even look at his face. He was right; I was so very disappointed in him. I let out a huge sigh and told him so. "It's not that you dropped out of school; it's that you lied to me."

"You wouldn't have understood. You're much stronger than I am." I wondered if he was correct. Would I have comprehended what he was going through or would I have pushed him? The rain pounded against the window as Alan continued. "You're like a dog with a bone," he said. "You trudge ahead. You never give up, even when something is difficult, like when you failed the chemistry mid-term in your junior year. You studied harder than I ever would have because failure is something you will never accept. I admire that, Carolyn. It's just not me."

"So now what? You'll get drafted."

"Not necessarily. I'm thinking of going to Canada."

"Are you out of your mind? I'm not moving there." Alan shrugged and looked out the window as if he could see Montreal through the deluge outside. It made me boil.

"Look at me," I yelled. "Tell me everything. Where've you been every night? Who've you been with? Is she going to Canada with you?"

My husband–the man I trusted–the man I thought I could depend on–raised his head a little. His eyes remained downturned as he said, "The racetrack. There's no other woman, Carolyn. Just the horses."

I collapsed against the back of the chair, relieved he wasn't having an affair. But gambling? That was dangerous, especially the fact that he had hidden it from me. And where was he getting the money from? I doubted it was from his little salary at the book store, which I assumed was put away to pay off last semester's loan when he absolutely was in school. Of that, I was certain. He'd passed his classes, though his grades were not as high as he'd hoped they would be.

"So you used my money to place bets," I said, more of a statement than a question. I was pissed.

He thrust his shoulders back and, with all the bravado of a gunslinger, answered. "Yeah. And I won a bundle. Where did you think I got the money for that watch you're wearing?" He pointed to the Movado he gave me for our first anniversary last June. He must have been gambling then, too, I realized. How long had this been going on? "Or when I took you to The Top of the Sixes on Valentine's Day or the orchestra seats for *Hair* last Saturday night."

I didn't know if I wanted to cry or scream. I got up and paced the floor. I sensed his eyes following me and then he pleaded with me to sit and talk to him. I waved him off. Words were not possible.

All along, I had thought Alan squirreled away a little of his salary every week to save up for those special evenings. Neither of us ever bought ourselves anything new. We had hand-me-down furniture from my parents, and a meal in Chinatown was big spending. I remembered how shocked I was when he gave me the watch. I loved him and was so touched that he took his small earnings to buy me something I'd never dreamed of owning at this point in our lives, and I felt awful I didn't have an anniversary gift for him. He didn't mind. He laughed and said, "I'd probably have known anyway, since I take care of the checkbook." Oh, what a mistake that was! And I thought I was doing the right thing letting him be in charge of our finances. I didn't want to emasculate him. Living off my salary was enough. If only I had asked him then where he got the money, maybe we wouldn't be going through this now.

I stopped and looked at him. "Lies. All lies," I said. "Telling me you're in school. What about those other weeks, when you weren't flush with winnings? I'll bet you lost plenty."

"Some," was all he said, as if it didn't matter.

I hated that attitude. He was never so cocky before. How could he imagine I'd never find out? Was he an idiot, or was he so addicted he couldn't think straight? That all that mattered were the ponies? I couldn't look at him anymore. I wanted him out. He begged me to let him stay, but I would never trust him again, no matter what he said. I could not look at his deceitful face. Another woman would have been easier to deal with. This was our whole life, our dreams, and he just tossed them on a win, place, or show. I slammed the door behind him and ran into the bedroom, threw myself down on the bed, and fell apart.

***

I rang Kate's doorbell and, getting no answer, I knocked. Kate's face appeared in the square window on top of the door. I heard the click as she unlocked it and opened it just enough to fit her body–not an inch more–her eyes narrowed, her yellow-paint-stained fingers fiddling with her collar. I sensed she was wary, wondering what I was doing on her doorstep, then realized it was my own guilt poking me. She had no reason to be circumspect.

"I hope I'm not disturbing you," I blurted out. "I'm leaving later this afternoon and wanted to make sure you were okay." That wasn't really a lie; I truly was concerned, even though that's not why I was there. "I know looking through the pictures yesterday was hard for you. I understand. As much as they may be comforting, it hurts knowing photos and memories are all we have left of our loved ones."

Kate pulled her shoulders back and assured me she was fine and that she was sorry for crying. The statement was short, quick, no embellishments. I winced. She had been so nice and open with me yesterday until I pressed her about the genealogy. Was that why she was so cold now? I tried hard to keep a smile – to no avail. I didn't want to lose her. Not now, when I had just found out we were family. She must have seen how upset I was because her demeanor changed right away. Kate opened the door wider and my mouth softened.

"Come in, dear. You're not disturbing me." Her voice had a much more friendly tone. "I just finished washing my brushes and was going to make something to eat. Why don't you join me?"

Kate sliced bagels while I set the table. A little while later, while I was spooning chicken salad on my sesame-crusted bagel, trying to calm the thundering in my chest, I asked Kate if she remembered our conversation from yesterday. "We wondered if our families came from the same town–if Minsk and Minsk Gabernia were the same place." Kate nodded as she bit into her sandwich. "So," I continued, putting the serving spoon back in the bowl, "did your grandmother ever mention the name Roth?" I wanted to sound casual, like I was merely making conversation, though I was dying to hear her response.

Her eyes opened wide. She pulled her mouth off the bagel and, holding it in midair, asked, "Why?"

"Because that's my mother's maiden name." There, I'd said it. The thundering ceased. One weight lifted off my chest. More were still pressing hard.

"That's *my* maiden name," Kate said and licked a smear of chicken salad off her front teeth. I forced a fake look of astonishment. She giggled. "Another coincidence, isn't it? Seems like we have many." Her bright, smiling eyes told me she thought this was funny, not as significant as I did. "You know," she said, "Roth is such a common name. Between Rothstein, Rothberg, and Rothenback and so many others that were shortened, I'm sure there were many families with that name from Minsk."

"But did they all come to the states in the early nineteen hundreds? That's when my mother's family came over.

She shrugged, as if it didn't matter. "I don't remember my grandparents having any friends named Roth. There was my father's family, though they weren't friends. She barely ever talked about them. They weren't in New York. After he died, which I was told was shortly after my mother died, the family moved to Chicago or St. Louis. Somewhere in the Midwest. That's when I went to live with Grandma Ida and

Grandpa Harry. They wanted to raise me. They always said they couldn't bear having me live so far away. I guess my father's parents didn't give a hoot. They just up and left and good riddance to me." I was amazed there wasn't an ounce of sadness in Kate's face, just disgust. Her lip curled, her nose wrinkled. "My grandparents made me keep my father's name–to honor him, they said–though I always thought of myself as a Pearl–their name.

Just as with the cameo, it looked like I'd come to another dead end. Roth was a common name and my mother's family lived their entire lives in the Bronx, not the Midwest. So the name was just a coincidence.

Kate moved the conversation from family names to recollections. "You asked if I was okay," she said lifting the bagel. "Well, after you left yesterday, I was filled with memories. This wasn't one of them, though, but I do remember my first bagel here on the west coast. So disappointing!" She took a bite, chewed, and swallowed, looking past me as if I wasn't there. She wiped a bit of mayonnaise from her lip and came back. "You know, dear, after my daughter died, my paintings were all dark. The first one I did actually had a dead bird in it. It was of a lone tree, a Joshua tree from the national park in Arizona where I loved to go. I painted it on a black canvas with dead branches, no leaves, just a solitary tree all alone except for the one dead red cardinal. I chose that bird particularly because I had fond memories of watching them from my bedroom window in Greenwich Village where I lived when Beth was born. I used to nurse her and follow them as they flew from tree to tree. Later, I stopped painting dead things. Still, all my work was gloomy in browns and blacks, dark green, and charcoal gray. In fact, when Robert called to tell me about you and the painting of my grandmother, I'd been working on a rainy scene, and this morning, I put it aside.

Somehow bright colors found their way onto the canvas. Shades of yellow and orange."

"What are you working on, can I ask?"

"I'm not sure exactly how it'll end up. For now, it's Washington Square. Carolyn, as I said, meeting you and seeing my grandmother again, I've been washed in memories. Some pleasant, some not so. You know that peach dress in the painting?" she asked. "Well, I used to dress up in it and clomp around the apartment in Grandma's shoes with her beads draped around my neck and a pocketbook clutched in my hand. And the crystal bowl in the painting? Remember it? That's the same bowl in my sun room with all the sea shells in it."

The phone rang. Kate let it go. It stopped after six or seven rings, then started again a moment later. After a few rings, Kate pushed her chair back and grumbled as she went to answer. "Oh, hold your horses, I'm coming. What's so important?"

Being in the kitchen, I couldn't help but hear her entire side of the conversation, even when she took the phone into the hall.

"Yes, she is legitimate," Kate said to the caller. "Really, I am fine." There were some moments of quiet when the caller must have been talking. I realized she was talking about me, maybe to the woman who had Googled me, and the word legitimate made me uncomfortable. I hadn't mentioned genealogy, but I was not legitimate either. I was going to continue researching her family without her consent. Then I heard her shout. "No! She didn't even want a painting. I had to insist." Kate sure sounded emphatic. I imagined the caller asking if I expected a refund for the painting. Again, Kate was quiet and then she laughed, as if she couldn't fathom what the caller was saying. "No, dear, I do not need you to come over." Her tone got real testy.

"What? You're gonna protect me? You got a Glock or a Wesson?" I almost burst out laughing.

Kate came back in the kitchen and banged the phone on the hook. "One of my friends," she said. "Just checking up on me." She was shaking her head with a look of disbelief. I kept quiet, not wanting her to know I was listening, but I sure did enjoy her sense of humor. Her friend obviously did not trust the strange woman from New York who was returning a painting. Kate sure set her straight. The saying "You can take the girl out of Brooklyn, but you can't take Brooklyn out of the girl" fit her perfectly.

After lunch Kate brought out the photo album she had shown me the day before. "I had such a wonderful time yesterday looking at these pictures," she said as she pulled a chair next to me and sat. She opened the book and flipped through some of the crinkly pages. "I kept looking at these photos, letting my mind wander, and then I noticed this one." She pointed to a black-and-white of a pregnant woman whose hand seemed to be reaching down and to the side, as if it was holding another hand. "This is my mother. It's odd, isn't it? It's not the same size as the others."

She was right. It looked as if something had been cut out of the picture, right where her mother's hand ended.

"My grandmother told me I was in the picture, too, in my mother's belly. I imagine my father didn't like his photo taken, so he cut himself out. Or maybe this one was developed differently and he got cut out by mistake."

My thoughts moved in another direction completely. There were some square pictures and some rectangles, though no photo as narrow as the one of Kate's pregnant mother. Was she holding my mother's hand? Mom was about a year and a half older than Kate, and she had once told me she was about that age when her mother died, which to me was so incredibly sad. I couldn't imagine not having any memories of my mother, especially now, when I was clinging to remembrances of the active woman she used to be who loved life. Not to have known your own mother is like not knowing a part of yourself.

Like a truck barreling down a hill, the name Roth careened back at me. Sure, it might be a common surname, but there were just too many coincidences to ignore it even with the Midwest discrepancy. My adrenaline kicked up. I was excited yet scared at the same time. I needed Kate's birth certificate. With that, I would learn her parents' names. Were they the same as my mother's parents?

CHAPTER 13

Eighty-Six Years Earlier

It was a busy afternoon on Fourteenth Street. Shoppers hurried by while Jack and Lena stood outside the automat in their cloth coats and hats. They both left work early on Wednesdays to go to their respective classes, Jack at the Pace Institute of Accountancy and Lena at Hunter College, from which she would be graduating the following year. A black Model T Roadster drove by leaving a trail of stinky gas fumes. Lena wiggled her nose. She stepped forward for a better look at the blue Dodge coming down the street. She liked the running board and turned to comment as a police paddy wagon sped by. Jack pulled her back from the curb. "Jeez, Lena, be careful." With an arm around her waist, he led her toward the buildings lining the avenue. "I wish my sister would get here already," he said.

Lena was about to agree with him when she noticed a full-figured woman turning the corner wearing a cloche with a mushroom brim. It was trimmed with a ribbon of rosettes and she was holding a young girl's hand. "Is that Teckla?" Lena asked, looking up at Jack. "And Nan? You didn't tell me Nan was coming, too." Jack's nod sent her hurrying down the street to meet them.

Teckla's arms opened to greet her. "It's so wonderful to see you again," she said, wrapping Lena in a hug. "I'm so glad my brother arranged this."

Lena kissed Teckla on the cheek and told her she was also glad. In truth, she was relieved—and thrilled—Jack had finally let someone in his family know they were together. She stepped back and smiled at the little girl standing next to her mother. "And this must be Nan. I can't believe it. The last time I saw you, you were a baby. Now you must be about ten or eleven."

Jack arrived at Lena's side in time to hear her last two sentences. He turned to his sister, his body rigid, his brow lifted in question.

"Yes, Jack," Teckla said. "Lena did meet Nan once. I visited the Pearls one time after Mama made her declaration never to see them again."

Jack shot a look at Lena, then back at his sister, his breath loud and fast, his teeth clenched. Lena did not understand why he was so incensed. What was wrong with her having seen Nan? It was such a long time ago, and she remembered how disappointed she was that Jack wasn't with them.

Teckla ignored her brother and looked directly at Lena. "I'm sorry it was only once," she said. Lena waved her hand to stop Teckla's apology, and Jack cut in, sounding like a prosecutor questioning a defendant.

"Did Mama know?" So that was it, Lena thought. He's protecting his mother. Otherwise, why would Jack care?

"No. I couldn't bring myself to tell her." With an apologetic look she turned to Lena. "That's why I never visited again. But I'll never forget that day. It was right before Thanksgiving. Nan was about a year old and I bundled her in her new navy blue coat and leggings." She tousled her daughter's curls. "We took the subway all the way from the Bronx to Brooklyn, and your mother made us a wonderful lunch. She even remembered the cookies I loved. The ones with the powdered sugar dusted on top."

"And I'll bet Nan would like a cookie now," Lena said, hoping to drop the discussion of the Roth-Pearl argument. She appreciated that Jack was close to his mother, although this obvious irritation with his sister's secret was going too far. Did he not see how wrong Rebecca was? A few days ago, when Jack mentioned they would be getting together with his sister, Lena was thrilled he had finally let a family member in on their clandestine relationship. Still, she worried he would never tell his parents, and if he didn't, what was their relationship all about? Lena offered her hand to Nan. "I know I would like a cookie, or maybe a baked apple," she said smiling at the little girl. "I've got to eat something before class. Let's go inside." Nan's face lit up. She placed her hand in Lena's and together they walked into Horn & Hardart's.

The foursome stood in front of the glass and chrome doors peering at the cakes and puddings on the shelves inside. "Can I have that one, Mommy?" Nan asked, pointing to a tall glass filled with creamy rice pudding.

"Certainly." Teckla dropped a nickel in the slot. Like magic, the door opened and she let Nan pull the dish out.

"Can we do that again?" Nan said. "It was fun."

"Absolutely," Lena said. "You can put the coin in for me." She showed Nan the slot for her baked apple and watched as the little girl carefully slipped the nickel in. Nan's delight was infectious as she pulled out the plate with the apple treat. "Now, let's get some milk for you and coffee for me." The two walked off like best friends.

Seated next to each other, Lena and Nan shared their treats. Lena spoke with the child while keeping a close ear to Teckla and Jack's conversation.

"You've got to tell Mama and Papa," Teckla said. "If you and Lena are really serious, you've got to prepare them."

"I know. I will."

Lena's pulse jumped. She moved a little closer to Nan and scooped up a spoonful of the warm cinnamon apple as if she had not heard. She didn't dare look at Jack. "Would you like some more?" she asked the child, but as she enunciated the question, she wondered if Teckla really knew what was in her brother's mind. Jack had never mentioned marriage to her. He hadn't even said he loved her, though Lena was certain she was in love with him, and she knew this was more than the crush she'd had on Jack as a kid. He made her feel beautiful. He was always so attentive, and she adored the way his eyes crinkled at the corners when he smiled, like he was enjoying every word that came out of her mouth. And when he kissed her mouth–oh, nothing was ever so delicious. Lena slipped her arm around Nan's shoulders as they dug into the sweet treat together and thought maybe–just maybe–Jack had confided in his sister– that Teckla wasn't imagining things. The idea made her so happy she wanted to hug everyone in the entire restaurant.

***

The cash register drawer closed with a soft thud. Lena pulled the receipt from the paper roller and dropped it in the customer's bag, then handed the woman her four dollars change. The morning had been so busy she hadn't had a chance to say hello to Jack, and she was desperate to see him after what she overheard yesterday at the Horn & Hardart. Lena had left the automat first to get to school so they hadn't had a chance to talk since. Telephone lines were shared with the entire neighborhood and someone was always waiting to make a call with the operator's assistance–and probably listening in to the one in progress–so Jack never phoned her. All of their communication happened in person, and she prayed that today he would say something in reference to his conversation with Teckla. After all, he *had* told his sister he was going to tell his parents about them.

Finally, there was a reprieve from the slew of customers at her counter, yet this woman was taking so much time slipping the bills into her calf-leather purse that Lena wanted to grab it and shove them in herself. From the corner of her eye, she caught Jack's wave motioning her to come over. The moment the lady was gone, Lena hurried across the aisle.

"I'm sorry, sweetheart, for beckoning you like that. I can't leave my post for another half hour. Can you take a coffee break then?"

Lena assured him she would. No matter what, she would make it work.

Thirty minutes later, on the dot, Lena met Jack in the employee break room. He poured them both a cup of coffee from the electric percolator, looked around the empty room, and then said, "Will you come to *Shabbos* dinner at my apartment?"

Lena almost spilled the entire cup of hot liquid all over herself. Shock and excitement all mixed together. His apartment meant his parents' apartment. Unsure of her ability to put a whole sentence together with her heart pounding so hard, she simply asked, "Tomorrow night?"

Jack shook his head. "No, next Friday. I told my parents all about us and let them know it was very important to me that they welcome you." Open mouthed, Lena stared at his adoring eyes. She was too stunned and too excited to talk. "My mother agreed, but she needs more time to get ready." Jack smiled. "For dinner, I mean, and maybe," he lifted his shoulder a bit, "to get used to the idea of us. So will you come next Friday?"

"Absolutely." Happy tears filled Lena's eyes. With the tip of his finger, Jack gently wiped the salty wetness from her porcelain skin. "I love you, Lena Pearl," he said and cupped her bright smile in his hand and kissed her lips, long and deep.

Her body tingled. It was the first time Jack had said those three special words she longed to hear. With the sweet taste of his tongue lingering in her mouth, Lena slipped her arms around him and nestled her cheek against his chest. "I love you, too, Jack Roth.

After work, Lena hurried home, anxious to tell her mother everything. She burst through the door, threw her purse on the hall table, and ran into the kitchen. Ida was preparing a meatloaf, her hands covered in freshly chopped chuck from Harry's butcher shop. Lena scooped two fingers full of the tasty raw beef, gobbled it down, and let the words pour out nonstop.

"Slow down, *shayna*. You mean Rebecca invited you to dinner?"

"Yes, though I think Jack might have twisted her arm a little. He said he made it clear to her that if she didn't accept me, she'd lose him."

"Oh, sweetheart. I'm so happy for you, but she's not the person to threaten. Watch your step with her. I doubt you will, but be sure you never come between Jack and his mother. He's the sun, moon, and stars to her." Ida washed her hands and wiped them dry. "Come, sit. I want to tell you why Rebecca dropped our friendship eight years ago."

Seated across from her daughter at the kitchen table, Ida explained the argument the night of the pinochle game was not actually what caused the rift between their families. "It was the last straw," she said. "You see, on the Saturday before, Papa let Karl go. Remember Uncle Karl worked in the butcher shop on Saturdays? He wasn't making much money as a presser, so Papa took him on one day a week. But Uncle Karl wasn't very dependable. There were times he didn't show up and blamed it on Rebecca, saying she didn't like him working on *Shabbos*. Papa knew better. Karl was at his club, not in shul. So on that day, when he came late to work, Papa said he could stay, but after that he didn't want him back."

"Good for Papa. Karl deserved it."

"Oh, honey, there's so much more to it. Before we left Russia, Karl and Papa had talked about going into business together in New York. They had high hopes for a huge success and talked about it constantly. By the time Karl came over, though, Papa already had the store and it was doing very well. He didn't need Karl. And, several years later, when Papa started talking about opening another shop, in Williamsburg, Karl was sure he'd run that store." Ida shook her head hard from side to side. "That was not Papa's plan. You can imagine how outraged Karl was. Rebecca too."

"So they just cut you off, dropped a lifelong friendship?"

"Not immediately. Papa said Karl screamed at him, said he was a good-for-nothing friend. They almost got into a fist fight. The other men in the shop pulled them apart, afraid one of them might pick up a butcher knife. Your father probably did not tell Karl in the nicest way, and I am pretty sure Karl's accusing Papa of cheating during cards was his way of saving face. That way, Papa looked like the bad one, the guilty party. Karl wouldn't have admitted he was in the wrong, and certainly Rebecca never would have, either. You see, in Minsk, we were all the same. None of us had much money and we were all afraid for our lives with the pogroms. Once we got to America, though, everything changed. And don't forget," Ida pointed her finger in the air. "We had the money to come over together–the Roths didn't."

"What do you mean? I thought they were always here."

"No. Karl left for England before we sailed for New York. Rebecca was jealous that we had the money and they didn't. It was there that he worked to make enough money for the passage, but it turned out it was only enough for one person. Again, Rebecca had to wait. About three years after he came to New York, Karl finally sent for his family. His brother helped him pay for it, and when they arrived, all eight of them lived in Karl's brother's three-room apartment. Karl, Rebecca, the children, and his brother's family. That's three rooms total, sweetheart, not three bedrooms." Lena's eyes opened wide. She couldn't imagine being so cramped. "And shortly after, we were fortunate to be able to move out of that neighborhood." Ida's face pinched. "There was always a stench from the horse droppings in the street and the outhouse in the back alley, and you had to keep your windows closed even in the heat."

"Outhouse? They didn't have a bathroom?"

"No. Tenements in those days didn't have indoor plumbing. It was smelly and noisy all the time. There were chickens clucking in the street and men shouting out, selling their wares." Lena looked around their brightly painted kitchen with yellow speckled linoleum on the floor and thought about the fresh air that blew through her bedroom window and the trees lining their Brooklyn street and their own toilet in a black-and-white-tiled bathroom. She understood Rebecca a bit more and was even sympathetic toward her.

CHAPTER 14

Eighty-Six Years Later

I left Kate's house and drove directly to Hertz, dropped off my rental, and took the shuttle to the airport. Like a dog with a tick, I couldn't shake the odd-shaped picture of Kate's mother from my mind. While sitting at the gate waiting to board, I opened my laptop and found the site for Jewish genealogy. Armed with Kate's maiden name, I was ready to begin my search for her birth certificate, even though my stomach clenched every time I thought of it.

Jewishgen.org asked me to create a password. I used my usual with letters and numbers and registered. I clicked "Get started" and felt like I was running a race. I was definitely going to be the hare, not the tortoise.

The link took me to "Family Tree of Jewish People." I was making progress. After several more clicks I got to a list of names, all Kate Roth, and scrolled through by date of birth. Not knowing her exact date, I began clicking on any listed as living or with a birth date in the 1920s. Four more clicks and I was there. Kate Roth Hemple born in 1926 married to Irving Hemple, one child Beth Pearl Hemple. Damn. The space for Kate's parents' names was left blank. Other than a note in small print on the top of the page that read "Contact the person who submitted this data by email," there was nothing else. I assumed Beth was the person to contact. I filled out the form anyway and clicked Send. The site didn't post an email address; I guess it was all done internally.

My flight was announced. I closed the laptop and kept my phone open to email, fiddled with the settings so I'd hear the chirp when a new one came in, in case it was from JewishGen or whoever filled out Kate's data. Usually, I don't like getting those notices. They annoy me especially when I hear everyone else's phones tinging and binging. It's my own little temper tantrum, I guess. "No! I don't have to be connected every minute of the day." But this time was different. I really wanted that reply and would keep the phone on to the very last second when the flight attendant insisted I turn it off.

I hoped JewishGen would work–that perhaps it was Ben, not Beth, who had filled out the information. If it was Beth, it would be a dead end. As we started our march to the Jetway, I heard the ping. At least it didn't sing "You've got mail." I was pretty adept at reading and walking at the same time, so I looked like every twenty-something walking the streets of Manhattan, eyes glued to a rectangular screen. Shit! Jewishgen responded that my email was undeliverable. I guess my whispered expletive was louder than I intended because the mother of a little girl standing in front of me turned and gave me a dirty look. With nothing more to get from the website, I shut the phone and slipped it in my bag. Beth was dead and no one had posted any more information on Kate Roth Hemple. My next step was a trip to lower Manhattan where all the records were kept: birth, death, marriage, divorce. All sorts of records.

It was a bumpy takeoff. The rest of the flight home was smooth, though no one would know by looking at me. I tried to calm myself by reading. No luck. I tried Continental's In-Flight magazine. I leafed through *SkyMall*, staring at stuff I wondered what I would do with if I decided to buy, and then picked up my novel again, but nothing took my mind off the name Roth even though I knew it was common. I'd worked with a woman named Nancy Roth and she wasn't related. We had Roth neighbors in New Rochelle and they weren't related. So why were my insides convulsing over Kate's maiden name? Chicago, St. Louis be damned. I didn't care where her family had moved to; I was certain there was a connection and I had to find out what it was.

The next morning, my clothes still in the suitcase, I headed to Manhattan. In Grand Central, I switched to the subway and twenty minutes later exited at Worth Street heading to the Department of Mental Health and Hygiene. I felt like one of those vibrating chairs at the nail salon, every inch of me quivering, and I had to remind myself to slow down. I'd probably come up with nothing.

The imposing brass doors opened onto the ever-present post-9/11 security. My shoulder bag waited its turn on the rubberized track, then slid through the scanner while I wondered if I would have a cheerful or churlish guard checking me as I walked through the X-ray. Power seems to go to their heads the minute they don a security uniform. I was shocked. My friendly "Hi" actually got a smile in return. This was going to be a good day. An elevator ride to the third floor left me at the room where birth certificates were housed.

There was a short line. It was only 10:00 a.m. I waited my turn, shifting my weight from side to side. Why waste the time? The more one fidgets, the more calories one burns. That's what I always told my exercise class, though that was not the only reason I was fidgeting.

The plump, frosted-haired woman asked for my photo ID. All I wanted was Kate's birth certificate so why did she need that? To prove I'm a citizen? What difference does it make? Like a good little robot, I pulled my license out of my wallet and handed it through the window.

"What year are you looking for?" the woman asked, standing straight and tall, shoulders pulled back in a very official manner.

"1926, I think." Her head tilt made me continue. "I'm doing genealogy research. I'm not positive of the year she was born, but... yes, '26 is a safe bet. Can you help me?"

"So this isn't for *your* birth certificate?" Her tone was the one bureaucrats always use to make us peons feel inferior. "You know," she said, all puffed up with pride, "I'm not allowed to give you someone else's certificate unless you have their permission."

My quiet "Oh," must have given her reason to change her tone. She became the friendly neighbor. "Don't lose hope, honey. If the person whose record you're looking for is deceased, I might be able to help a little."

"Yes. Yes, she is." I did not like lying and, certainly, did not want to curse Kate's life, but I had to get that information. If only Kate had told me her parents' names, I could have avoided this whole scene and gone right for their birth certificates, rather than reading their names on Kate's. Maybe I was jumping into this too quickly, not thinking things through. But I was there in the building, so why not continue and leave Kate alone?

The woman handed me the official request forms which I filled out sitting on an uncomfortable metal folding chair along the wall. Name and city and state were no problem. As to date of birth, all I could write was 1926, if my hunch was correct. I didn't know the date of my maternal grandmother's death, just that Mom was about a year and a half old when she died. I lifted the pen, midstream, and thought, "But the baby died too." Oh, I was so confused. One part of me was so sure I'd find out Kate and Mom were sisters and that I would be able to bring them together. I so much wanted to do that, for both of them. To be in your eighties and meet the sister you never knew existed would have to be wonderful. Then another part of me said it was not possible. I finished filling in all the blanks I could and handed it back to the woman. "That's all the info I've got," I said and poured myself a cup of tea from the electric pot on a corner table. While I waited for Kate's birth certificate, I took out my phone to check email, then read the front page of the *Times*. It seemed like fifteen hours, even though it was only fifteen minutes when my name was finally called.

"This is a copy of the birth certificate you're seeking," the clerk said as I stood in front of her window. She used her official voice again. "I can't let you have it. You can stand here if you want and read it."

There were the names I wanted. Kate Mildred Roth. Date of birth, September 17, 1926. Place of birth: New York City. The borough was listed as the Bronx. But Kate said she grew up in Brooklyn. Below those boxes were the two names I was really looking for, the names of Kate's mother and father.

I read the two names then brought my face closer to the document. Had I read them correctly? Right there, printed in black ink was Father: Jack Roth and Mother: Lena Pearl Roth. I sucked in a breath so loud everyone turned. The clerk asked if I was all right. Unable to put words together, I nodded, a very slow up and down with my mouth hung open. My mother's father was named Jack Roth and her mother was Lena, though I had no idea of her maiden name. All these coincidences shook me hard. Kate's mother's place of birth was listed as New York City and her father's as

Minsk. She and I had already gone over that similarity, but I had no idea where my maternal grandmother was born. And I had no idea of the date of her death, or Kate's mother's date of death. I had a lot more digging to do.

"I'm sorry," the clerk said, startling me. "There are others waiting."

I peeled my eyes off the document and looked over my shoulder. There was a line of people, all eyes glued on me. I slid the copy of Kate's birth certificate toward her, said a quiet "Thank you," and walked out the door.

The elevator doors opened, and I elbowed my way in, pushing everyone else aside. I punched the button for the ground floor and, when my feet hit the pavement, hurried to Chambers Street. Three short blocks later, I arrived at a French Château shoved in between cement office buildings and coffee shops. The Surrogate's Court of New York City. It housed the Municipal Archives where I would find Lena Pearl's death certificate.

"Roth," I said to the man with the receding hairline seated behind the desk. "Lenapearlroth."

"It's okay, miss. I have all day." He smiled. "Take a breath. I'm sure we can find what you're looking for."

I started again, slower this time, more in control. "I'm looking for the death certificate for Lena Pearl Roth."

"What year?"

Crap. Why'd he have to ask that? "1926, I think." That would be the right year if my mother actually was eighteen months old or thereabout when her mother died. And Kate was born in '26 and she claimed she never knew her mother, so she must have been a baby when Lena died.

"You think? You don't know? All right," he said and motioned to the chair at the side of the desk. "Have a seat. I'll be right back."

I waited and looked around Room 103. There was a picture of President Obama hanging on the wall and photos of old New York City streets with vendors selling wares from their carts. A black-and-white shot of the World Trade Center, its towers standing tall and proud, caught my eye and brought back memories of that day nine years before when two airplanes turned a clear sunny day to ash. This was a sunny day too. Would this information burn me? Would I find out something I didn't want to know like Bill had when he met his half brother? That was always a possibility when digging into a family's history. I stared at a framed shot of the Statue of Liberty and imagined my great-grandparents, Karl and Rebecca, seeing her come into view as their ship neared the shore bringing them from their Europe of pogroms to the freedom of the United States. And I wondered who my other great-grandparents were, the ones my mother never knew.

The man returned carrying a box of microfilm and brought my thoughts back to present day. "Here, take this over to the counter. I hope it's what you're looking for."

I fed the first roll in with shaky hands. It got all tangled up. I was petrified I'd rip it. This might be the only copy. "Excuse me." I looked over toward the clerk. "Could you please help me?"

He came over and threaded it through. "This happens a lot. Take your time. Hold the film taut and it'll slide right through."

He was right. I scrolled through the names. Lena's was not there. I told him and he brought me another box. This time, loading the film was smooth. My breath was not. "Calm down, Carolyn," I mumbled. "Take your time."

I started with the "Ps" for her maiden name even though I had checked them before. How many boxes would I have to go through if they repeated the same letters in each?

There were Pearles and Perlmans and even Pearlmans with an "a," but no Pearl. I switched to "L" then remembered nothing was ever listed alphabetically by first name so I checked the "Rs." Raskin, Raymond, Regen, Rich . . . I kept scrolling down. There were so many names that began with "R." Rivera, Rosen, Rosenberg . . . And then I saw it. Roth. Lena Pearl Roth. I read it twice to make sure. Yes, my mother would have been a year and a half old. The date of death was September 17, 1926. I stared. At first my mind went blank, then all sorts of thoughts came crashing in, bombarding each other. That was the date Kate was born. Did she say her mother died in childbirth?

After a few moments trying to quiet the brass band in my chest I brought the box back to the clerk. The air was heavy. My mind tried to grasp what I had just read. The clerk reached for the box. It slipped from my fingers.

Was this the Lena I was searching for? I walked out into the sunshine not appreciating the blue sky at all. My stomach rumbled and not only from nerves. So anxious to get started today, I hadn't had anything for breakfast except the cup of tea on the train and the one while I waited for Kate's birth certificate. A glance at my watch told me I had another two hours before the next train to Tarrytown. I wished it were sooner. I had to get home and find my mother's birth certificate to read her mother's maiden name. If it was Pearl, then I would know for sure Kate was my aunt, and I would have to tell her and admit I had gone behind her back. A chill ran through me just thinking about it. I headed to the subway to get back uptown.

At a deli near Grand Central, I ordered a grilled Swiss and bacon on rye, and watched the people hustling down the street from my seat at the window. I thought about all those times my mother and I had come into the city–all those train rides into the bustling station and how we walked this same street heading across town to the theater or uptown to a museum. I wished we could do that again. And I wished I could call her right now and ask her mother's maiden name, but she no longer answered her phone. Tomorrow, I would.

On the subway, I realized my grandmother's maiden name possibly might not be Pearl and I finally calmed down. There was no reason for me to get so worked up. There was no way Kate and Mom had the same mother. My grandmother died in childbirth as Kate's mother obviously did, but so had the baby. Still, I had to find my mother's birth certificate. I would need that maiden name for my genealogy search. And I still hoped Kate and Mom were somehow related and that my research would bring it out. I wanted so much to bring some fun, intriguing news to Mom. And I wanted to be part of a family.

CHAPTER 15

The moment I got home, I hurried to my den where I kept Mom's important papers. The clear plastic container holding them sat on the floor exactly where I'd left it several weeks ago. I plopped down and began sifting through its contents: copies of income tax forms, the certificate of completed mortgage, EOBs from the insurance company, my father's death certificate, Mom's passport, and, ensconced in a small white envelope, her birth certificate. Her name was on top, Sarah Hannah Roth, with her father's name below, Jack Roth. I already knew that. Directly opposite his was her mother's name. My mouth went dry. I read it again to make sure I wasn't imagining things. In black ink on a white background was the name Lena Pearl Roth. I tried to swallow. My entire body was numb. I read the name a third time, then jumped up and paced the floor. Kate and my mother were sisters. It had to be. No way was there two Lena Pearls who married men named Jack Roth. It just wasn't possible. But why weren't they raised together? I told myself to calm down. That was ridiculous. It wasn't possible. I examined the papers again, not knowing what I was looking for, hoping there would be a clue of some kind. I didn't find anything.

I flopped down on the couch and suddenly burst out laughing. Nervous laughter, as that odd picture in Kate's scrapbook zoomed back at me again, the one where her mother's hand was stretched out holding onto something. It was! She was holding my mother's hand. It had to be. The ages worked out perfectly. I was so keyed-up over my discovery and the fact that I would have a family, yet, at the same time, I could not suppress my turmoil over how to tell Kate. First, I would have to admit I had gone behind her back. With this news, Kate would surely ignore that fact. Or I hoped she would. Otherwise ... But I did not want to think about that. It was too upsetting. And as to my mother, she would have something new to bring her joy–a sister she never knew. The news would make her happy; I was sure of it. I decided I would fly Kate to New York as soon as possible just to see my mother's eyes light up again. I was sure bringing them together would give Mom a reason to live, to fight, to walk again, to smile again. And then, as swift as a tsunami, my fevered enthusiasm crashed. I felt hollow, like a chunk had been ripped from my chest, with the realization that for years–for decades–lies and secrets had infested my family. Why? The only person alive who could answer that question was Nan. I went to bed hatching another plan. I would call Nan in the morning and then, equipped with the truth, bring the sisters together. I slipped under the covers telling myself they would be thrilled with the news.

It was only 6:00 a.m. and I was wide awake. I reached over to the lamp on my night table and turned it on thinking reading would help. Nothing else seemed to get me calm enough to fall asleep. On and off, all night I did relaxation breaths and counted backwards. Nothing helped. I could not stop thinking about Mom and Kate. I was convinced the news would be as wonderful as I imagined for them and not rip them apart as the lie was doing to me. I opened the book and started to read. After two paragraphs of having no idea what I was reading, I lay it face down on my lap and stared straight ahead composing conversations in my mind: what I would say to Nan, to Mom, and to Kate. As if it could sweep the tension from my mind, an early spring breeze floated through the open window. I looked at the clock. It was only 6:30, the sun wasn't even up yet, and my eyes still refused to close. I opened the book again. Sometimes, when I got involved with fictional characters, I was able to relax and then, when I came back to what was troubling me, I would have a better idea how to handle it. I needed that to happen because I was at a loss as to how to bring this shocking news to Kate without her turning against me. Although I told myself she would be happy with it, I could not kick that thought from my head. Then the phone rang. My hand flew across the bed and grabbed the receiver.

"Carolyn, I'm so sorry to call this early." Grace's voice was gentle. "Your mom isn't doing well. You should come over as soon as possible. Her breathing is very weak."

Blood raced through my veins. Not now, I thought, as I tossed the covers aside and jumped out of bed. Not when I had good news. It was normally a twenty-minute ride to Maple Valley from my condo, but that morning, without even realizing I was making right turns and lefts, I pulled into the parking lot in fifteen. I threw the gear into park, clicked the doors locked, and raced in.

That same trepidation—the one I felt every time I entered Mom's room—grabbed my chest again, this time especially hard. My question was answered immediately, though. Mom was asleep. Oxygen pumped through tiny plastic clips attached to her nostrils. She looked peaceful, but she was not sitting up and smiling as I'd always hoped to find her, and she was not staring into space with a frown either, which I understood but was not used to, and her telephone wasn't against her ear where it always was before she came here. It was in its cradle.

Over the past two and a half months I had watched my mother go from a woman whose lips were always glossed a soft coral, whose hair was done religiously every Friday, to the woman lying in bed, hair matted, gray roots showing through the red dye, lips chapped. With my pasted smile, I walked over to the side of the bed. "Hi Mom." I hoped the false cheer would come through, in case she heard me. Then I bent over and kissed her on the cheek. It was cold and dry. Her eyes remained closed. I wasn't sure if she aware I was there. All thoughts of telling her about Kate evaporated. This was not how I wanted to present her with a sister she never knew. Instead, I opened the top drawer of the metal bedside cabinet and pulled out her blue comb with the pick on the end that rested next to her bridge. She had lost too much weight over the last two and a half months and it no longer fit. Who knew you could lose weight in your mouth? I was astounded when she told me, a few weeks ago, "I'm not wearing that thing, Carolyn. It hurts too much." My mother *never* went without her teeth!

"Mom, I'm going to comb your hair. It needs a little teasing," I said, taking a soft, thin strand between my thumb and index fingers. The aide had left mom's bed in a reclining position, as if she was resting, so it was easy to comb her hair. In the past, the teasing and hair spray had camouflaged the wispiness of her thinning locks. I played hairdresser and tried to duplicate the style, careful not to pull too tightly on her scalp. The pick helped me pouf it up. Who was I satisfying, I wondered. Me or Mom?

"Are you thirsty, Mom?" No answer. Her lips were so dry, she had to be. I took one of the cotton tipped sticks that looked like a lollipop, dunked it in some water and ran it along her lips. Mom opened her mouth and clasped onto the wet tip like a baby nursing at her mother's breast. I re-wet the stick and tapped it on the white caked sides of her mouth, then let her suck it dry again.

This isn't right. I am not supposed to be your mother. I want my mommy back. I want to go out to lunch with you, go shopping . . . I shook my head. Stop it, Carolyn! I had to clear out all those thoughts. They did not do me any good. I pulled the ugly armchair next to the bed and sat.

With Mom's clammy hand in mine, I sat in silence staring at her expression. She looked calm. She was breathing easily with the oxygen in her nose and I was glad of that. Before I entered the room, Grace had told me Mom could hear what I was saying. I wasn't sure. I couldn't tell if this was a real sleep she was in, just very deep, or something else. Anyway, I figured this was a good time to tell her all the stuff I wanted to be sure to say.

"Mom," I started slowly, "you've been the best mother any girl could have, always so understanding, like a friend and a mom all rolled into one." I stopped for a moment to see if she was listening, but couldn't tell. I leaned in a little closer, my hands resting on the edge of the bed. "I know you weren't thrilled with Stan. You knew he'd never marry me. I did too, but didn't want to admit it. I thought maybe once his wife died . . . I'm sorry I yelled so much, I just didn't want to hear it. I did finally take your advice. Remember?" Mom didn't answer. I kept on hoping Grace was right about her still being able to hear me. "I never went to the hospital to see him. You were right–his kids didn't need that." I stopped talking for a moment and closed my eyes. Memories flashed across my mind like a beautiful movie. "But, Mom," I sighed, "I never got to kiss him goodbye." My eyes welled up. Was it for Mom or Stan? It didn't matter. I lost him five years ago and was losing her now. I drew her hand to my mouth and kissed it, then lowered it to the edge of the bed and held it there. My iPhone pinged. I didn't want to let go. The text would have to wait. I took a breath and found the courage to say what needed to be said. I had heard of other women who sat by their mother's bedside saying similar things, but I never imagined myself actually uttering the words.

"I'm okay, Mom. I want you to know that. You can go to Daddy, if that's what you want." I swallowed the lump in my throat. "I know this is hard for you; it's not the life you want. So if you've had enough, it's all right. I'll be fine."

I sensed a little pressure on my hand. Maybe it was more hope. I so wanted to believe she heard me. I stroked my mother's bony shoulder with my free hand and sat back. I was never able to speak directly of death to her. Not her death. Not since she came to Maple Valley. Maybe she did hear. Maybe she did understand.

The phone pinged again, that insistent second ping. My shoulders tensed. I remained staring at Mom's pale, closed eyelids. They'd never again feel the soft brush dusting them with blue shadow. My thumb gently slid up and down her hand, tracing from knuckle to wrist as I thought about what Grace had said, that she could go on like this for several days. My chest rose and fell with every anxious heavy breath.

Bereft of words, I slid my hand from Mom's and slowly pulled the phone from my pocketbook, looked back at Mom, then read the text. "Call me." It was from my realtor. My stomach churned, fearing it was bad news that the buyers wanted out. I did not have strength for any more problems.

I sat for a few more moments deciding whether or not to say anything about Kate. Sadly, there was no sense anymore. I leaned over and put my lips close to her ear. "Mom," I said, maybe a bit louder than usual. "I've got to go now. I'll be back this afternoon." Then I kissed her forehead, stood up, and said the words I, unfortunately, had not said often enough. "I love you."

Maple Valley's automatic doors closed behind me. I looked up at the clear blue April sky. It was too beautiful for such a sad day. The only upside was that I was wrong–the buyers didn't want out of the contract. They wanted to push the closing date up. I assured my realtor the house would be ready, that I only had to switch the date with the people running the estate sale. Other dates would have to wait, I realized, but that was not her problem.

I stopped at the diner on North Avenue instead of heading directly home, desperately needing a strong cup of tea. I hadn't eaten anything yet and ordered scrambled eggs. Not really able to swallow even a forkful, I pushed the yellow pieces around the plate and thought about Nan and Kate. I would wait a few days to call Nan, until this new situation with Mom calmed down. And I doubted I would bring Kate east. Mom was not likely to improve. Oh, God, I hoped she wouldn't linger too long. She'd have hated that. Then a pang of guilt seared through me.

After paying the bill, I got back in my car. As I pulled out of the parking lot and turned right onto the avenue, another realization hit me, as if someone had thrown a bucket of cold water smack in my face. Once Mom died, I would have no reason to come back to this neighborhood again. After so many years, I would have no cause to drive down this street, to turn these corners. Other people would be living in my childhood home. I stopped at the red light right next to the bank where my mother took me to open my first savings account. The dry cleaner where Daddy used to take his shirts was across the street. Bubbling tears clouded the light as it turned green. I gulped them back, to no avail, as I crossed the next intersection. The stationery store was gone. So was the ice cream stand where I used to go with my parents on summer nights and where, as a teen, I hung out with my friends. In the exact same location was a new apartment building dressed in an old-fashioned façade that evoked simpler, more innocent times.

My cell phone rang as I was about to turn onto the Sprain Parkway, heading home for a few hours of some desperately needed sleep. I clipped the Bluetooth to my ear and tapped it on.

"What?" I heard myself ask the question, though I knew what Grace had said. "A few minutes ago?" I listened as she explained that Mom wasn't alone when she died–that she was at her side stroking her brow as the hospice nurse monitored her pulse.

"She just slipped away, Carolyn. Very peacefully."

A volcano of emotions erupted in me. I made the next U-turn and rushed back to Maple Valley. A heartbreaking sadness seeped from my every pore while a dry lump formed in my throat. I held the steering wheel tight, berating myself for the feeling of relief that washed over me even as my eyes welled up.

CHAPTER 16

The first person I called, as I was driving away from Maple Valley for the last time, was Anita. She jumped into action taking care of the details: phone calls to my friends, food for after the funeral, paper goods, and anything else she thought important. She offered to go to the funeral parlor with me, but I needed to do that by myself. I did not want hers or anyone else's suggestions about which casket I should buy or what prayers should be said or how the obituary would read.

I met with the funeral director in the afternoon. He instructed me to go to Mom's house and pick out an outfit to bury her in. A shiver ran down my spine, but it had to be done. Her cornflower blue skirt and jacket, the ones that matched her eyes, always brought compliments so I grabbed them from the hanger. She wouldn't need shoes and I certainly was not burying her in any jewelry. "You'll look lovely, Mom, I promise," I said to the air.

I remembered when my parents came home from my great-grandmother Rebecca's funeral. Since I was only eight at the time, they thought I shouldn't be there. Instead, I spent the day with my friend and her parents unaware that I should feel sad. It wasn't as if I'd lost a cuddly grandma.

***

"Mommy, what do people wear when they're buried in a casket?" I asked. "What's Great-grandmother wearing?"

We were sitting next to each other on the couch in the living room. She had her stockinged feet up on the cocktail table like she always did when she was relaxing. Cousin Nan was in the kitchen with my father, cleaning up. Everyone else who'd come back to the house after the cemetery had already left.

"She was buried in a shroud," Mom had said, examining her nail polish. "Not everyone is, but Aunt Teckla said that's what she would have wanted."

"What's a shroud?" I asked, my knees tucked under me. I was fascinated with all the requirements. We had not covered the mirrors, like some people do, and Aunt Teckla sat on the club chair all evening, not on an uncomfortable wooden box as immediate family members are supposed to, if they follow custom.

"It's a plain white covering for the body, usually linen," she said. "It can't have any pockets or buttons or zippers." She turned to me with a smile. "It's the way it was done in the old country, and some people still observe that rule. But I don't like it."

I asked why not and she simply lifted her shoulders and said, "I think you should always wear something pretty." She gave me a kiss and told me to get ready for bed.

Later, while I was upstairs reading, tucked under my lemon-yellow comforter, I heard Nan's and Mom's voices through the heating vents.

"I didn't even put lipstick on her or comb her hair," Mom said. Nan remarked that Mom didn't sound sad. "No, I am," she answered. "I'm sad when anyone dies. If I'm honest, though, I doubt I'll miss her."

I thought that was really cruel, so when Mom came in my room to say goodnight I asked why she wouldn't miss Great-grandmother Rebecca. "Even though she's the only mother I ever knew," she explained, "she was tough. She probably loved me. Cousin Nan says she adored me when I was a baby, though I don't remember that." She kissed me goodnight and turned to leave. The scent of White Shoulders trailed behind her as always. She stopped in the doorway and turned back. "I suppose Aunt Teckla might miss her," she said. "She is her real daughter, but I never saw any affection between them."

***

Back at home, I made myself a cup of tea and opened Mom's address book. Nan was my first call, though I was not about to mention Kate Hemple at this time. Maybe during Shiva I would get the chance to talk to her. But what if she wasn't lucid? That thought hit me hard. All along, I was depending on her to reveal the reason for the family secret. But she was ninety-five. She might have dementia.

Nan answered after several rings. She sounded sharp. Oh, how I admired elderly women who were still active and bright, like the women in my class. I asked how she was faring, before blurting out my devastating news, and words flowed from her lips nonstop. She told me about her aquacise classes and that she was reviewing the next selection for her book club and was absolutely passionate about never missing the current events club meetings on Friday afternoons. Finally, she asked about me and I told her about Mom. There were tears in her voice when she responded and I swallowed mine. I refused to let myself break down. Oh, how good it would be to feel safe enough with someone to be completely genuine. Mom and Stan were the only people I could ever do that with. After we hung up, I called some of my mother's friends, and they promised to spread the sad word to everyone else.

I knew I should try to rest a little. I was totally drained, but it was not about to happen. I didn't know what to do with myself. I could not sleep, did not want to eat anything, didn't really want to watch television, and could not focus on a book, so I sat at the piano in my living room. I didn't have a painting to talk to, to tell how alone I felt, that there was a deep empty hole inside me. As much as I liked my photographs, none spoke to me like my lady, and I no longer had her. That was okay, though; I was glad she was with Kate, and anyway, I was not a kid anymore–I no longer spoke to paintings.

Trying to clear my head, I played songs in the *Billy Joel Songbook*. The phone rang in the middle of "Just the Way You Are."

"Oh my gosh!" I said when Nan's daughter announced herself. I didn't recognize the voice. She was my older cousin and we were never close. We barely knew each other, with her having grown up on a kibbutz in Israel and then coming to the states for college. She was at Brandeis studying for a career in education while I was riding bikes and playing jump rope. After she graduated, she got married, Nan joined the Peace Corps and moved to Guam, and we lost touch with her daughter. Nan was no longer in New York at the time, so her daughter never came to holiday dinners. I was glad she called now. It sure felt good having family reach out to me.

"Thank you," I said after she offered her condolences. She kept talking letting me know she would be bringing her mother to the funeral, that she knew how important it was for her to be there. Nan and her mother Teckla were the two people who kept my mother sane throughout her childhood. After my parents married, my mother wanted to get out of the Bronx, away from her grandmother. "To escape," she once told me, though she had to wait until they could afford it. Mom claimed Rebecca always had something to say about what she was feeding me or how she kept house, and she didn't even approve of the way Mom ironed! "If I could have, I would have moved cross-country," she'd said. Great-grandmother could barely speak English, but she certainly made her opinions known. The night after Rebecca's funeral Mom had told me, "If it wasn't for Aunt Teckla, I'd probably be speaking Yiddish now."

Funerals and weddings bring families back together, and the closeness lasts about a day. We say we'll stay in touch–"I'll call you; you'll come for dinner." –but we never do and that's a shame. I decided I would change that. From this one phone call, it appeared as if I did have a family after all and that realization helped get me through the rest of the weekend. The family might be from my father's side, but I was warmed knowing they would stand with me beside my mother's grave on Monday. And soon, I would embrace my aunt from my mother's side of the family. From the deep depth of my sadness, something positive had surfaced, and the late afternoon sun, streaming through the window, warm my despair a bit.

CHAPTER 17

As the gravediggers lowered my mother's casket into the soft ground, Nan stood next to me, holding my hand. The rabbi recited Kaddish, the mourner's prayer, and we read along sharing the paper with the transliteration printed on it. A soft breeze blew, rustling the new green leaves on the trees edging the cemetery, singing a mournful song. As custom requires, the rabbi then picked up the shovel and sprinkled the first layer of dirt over the casket, performing the great mitzvah of participating in covering the lowered coffin with earth. He then handed the shovel to me, looked into my eyes, and raised his brow in question. I always thought this was the most striking, painful part of a Jewish funeral, and now recognized that it was the last act of kindness that I could do for my mother, as the rabbi had explained the night before. He had come by to talk to me about the service, and I mentioned my reluctance of throwing the dirt. He'd said, "Your mother has no more earthly needs now. There's nothing we can give her, although we can see that her body is honorably and properly buried." I scooped up a bit of the soft brown earth, turned, and watched it trickle down. It made a soft thump as it hit the pine box, its echo a haunting sound of finality. The deep desolation that consumed me could not be covered up, as my mother's grave was, by this honorable act.

I was afraid to let Nan have a turn; she might lose her balance, so I held out the shovel expecting her daughter to take it from me. Though not immediate family either, she was the only other relative available to do the honors. Instead, Nan stepped forward and dug the shovel into the pile of dirt that had been excavated to create the gravesite. After that, Mom's friends and mine came forward. When the top of the coffin was covered, everyone performed another custom. They made two lines giving the immediate family a path from which to exit. I stood and watched, heavy with the finality, knowing I was the only one to walk along that aisle. The reality pressed on my shoulders like a massive weight. Then Nan walked up to me, slipped her arm through mine and led me through the passageway. My heart swelled, thankful I was not alone.

From the cemetery, we all drove back to my condo. I tingled with warmth as I stepped through the door and saw the table laid out with platters of smoked salmon decorated with salty capers and bowls filled with whitefish, tuna, and egg salads accompanied by straw baskets brimming over with bagels and fresh seeded rye bread. There were enough cakes and Danish pastries to feed the entire neighborhood and dishes of pickles and olives, hummus, and chopped liver. A large, colorful fruit platter held center stage. Several women from my class had offered to set up the food while I was at the funeral. I just never expected such bountiful fare. I had only ordered lox and bagels from the deli.

The robust aroma of freshly brewed coffee filled the dining room. I poured a cup and brought it to Nan, seated on my club chair in the living room. She thanked me and clasped my hand. "We were like sisters," she said, and I teared up, understanding how much she also missed Mom. I wasn't the only one.

Just then her daughter walked in with her Louis Vuitton pocketbook slung over her shoulder. "We can't stay long," she said, her voice curt. "I've got to get my mother back to Riverdale then get over the Whitestone before rush hour. Come on, Mom, put your coffee down. Let's go."

I was pissed. If the tables were turned and it was me bringing my mother to her mother's funeral, I wouldn't be concerned with bridge traffic. Families needed to be together at times like this, and I thought we were one. Now it did not feel like that. Again, tears pooled my eyes. No matter how hard I tried to keep my composure, they had their way of cutting in. Nan reached over and clasped my hand. I took that to mean she understood how I felt and was sorry she had to leave.

"I'm going to call you," I told her. "We'll go out for lunch."

"Sarah would like that," she said.

I swallowed hard, hearing my mother's name.

The morning after the funeral, I put up a pot of coffee and got ready for Shiva. Traditionally Jews are supposed to sit Shiva for a week. I only sat for three days. I'm not traditional. Anita and Bill came every night, along with former colleagues of mine and members of the synagogue and, during the days, Mom's friends dropped in, thus the coffee. I was so touched that the women in my class came back, but I did not see Nan or her daughter again. At her advanced age, I was willing to excuse Nan. Her daughter, though . . . It would have been nice if she'd have come. Obviously, not having to cross a bridge was more important to her than family. At times like this, being an only child really sucked.

It used to make me bristle when I heard my high school students say something sucked. They used the word so casually. Somehow "suck" morphed into another definition and became accepted. And for this, it was so perfectly succinct.

After three long days, the last of the people offering their condolences left. It was only five o'clock in the evening, and I figured it was a good time to call Nan. The phone rang seven times and I was ready to hang up when she finally answered. She asked how I was getting on and I answered, politely, but all I wanted was to ask about Lena Pearl having two daughters. It took everything in my power to let her chat and not interrupt. Finally, I had an opening and reminded her of my offer to take her to lunch.

"Oh yes, I would love it," she said. "When were you thinking of? I have a very busy schedule."

How busy could a ninety-five-year-old woman be? "How's tomorrow?" I would have gone right then, if it wasn't so late.

"No, that doesn't work for me. And the next day, I'm going shopping. They take us by bus to a little grocery store in town. I like to have some fruit in the refrigerator, even though all my meals are taken care of."

As frustrated as I was, I kept my cool as we tried to come up with a date. Nan was an incredible woman. Here she was at ninety-five schlepping on a bus for an orange. She was always a tough one. During Israel's fight for independence and for several years after the state was formed, she lived on a kibbutz with her husband and daughter. She was widowed young, spent some years with the Peace Corps, and eventually came home to New York. Yet, throughout all the years, she kept in touch with my mother. Her letters, on that blue onion skin paper, told tales about her teaching the native children to read and write and to play softball and kickball. Finally, we settled on meeting at her present home after lunch two days hence. I let her know I was doing some genealogy and it was confusing.

"Confusing? What's confusing about the family? They came here from Russia and made a decent life for themselves. They never got rich but they weren't poor either. They were comfortable. We were comfortable. As a child I didn't know any different." She kept talking and I hoped she would give me some kind of hint, some kind of answer to the name on my mother's birth certificate. "There was Grandmother Rebecca and Grandpa Karl," Nan said, "and my mother, Teckla, and Jack, her brother. He was your grandfather you know. He died very young. And . . ."

Her voice trailed off. I wasn't sure if she forgot other relatives' names or stopped talking on purpose. I didn't dare interrupt her train of thought in case she would say something about Lena or even Kate.

"Anyway, Carolyn," she said after what seemed like a long silence yet really was only a moment, "we'll talk about the family when I see you. I hope I can help you sort things out."

So did I. Nan wouldn't have information about my mother's ancestors since they were not her family. She would know about Lena, though and it was time I learned it all.

CHAPTER 18

Eighty-Six Years Earlier

Lena stood in front of the ladies room mirror and turned her head right and left, checking how she looked. She leaned over the stained sink, peered in a little closer, and pinched her cheeks giving them some color. It had been a long day at work, and she wished she had time to go home and freshen up, but Rebecca was adamant about dinner time.

As thrilled as she was ever since Jack had invited her to *Shabbos* dinner, Lena could not stop the rolling, fluttery feeling in her stomach. Her mind kept going to the worst case scenarios. Rebecca would slam the door in her face or maybe just not speak to her. Uncle Karl, if he deigned to sit at the same table, wouldn't look at her. Jack kept telling her to relax, that all would be fine. "My parents are looking forward to seeing you," he said every time she voiced her fears. But were they looking forward to having her as a daughter-in-law? Having her parents as their *machatunim*? If they refused to be friends, how could they ever be a family? But Jack had not proposed, so why was she thinking all this?

Lena frowned and berated herself. Be happy you got invited to dinner, she told her image in the mirror. You wanted Jack to tell his parents about you and he did, and he said he loves you. Give him time. This is the first step. She reached in her bag, pulled out a metal lipstick tube and applied the new daring shade. With a tissue, she blotted her lips softening the bright red color. She didn't want to give the impression of being a flapper. Rebecca would never approve of that. She tossed the ruby colored Kleenex in the trash and went to meet Jack at the employees' door.

Jack held Lena's hand as he turned the knob and pushed the apartment door open. Lena recognized the mahogany hostess table with the dark green leather top. It stood in the foyer welcoming her, as it had years ago when she was a little girl visiting the Roths in this same apartment shortly after they had moved to the Bronx. The same red tufted sofa sat against the living room wall, faded after all these years, just like her Uncle Karl who was standing in the middle of the living room, his arms open wide.

"Look at you, Lena," Karl said. "So grown up." He reached forward and clasped her hands. "Can I give you a kiss, or are you too old for that now?"

"Oh, Uncle Karl. It's so good to see you again." Lena leaned in and kissed his stubbly cheek feeling her eyes well up. Jack stood by her side; a smile filled his entire face. She turned toward his mother and reached out her arms. "And I'm so happy to see you, Mrs. Roth." Rebecca's wrinkled hands remained at her side though she did offer a slight grin. "Thank you for inviting me for *Shabbos* dinner." Lena drew her arms back to her sides where they would obviously remain.

Teckla, her husband, and Nan stood behind Rebecca watching the long-awaited greeting taking place. Lena felt their stare. She wondered why Mrs. Roth still looked like she'd sucked on a lemon and why she was scrutinizing her outfit. Rebecca used to do that to Lena's mother, even accusing her one time of being a fancy-schmancy lady now that she was in America, though she had said it in Yiddish.

Nan pushed her way in between her grandmother and Lena and grabbed Lena's hand. "Come, I want to show you what I made," she said. Her patent leather shoes clomped against the bare wood floor, and Lena had to shuffle quickly in her heels to keep up with the ten-year-old.

"Not now, Nan," Teckla called to her daughter, who was hurrying down the hall. "You can show Lena your picture later."

Jack cut his sister off. "Let her go. Lena loves children and Nan seems to adore her."

Teckla followed her mother to the kitchen, and Jack and his father moved to the dining room table to sit and wait for dinner.

"So you said you've seen her parents, right, Jacky?" his father said. "And they treated you well?" Lena wasn't able to hear Jack's response as she headed back from the bedroom where Nan had shown her the picture she had drawn of the two of them sharing a baked apple. She assumed he gave his father a look that said "Of course. Why wouldn't they?" Her parents already had Jack to dinner, before Rebecca had invited her here. After all, she thought, that's how they treated him when he was a child and the two families were friends. Wouldn't his parents do the same–treat her well? So far, from the way he welcomed her, it seemed Uncle Karl would. It was too soon to tell about Jack's mother. As relieved as Lena was about Karl, she was distressed over Rebecca with her unopened arms.

The fresh, woodsy scent of mushroom barley soup drew the rest of them to the table. It looked thick, rich, and delicious and Lena said so as Rebecca poured a ladleful in her bowl. "Jacky's favorite," she said looking Lena in the eye. "Better than kreplach." Rebecca knew Ida's favorite choice for *Shabbos* soup had always been chicken with those sumptuous, crescent-shaped, meat-filled dumplings floating in the savory broth. Was she trying to outdo her? Was she making food a contest? Lena was not about to take the bait, as she hoped this would be the first of many dinners together. Jack quieted her nerves with a tender touch to her knee. His chair was next to hers, and he moved it a little closer. Teckla, seated on the opposite side of the table, crinkled her nose at Lena. With a little wave of her hand, Teckla let her know not to worry about Rebecca's remark. Those little touches and Nan's chatter broke the tension.

As children do, Nan peppered Lena with questions throughout dinner about her favorite things, especially actors. "Did you see *The Thief of Bagdad*? Don't you love Douglas Fairbanks? Isn't he romantic? Someday I want a handsome man to rescue me, and then I'll marry him."

Everyone around the table laughed except Rebecca. Jack translated for her but Lena thought his mother understood what they were saying; otherwise, why were those wary eyes peeled on her? Did Rebecca want to judge how Lena would act toward a child or how she would react to the word marry? Teckla made up a story about finding husbands on magic carpets and in crystal balls and even Karl added to it with handsome princes rescuing maidens. In addition to his mother's, Lena sensed Jack's eyes on her. If he was her prince, she wasn't sure what he was rescuing her from. Certainly not his mother with her puckered face.

"Let me help you with the dishes," Lena said when dinner was over. She stood, lifted her plate, and reached for Jack's.

"Nah, nah." Rebecca waved her hands. "*Gey, gey mit de kind.*" Lena understood Mrs. Roth wanted her to stay with the little girl, but she needed some time alone with Jack's mother, to give her the opportunity to ask any questions she might have and for Lena to assure her she loved her son and hoped they could all, despite what had happened, be friends. Lena continued clearing the table, going back and forth between the dining room and kitchen while Rebecca murmured in Yiddish. It was obvious she did not want Lena's help when she grabbed a pile of plates from her hand.

Lena would not let that stop her. She had to win the woman over and trusted working together in the kitchen would help. Isn't that where women bonded? She remembered the laughter that filled her mother's kitchen all those years ago when Rebecca and Ida washed dishes together while everyone else sat satiated on the living room sofa. Wanting that same relationship with the woman she hoped would be her mother-in-law, Lena strolled into the kitchen, stepped up to the sink and ran the water. Just as she was pouring the Super Suds detergent, Rebecca walked in, slammed down the dishes, and grabbed the box of soap.

"No, no. *Gey avek.* I'll do it."

"Please, let me help. It's a lot of work for you."

Teckla walked into the kitchen carrying the big platter that had held the roast chicken. "Lena, please, don't argue, it's not worth it." Jack came in behind her holding empty vegetable bowls. "I'll help my mother," he said. "Nan's waiting for you."

Lena shrugged. What could she do? She went back out to the dining room.

Nan had the checkers game open and ready. Her red pieces were laid out. "Please play with me, Lena," she said.

Lena sat and smiled at the little girl who obviously was infatuated with her and placed the black checkers on her side of the board. As Nan made her first move, Lena heard muffled voices coming from the kitchen–Jack's, his mother's, and Teckla's. She kept her eyes glued to Nan's round piece and remained silent, hoping Nan would do the same. Oh, how she wished she was sitting closer to the kitchen door.

"Your turn," Nan said. She repeated the phrase with more emphasis, forcing Lena to sit up straight. Feeling admonished, as if a teacher had caught her daydreaming, she picked up her piece and moved it one space forward. Nan took her turn and Lena forced herself to focus on the game. Karl sat across the room on the sofa stuffing tobacco in his pipe. The sound of the match against the flint irritated Lena. Nan was humming, holding her checker up while deciding where to place it, and Lena had to hold her tongue. Every sound was annoying, forcing her to listen harder. She shoved her chair a bit to the left. It didn't help. She just was not close enough to the kitchen door. Nan placed her piece on the game board and stopped warbling. Lena relaxed and looked for a spot to put hers when the voices from the kitchen escalated.

"Mama, Mama, sha sha. Calm down." Jack's words became garbled, but through the Yiddish, Lena definitely heard Jack say two words in English that made her forget the black checker piece in her hand. "Marry me." Her ears perked up like a puppy's. The rest of Jack's discourse was silenced. Rebecca interrupted and her voice was not as sweet as Lena would have liked. She didn't understand what the woman was saying. Then Teckla's voice came through. She sounded like a mother trying to stop a toddler's temper tantrum. The tone softened. There was some more Yiddish and then Jack's voice came through with a great deal of emphasis. "Of course I'm going to stay in school," he said. "Why wouldn't I?"

Those were the last words Lena understood or could decipher. She had to pay attention to Nan, who was peering at her, but she wished it was time for Jack to take her home. It was a long ride back to Brooklyn on the subway. Would she admit she overheard his conversation with his mother? And would she ask him why he used the words "marry me"? Was his full sentence "I'm not going to ask her to marry me"? With every cell in her body she hoped that was not the case. He had assured his mother he would stay in school, but they could marry without him leaving. Getting his degree meant a great deal to Jack. She knew that and besides, Lena planned to stay in school. It would be the same as it was now. They would work together and go to school, except at night, when they came home from their classes, they would go to sleep in the same bed with their arms around each other. Lena felt all dreamy thinking about that and imagined waking up each morning wrapped in his embrace. Oh, how she prayed the words he spoke before saying marry me all led to a beautiful future.

Jack paid the two nickels, one for himself and one for Lena, and they stepped into the subway car. With few passengers traveling at night, they were able to find seats rather than having to stand holding on to the overhead metal straps like she did everyday going home from work. Lena sat erect on the yellow seat, her feet planted on the floor.

"Lena." Jack took her gloved hands in his. "Sweet Lena." He kissed the ivory lace that covered her palms, one kiss on each. Lena moved a bit closer and waited for him to say something more. Jack only stared out the windows on the opposite side of the car. The rattle of the wheels on the IRT—the clinking and clacking as it travelled underneath the city—were the only sounds she heard. One passenger was reading the *Times*, another looked like he was dozing. The woman seated a few seats down the row on the opposite side fussed with the feather in her hat, and the man beside her fidgeted with his gloves. Lena wondered if they'd had a row. She and Jack never fought. He was the most amenable man she had ever met, except for the time outside the automat when he was so cross with Teckla for visiting her mother all those years ago and keeping it a secret. But, Lena thought, he was protecting his mother and he never did raise his voice. Even that night, when she overheard him from the kitchen, he spoke emphatically. He never raised his voice to his mother when she probably would have if the circumstances were turned. And she was so anxious to know in what context he had said those two words to his mother. Her stomach wouldn't stop churning.

Lena looked at the man she loved. He had a serious expression on his face, like he was trying to figure out a difficult problem. She had to lift her chin to see his eyes. The felt cloche she wore came down to her brow and made viewing anything at eye level difficult. "Are you all right?" she asked.

Jack nodded and turned to her with a slight smile. "I was thinking about the conversation I had with my mother tonight," he said.

Lena's heart raced, yet all she said was, "Oh." She pressed her lips together then turned her eyes to the woman with the feather in her hat as if all was natural, as if she was just looking around the subway car and her heart wasn't about to jump out of her chest.

"Lena," Jack said. She waited for him to find the words he seemed to be looking for. "This isn't where I wanted to say this, but I can't hold it back." Lena turned toward him and lifted her chin. She could barely breathe.

"Tonight," he began, "I told my mother I was going to ask you to marry me." Lena looked up. Their eyes locked. She felt her face light up as bright as the sun in July. "Is that a yes? You'll marry me?" Jack asked.

So excited, thrilled, words wouldn't form. All she did was nod, and nod, and keep nodding until finally she answered, "Yes, yes. Absolutely, yes."

Jack wrapped his arms around her and planted a big kiss on her lips, not caring a whit for the other passengers. "When we're alone, I'll get down on a knee and do this properly," he said. "I promise. And I promise I will make you the happiest woman alive and never let any harm come to you."

Several days after Jack's marriage proposal, Ida phoned Rebecca. Lena sat at the kitchen table waiting to hear the result of the conversation, hoping Jack's mother would agree to meet with her parents to discuss wedding plans. The luscious aroma of chicken soup perfumed the kitchen, and Lena wished for the two families to blend together again as sweetly as the fresh carrots simmering in the pot.

Ida hung up the telephone and turned to her daughter. "That went well," she said. "Rebecca still sounds cold and distant; however, she's willing to get together for the *kindela*, as she said. As long as it's for the children, she's willing to make peace, just never forget why Rebecca acts the way she does."

Lena remembered all her mother had said about her father firing Karl and the jealousy Rebecca held. At least she didn't hang up, Lena thought. That was a positive sign. Lena had high hopes that the two families would meld into one again and celebrate the engagement without any more arguments.

***

Lena and her parents climbed the steps from the subway. Leaving the dank air behind, they emerged to the fresh scent of spring. As they walked the two blocks to the Roths' apartment, Lena took in her surroundings. There was Molly's Notion Shop then Jake the Tailor. The green grocer was next to the fish market, and at the corner, the delicious aroma of freshly baked bread reminded Lena that, in spite of her nervousness, she was hungry. She looked up at the apartment buildings with their fire escapes and fluttering curtains in open windows and smiled at the women pushing their baby carriages along the street.

Karl opened the door to Harry's knock and the two men stood staring at each other. Harry stepped across the threshold and broke the silence. "It's so wonderful to see you," he said, as he slapped his old friend on the back, as they used to do before a pinochle game cut them apart. Lena was proud of her father for making the first move, being the bigger man.

Karl stammered, blubbering words that made no sense as he returned the back slap, the way men, embarrassed to hug, showed their affection to one another. The scene brought Lena back to her childhood when Karl and Harry were close, like brothers, and her nervous heart slowed. Today was going to be fine. Then Ida came forward and embraced Karl. "Yes, it is good to see you," she said, "and for such a wonderful occasion." Karl squeezed Ida's hand and agreed. It seemed it took the children's engagement to bring the so-called adults to their senses.

Rebecca called from the kitchen. *"Kimme here. Los zein nish in hall."* Karl stepped back and waved them inside. "Of course, of course, come in," he said. "No need to stay in the hall."

Rebecca walked into the living room with an apron around her plump hips and a forced smile planted on her face. Lena took one look at that artificial expression and worried. Would she ruin what seemed to have been a good start? Lena stood in the background, as Ida walked over and hugged her old friend. Rebecca stood stiff, like stone. Thankfully, Jack appeared to ease the tension. He winked at Lena and kissed her on the lips. "Give her time," he whispered. "She'll come around." Then he kissed her mother hello and shook Harry's hand. "Come sit," he said and, with his arm around his future father-in-law's shoulders, led them into the living room. Rebecca turned and walked back into the kitchen without ever acknowledging Lena. It was as if she wasn't even there.

Lena looked around at the tattered furniture while the men took bets on how many home runs Babe Ruth would hit in tomorrow's Yankees game. Her mother was in the kitchen helping Rebecca who had refused Lena's help again. At least this time, she had a reason. "It's your special day," Rebecca told her, in broken English, when Lena offered. "Go sit. No work for the *Kah'-leh,*" she'd said. Lena wanted to hug her when she called her the bride. Unfortunately, Rebecca's tone didn't encourage any showing of warmth. Still, Lena was glad she at least recognized her and what this day was all about. One day soon, she hoped, Rebecca's frigid attitude would melt. Not only did Lena understand the reasons for Rebecca's jealousy, from the torn fabric on the sofa and chairs, she also realized why her future mother-in-law was so concerned about Jack staying in school. With his accountancy degree, he would have opportunities his father never had. Jack would be able to afford the nicer things. A large apartment, maybe on the Grand Concourse, the boulevard in the Bronx that echoed the *Champs-Élysées* in Paris, might not be out of the question. With Lena's teaching license and Jack's degree, they would have enough money to live in one of its stunning buildings, and Rebecca would be puffed up with pride when she told everyone where her Jacky lived.

Rebecca called everyone to the table. "*Kimme here.* Have a glass tea, some cake." Ida and Harry sat on one side of the oak rectangle, Jack and Lena on the other, and his parents on either end. Lena was aware of Rebecca's stare as she picked up a piece of the homemade cinnamon babka with her fork. The crumbs fell onto the table cloth. Lena scooped them up as fast as possible. "Oh, I'm so sorry," she said. "I made a mess."

"Don't worry about it," Jack said as he took her hand in his and gave it a loving kiss. Lena caught the disgust on Rebecca's lemon-sucked face. The realization hit her hard–she was Rebecca's rival, the obstacle for her son's love. Lena was certain Rebecca believed that and understood she had to assure Jack's mother she would never interfere between mother and son. Lena wouldn't put voice to her pledge, positive Rebecca would never admit to another jealousy, but she would demonstrate it in every way possible.

"They'll be married in our shul," Lena heard Rebecca say, which brought the bride back to the conversation going on around her while she dwelled on ways to prove she was not an obstacle. She understood the broken English well enough, even when Rebecca became more emphatic, insisting her whole family lived in the Bronx and basically said "we're not going to schlep all the way to Brooklyn when we have a shul right in the neighborhood."

"Weddings should be where the bride resides, not the groom," Harry said slapping his hand hard on the table. "You can't always get your way, Rebecca."

"Certainly, your shul is bigger, better, fancier." Rebecca threw her chest out and shook it all around. "Always the best for Harry."

"Mama, calm down," Jack said. "Lena and I haven't even discussed the ceremony yet. Don't get so upset."

"Upset? Me? Nah! It's always them. They have to do it their way." She pointed to Karl. "And what about your father? He doesn't count?" She tossed her hand in the air. "Harry just kicks him out, no job, forget the promises . . ."

"Please, let's not get started on that," Ida said with enough emphasis to shake the table. "Think of the children. The wedding."

"Right. The *kinder*," Rebecca mocked. "And they're getting married right here in the Bronx." She pointed an accusatory finger at Ida. "You don't even belong to a shul."

Lena pushed her chair back and stood. "Stop it," she shouted over their bitter voices. Like electricity cut by a storm, they silenced. Lena lowered her tone. "I'm the bride. Doesn't anybody want to ask me what I want? Where I want to get married?" Jack looked at his fiancée and then at all the faces around the table. He stood and put his hands on her shoulders, whether to calm her or force her to sit Lena wasn't sure. What she was positive of was not letting this argument escalate. "It's okay, honey," she said patting his hand. She looked at her parents and future in-laws. "Soon we'll be one family, and I don't want any more fighting. Please. It doesn't matter which borough we get married in, just as long as the four of you stand with Jack and me under the chuppah as loving Jewish parents *do*." She focused her eyes on Rebecca, then her father. "You all once cared about each other, or so I thought. Can't you simply get along now? Forget the past. We have a new beautiful future to look forward to."

Rebecca grumbled what sounded like "yeah, yeah, yeah," Harry nodded his head, and Ida smiled at her eloquent daughter. "And to let you know," Lena continued, "the Bronx is fine with me." She turned toward Rebecca. "I'm sure your shul is lovely, but Jack and I might want a larger venue." Lena knew the synagogue in Jack's neighborhood was tiny and old and separated the men and women by a curtain. She believed there had to be newer, more egalitarian places in the borough. Rebecca's tight jaw softened a bit as Lena continued. "Of course, Mrs. Roth, we'd want you to come see whatever synagogue we're considering."

Rebecca acquiesced and Lena was delighted. She'd made her first move toward a peaceful relationship with Jack's resentful mother, and later, as they stood at the door saying goodbye, a warm flush of love infused her bones. "One day, God willing," Harry said, elbowing Karl with a friendly nudge, "we'll be grandparents together. We'll have a bris maybe." Karl nudged him back, adding, "A bar mitzvah, too, if I should live so long." Lena felt a huge grin fill her face. Yes, she thought, we're going to be fine. They're already planning grandchildren. She crossed her fingers and made a wish. Please, God, no more arguments.

**

Lena stood under the clock in the middle of Penn Station watching hordes of people rushing from the ticketing office to the train platforms, their valises clutched tight. Her own brown leather one with well-worn straps and buckles rested on the floor at her side. Although it only held enough clothes for the weekend, it was heavy. She'd packed a bathing costume, as Jack had suggested, and a dress, mid-calf with a dropped waist, the style all the fashionable women were wearing. It was similar to the yellow one she had on for travel, and her straw hat matched both. A smaller felt hat nestled in the case next to the skirt and blouse she planned to wear on Saturday; and, as the weekend was daring, so were the trousers she thought she'd wear on Sunday. Two pairs of shoes rounded out her ensembles along with a nightgown, a robe, and all the other necessities. The nightgown had taken her the longest to choose. Ultimately, she bought a new one with a matching robe and pink silk slippers in the event she didn't share a room with Izzy's girlfriend, as she had told her mother she would.

When Jack first proposed the weekend, he hadn't said anything about the sleeping arrangements. She was so embarrassed by her naïveté when she told her girlfriend about their little vacation. "Are you kidding me?" Shirley had said. "That girl is sleeping in Izzy's bed, and Jack assumes you're going to sleep with him. You're getting married in a few months. Why wait? Lena felt herself blush, even when she agreed with her. Shirley had been sleeping with her boyfriend for months, and they weren't even engaged. And this was the 1920s; she'd be modern, if those were the actual arrangements.

"Sweetheart, I'm sorry I'm late," Jack said rushing to her side. A kiss on the lips right in the middle of the station made Lena smile. "I was studying for next week's exam." He picked up her suitcase. "Come on, let's go. We're meeting Izzy and Iris on the train."

Izzy's parents had a bungalow in Far Rockaway, and since they weren't going to be at the beach that particular weekend, the two couples were taking advantage of the free rooms. Lena had never been out to the Rockaways, the eleven mile barrier reef at the city's southeastern edge, the only oceanfront community in New York City. Coney Island was the only beach she knew. She also did not know Iris very well. In the six months since Lena first met Izzy, Iris was the third woman she'd seen on his arm, all of them heavily made-up with bright red lipstick and lots of eye makeup, true flappers. She was glad Jack was only Izzy's friend and not his double. Jack was steady, loyal, and a hard worker. Izzy? Well, his parents had the cottage and she was looking forward to the weekend.

Jack slipped his arm around Lena. As the train pulled out of the station he began to hum a familiar tune and Lena snuggled in close. He sang softly so only she could hear. "I'm just wild about Lena and Lena's wild about me. The heavenly blisses of her kisses fill me with ecstasy."

Lena squeezed his hand and he continued. "She's sweet just like sugar candy and just like honey from a bee . . ." Lena joined in with the chorus, changing the names. "Oh, I'm just wild about Jacky and Jacky's wild about me."

"Hey. What are you two lovebirds whispering about?" Izzy asked. Lena and Jack swayed side to side, his thumb sensually stroking her inner thigh, and entertained Izzy with a final chorus. "Oh God," he said. "You two definitely need your own room."

Jack gave Lena a questioning look. As an answer, she snuggled closer to him.

***

Lena's counter was quiet on this early September afternoon so she took the opportunity to go across the aisle to see Jack. He smiled at her and lifted his index finger indicating she wait a moment while he finished with a customer. As the man walked away with his package, Lena asked if they could grab a coffee together after work. The store, with everyone around, was not the place to give him her news, as anxious as she was to tell him. And she had qualms about how he'd react. She wished there was somewhere more private than a coffee shop.

"I've got classes tonight," Jack said

"I know, but please, I really have to talk to you."

"Why?" Jack teased. "Are you having second thoughts?"

Lena thought he looked adorable with his big smile and wide-open eyes. This, though, was too serious a topic to kid about. He'd realize that soon enough, and she was afraid he might not be smiling then. She kept her tone sober to let him know it was important.

"No. Of course not, although it is about the wedding."

Jack's grin switched to a look of concern. "So you've changed your mind," he said. "You want to get married in Brooklyn. Isn't it a little late for that? The wedding's in six weeks."

Already, from his inflection, Lena could tell he was worried about his mother's reaction and that irritated her. Rebecca had been adamant about their getting married in the Bronx. If Jack thought this was about the locale, well then, that was fine. She wasn't going to pursue this conversation on the shopping floor. He would have the rest of the day to consider how to oppose his mother, which he did not like to do, and take his bride's side of the argument. It definitely would be a fight, if the locale was the case. Once she told him what the issue really was, Lena was positive he'd have to deal with his mother's anger anyway, and she hoped he would be up to it. She needed him to be strong since she doubted Rebecca would accept the news of her pregnancy graciously. After all, they weren't married and nice girls were not supposed to do those things–at least that's what Rebecca probably thought. Lena knew otherwise. Not only could women vote now, they could smoke and drink in public, a huge change from only four years ago. They were equal to men, as the suffragettes shouted. Times were changing. Though she didn't know any personally, Lena was sure she wasn't the only good girl walking down the aisle with a baby in her belly. She certainly had not planned on this and wished it were not the case, but this was the situation and there was no way to hide it. Rebecca would have to deal. Or lie, if she so chose. Lena would not.

Thankfully, two women walked up to her counter looking for the salesgirl. "We'll talk later," she told Jack, as she hurried across the floor. "And you'll get to class on time." She hoped that was true. Lena was worried he might not be in the mood to focus on torts and constitutional law. Just as she was distressed, despite how empowered she felt in this new day and age, Lena was sure Jack would be too. She just didn't want him to be angry or resentful. Sure, the life they planned would be different, she thought as she greeted her customers with a fake smile. She was aware of that, but Jack loved her. They would get through this together.

Two hours later, Lena and Jack sat across from one another at a coffee shop on Fulton Street, a few doors from A&S. "Do you have a synagogue in Brooklyn?" Jack asked putting a sugar cube into his cup.

Lena looked down at the table and traced the pattern on the napkin with her fingers. "The problem is not which borough we have the wedding in," she said, rustling her courage up. She lifted her head to look into the eyes of the boy she'd had a crush on since she was eleven years old and dreamed of marrying one day, though she never believed it would actually be possible. Now, these were the eyes of the man she loved, the man she would soon call husband. She prayed he wouldn't be overly upset when she said, "It's that I'm pregnant."

Jack fell back against the booth and his jaw dropped. Relieved the words were finally out, one huge weight lifted from Lena's shoulders. Another still pressed as she waited with trepidation for his reaction. Dissonant sounds surrounded them—the clink of silverware, hushed voices and some louder ones, waitresses' footsteps, and the swoosh of the door as it opened and closed. Around their table it was silent until, finally, Jack said, "Wow, that's not what I expected. Are you sure?"

Lena tensed. Every muscle tightened. Was he doubting her? "Of course," she said, maybe a bit too curtly. She made herself swallow the irritation, not wanting to give him any cause to be angry. So far, he sounded more stunned than anything else, which made her glad. She forced her shoulders to relax and leaned forward to be closer to him. "I waited to tell you until I was. I haven't been to a doctor, but I'm pretty positive I'm two months gone, probably a bit more."

Jack cocked his head in thought. "The Rockaways," he said. "It must have been, if you're calculating correctly." That aggravated her too. She knew how to count. She was the one who'd missed two menstrual cycles. Other than that weekend in June, there were only three more times over the summer when she and Jack had slept together, and they were all in August. If it wasn't for Izzy giving them his apartment, they would never have had any privacy. That was one reason they were excited about having their own place soon. Without any parents in the next bedroom, they could be as frisky and spontaneous as they pleased, and they were both counting down the days. "I thought I was so careful," Jack said.

"I know, sweetheart," Lena said. "We just couldn't keep our hands off each other." She remembered how they had tumbled into bed that night, a little tipsy from the gin Izzy brought, hungry for each other. Originally, Lena was a little timid contemplating the sleeping arrangements for that weekend. Once on the train, cuddled next to Jack, all that bashfulness got tossed aside. It blew down the tracks mixed with the smoke from the locomotive, never to return. It was nineteen twenty-four and she was a modern girl. "Rather than changing where the wedding will be," she said, "we need to change when it will be. I don't want to be showing when I walk down the aisle."

"Damn it, Lena. I didn't want to start our life together saddled with a baby. You need to finish school and get a teaching job. All our dreams . . ." Jack had such a look of despair on his face. It frightened Lena.

"Please, Jack, don't be cross," she pleaded. "We can still do it all, just not right now. I love you. Isn't that what really matters?"

Jack let out a long, deep exhale until there wasn't a shred of breath left in his lungs. "Yes, of course," he said, and Lena suddenly felt as light as the dust floating in the air. She wanted Jack to hold her, to tell her everything would be fine. She sighed as he reached across and caressed her palm. "I love you," he said, his eyes hooded with sincerity and care. "We'll make it work."

The waitress came and asked if they wanted anything else. Without taking their eyes off each other, both shook their heads and she strolled away. Lena hadn't touched her tea and Jack's coffee was growing cold. He pushed the cup away as if it and the conversation were done. Lena thought all was going to be fine now until Jack said, "We'll have to live with my parents. Without you working, we can't afford our own place."

Lena removed her hand from his. She sat back, not liking this idea at all. "Why your parents and not mine?"

"It's easier that way," Jack said, as if it was obvious. What was easier? Lena wondered. Not having to tell your mother we're moving in with mine? She wished he had more backbone when it came to Rebecca. Maybe she should recruit Teckla to convince him again.

"Think of this, sweetheart," he said. "If we want to get our own apartment, then you'll have to work after the baby is born. You don't want to do that—or do you?"

"I wouldn't mind. Why shouldn't a woman be allowed to work, just as a man is?"

"Now you sound just like one of those suffragettes. And who's supposed to take care of the children when their mother is working?"

That made Lena stop. All along, she agreed with the women's movement. Being a college student and a working woman made her confident in the cause; however, Jack did have a point.

"You see the dilemma," Jack said. "Living with my parents will make your working easier. My mother will be able to care for the baby when the time comes, and she'll have my sister to help."

Lena realized it would be hard on her mother to care for the child on her own. At forty-two, Ida barely had the patience and stamina for a baby, especially when she would start walking and then running all over the place. Rebecca was the same age, but she did have Teckla. Still, Lena wasn't ready to agree.

"I've got to talk to my mother about it," she explained to Jack. "If she's willing, I'd rather live with my parents. But we're getting ahead of ourselves. First, we have tell them I'm pregnant."

"No one has to know." Jack was being emphatic. "We'll call the shul and change the date and tell our parents we didn't want to wait any longer."

"No." Lena sat up straight. She mustered all the confidence she could. Jack had to agree with her on this aspect or it would cause all kinds of problems she was afraid to imagine. "I'm going to tell my mother and you have to tell yours. Our families have finally made a truce," she explained, "and if your mother finds out later, on her own, she'll be furious we deceived her." Rebecca already believed the Pearls had deceived Karl about the butcher shop. Lena refused to be the one to invoke her wrath again. "I can't hide my belly from them," she said. "Some women may not show this early, but mine's already a little bump. In another month, it might too late. Please, Jack, tell your mother before she figures it out. I'm telling mine tonight."

***

On her way home, Lena tormented herself wondering how she was going to tell her mother. She never wanted to disappoint Ida and was afraid this unplanned pregnancy would. Lena wouldn't be able to finish school with a baby to take care of, and her mother so much wanted her to get a degree. While sitting on the bus, she thought about living with Rebecca. Would they get along? Would her own mother be jealous?

Jack had agreed she could tell her mother that night. He wouldn't tell his until after the ceremony. "It's just a few more weeks," he said. "I don't want her ruining our wedding day and you know she could." Lena agreed, figuring he needed time to rustle up his courage, and when he kissed her goodbye at the subway station, he said not to worry. "We're in this together, sweetheart, and you are correct–the most important thing is that we love each other and we're getting married."

The apartment was dark and quiet when Lena arrived home. In all her anxiety about telling Jack, she forgot that her parents were out this evening, at a friend's playing cards. Exhausted from her turmoil coupled with her pregnancy, Lena went right to her room, kicked off her shoes, and curled up in bed, still in her work dress. It was dark outside when she woke and her situation tumbled back at her. Pregnant was not how she wanted to start a marriage, and she still hadn't said a word to her mother. With her head buried in the pillow, Lena let the tears flow.

"*Bubeleh*, can I come in?" Ida said as she opened the door a tiny bit. "I heard you crying. Did you and Jack have a fight?"

Lena unfolded herself from the fetal position and sat up, hugging her knees. "Oh, Mama, I've got trouble," she cried.

"What sort of trouble?" Ida sat on the crumpled sheets, her expression filled with love and concern. "Whatever it is, you can tell me."

Lena knew she could always speak to her mother. Even when they disagreed, Ida kept a cool head and tried to understand her daughter's point of view, except for that time when Lena was in junior high and lied about skipping school after a neighbor had said she'd seen Lena on the Coney Island boardwalk during the day. Ida had insisted she always tell the truth. "Especially once you're caught. You only dig yourself in deeper when you lie about it," she'd said, and Lena finally came clean and admitted it was an exciting adventure and promised never to do it again. She hated seeing the displeasure in her mother's eyes. Oh, if only this was as easy a problem as cutting math class. Lena's face crumpled into tears. She might as well get it over with, she thought, and face her mother's reaction, whatever it would be. She took a deep breath and let the words out. "I haven't been unwell in two months."

"No bleeding at all? No spotting?" Lena shook her head. "You're nervous," Ida said, her voice full of compassion. "Oh, sweetheart, that happens sometimes. You're planning a wedding; you're working and going to school . . ."

"No, Mama."

Ida's soft smile wavered at her daughter's serious tone. "*Gottenyu*. You and Jack have been intimate?" Lena shook her head, tiny movements up and down, as she sniffed back tears. "And you're sure?" Again, Lena nodded. Ida pulled her daughter close and wrapped her in her arms. She stroked her daughter's head and the tears subsided.

"The past few days, I've been sick in the morning at work," Lena said, her face comforted against her mama's soft chest. The heavy weight of her secret lifted and floated away. "Then I knew I was pregnant." She pulled herself from her mother's embrace and wiped her wet cheeks. "Are you angry with me?"

"No, sweetheart. I'm just sorry. Some people will think it's terrible and say you had to get married although I know differently. These things happen. It's nothing new." She gave her daughter a loving smile. "It happened in my day too, and to nice girls like you." She placed her palm on Lena's cheek for a moment. The tender touch allayed Lena's anxiety even more. "I'm sorry because I would have liked you and Jack to have time together, alone, to solidify your relationship. Marriage takes a lot of work and as beautiful as it is to be a family, children do create stresses on the couple, no matter how much they love each other." All of a sudden, Ida pulled back. "Have you told Jack?" Her words came fast. "He loves you. You can't keep this from him."

Lena assured her mother she had. "I won't start my marriage with secrets," she said. "As you say, Jack loves me. He's wonderful." She told her mother what Jack had said about not telling Rebecca yet.

"Good idea," Ida said. "She could cause a great deal of trouble, and you don't want that. I don't trust her anymore. Sometimes there's a need for secrets."

"There's another problem, too, Mama." Lena pushed herself back to rest against the mahogany headboard and continued on explaining about having to live with either the Roths or the Pearls.

"As much as I'd love you to live here . . ." Ida said, getting up and walking to the other side of the bed. She climbed in next to her daughter as she used to do when she read her bedtime stories. "I agree with Jack, and not just because of

Teckla helping with the baby. Rebecca will never come here to visit, and she's going to want to see this baby." She patted Lena's tummy. "Even if I lived in the same building as her, she wouldn't step in my door anymore."

"But she used to always come here," Lena reminded her mother, and Ida explained that wasn't true.

"She came for holidays with Karl and everyone. Never by herself, not even when they lived on Rivington Street. Rebecca doesn't leave her neighborhood–hardly ever leaves her own apartment–and she'll make it hard on you. She'll want to see the baby, and you'll have to schlep up there with diapers and bottles carrying the carriage up and down the subway steps."

Lena pictured herself trudging up the steps carrying a huge bag along with a baby and carriage. As much as she hated to admit it, her mother was right. It would be hard. "What about you?" she asked, in all sincerity, concerned Ida would have to make the trip to the Bronx. Lena planned on being home for several months before going back to work, and she certainly would prefer having her mother with her rather than her mother-in-law.

Ida laughed and told Lena it was easier for her, that she was used to subways and didn't mind traveling alone. "Don't worry. I'll see the baby plenty."

Lena knew her mother was perfectly able. She was an American woman, and Rebecca, after almost twenty years, was still an immigrant down to the shoes she wore. Ida had recently bought a pair of Mary Janes in red with a two-inch heel while Rebecca still only wore heavy black oxfords like she had in the old country.

"Are you sure you won't be jealous, Mama? It would be so much easier for Jack to get to work from here," Lena said, realizing another reason they should live in Brooklyn.

"I won't let jealousy interfere," Ida assured her daughter. "I understand the situation and I don't want to cross Rebecca. Maybe it's my guilt."

Lena wondered what her mother meant.

"When Papa fired Karl," Ida explained, "I didn't agree with the way he did it and told him so. 'Business is business,' he said and it was separate from friendship. Unfortunately, Rebecca and Karl didn't see it his way, and when I brought it up, we argued." Ida's eyes glazed over for a moment, and Lena imagined her mother was remembering those trying times. Ida then looked at her daughter and with a slight smile continued. "After a while, I kept quiet. Homemaking was my job, the butcher shops were his. And, sadly, we lost a long-time friendship."

Lena was surprised by her mother's admission. She hadn't realized her father was as stubborn as Rebecca. She also understood how her mother had kept her marriage on an even keel for all these years while she disagreed with her father. She deferred to him, as she wanted Lena to do with Jack. "If you want," Ida said, "talk to Jack again about living here." With her finger pointed in the air, she made her point. "Just remember, Jack is used to making the long trip to work. He's been doing it for several years so that argument won't hold muster." She leaned over and kissed Lena. "It's okay, my *shayna*. We'll all make it work."

***

Three weeks later, Lena looked up at the onion-shaped dome on top of Montefiore Synagogue. The building resembled the shuls of Eastern Europe, which was why Jack's mother agreed to have the wedding in this reformed synagogue, on this crystal clear September afternoon, instead of the *shteeble* in their neighborhood. Harry reached for Lena's gloved hand and, together, father and daughter walked through the main entrance. Ida followed close behind, her treasured cameo pinned to her silk jacket. Lena looked back. Despite the fact of her pregnancy, her mother's face was lit with joy, matching her own elation. She was marrying her childhood crush.

Guests, gathered in the lobby, made their way into the wood paneled chapel. Men, in their striped, three-button suits and starched white dress shirts, all wore hats as was the custom. Some, not ready to give up their summer accessory, wore the straw Panama and others brought out their felt fedoras for the first days of autumn. The women looked lovely in their calf-length dresses, some even a bit more daring, bringing the hem just under the knee, and all without corsets. With bare arms and honey beige or the new rose morn colored stockings, they looked elegant yet comfortable.

Rabbi Katz stood under the chuppah facing the bride and groom with their parents angled on either side. Lena, in her lace and satin gown, held Jack's hand. A matching white hat perched atop her newly trimmed bob, and her soft brunette waves framed her lightly rouged cheeks.

The rabbi recited the betrothal blessings, and Lena and Jack took the traditional sip of sweet red wine. Then Jack took the ring from Izzy, his best-man. With his eyes on Lena, he recited, "Behold, you are betrothed unto me with this ring, according to the laws of Moses and Israel." He placed a plain gold band on the forefinger of his bride's right hand. Lena beamed. At that moment, according to Jewish law, Jack and Lena were fully married. The rabbi then read the *ketubah*, the marriage contract, which had already been signed by two witnesses prior to the ceremony, in its original Aramaic. He handed the beautiful calligraphy to the bride. The *Sheva Brachot*, the seven blessings, were recited over the second cup of wine, and Lena, to make Jack's mother happy, circled her groom as the rabbi recited each one, the way it was done in the old country. To mark the conclusion of the ceremony, the rabbi placed a glass on the floor and with shouts of mazel tov filling the chapel, Jack smashed it with his foot, drew Lena toward him, and kissed her ruby lips.

Yichud is a custom all Jewish brides and grooms appreciate. In a private room they have a few moments alone together without the throng of well-wishers kissing their cheeks, shaking their hands, and wishing them another mazel tov. Jack closed the door to the *yichud* room and pulled Lena close. "Now let's have a real kiss, Mrs. Roth," he said. They reached for each other with a fierce hunger, the intoxicating fragrance of Chanel No. 5 causing a stir in his loins, and lingered with their lips tight together, tasting the sweetness of their love, clasped in their shared dream. After a few delicious moments, Jack pulled back and smiled at his bride. He placed his hand on her belly, bent down and gave it a kiss, then stood and cupped her brightly lit face in the palm of his hands. "My darling, in six months we'll be a real family." Those words made Lena love him even more. All would be wonderful for the new Mr. and Mrs. Roth, she was sure.

A buffet lunch, catered by J. Russ National Appetizing Store of East Houston Street, was laid out in the social hall. Lena and Jack joined their guests to enjoy the silkiest smoked fish the five boroughs had to offer. Glistening whitefish, salt-cured lox, and smoky sable along with fresh herring fillets and pickles cured in a barrel filled their plates, and there was plenty of schnapps to drink for those who wanted to celebrate with more than soda water. Two hours later, when the doors closed behind the last of the guests, Lena turned to Jack and asked him when he was going to tell his mother about her pregnancy. She looked at her belly, thankfully still a tiny bump. "It may not be obvious now," she said, "but it will be soon and your mother is going to be furious if she finds out that way."

Jack looked hesitant. "Sweetheart," he said. "I can't promise she won't be now. Let's wait a little longer. Today's been so perfect . . ."

Lena assumed a brave stance, tall and straight. In the most lion-hearted tone she could muster she told him he had to tell Rebecca now. "I don't want to live in fear of her finding out on her own. And if she is furious, well, I can handle it." Nan approached and they both stopped talking.

Lena put a smile on her face and took Nan's hand, and the bride and flower girl trotted off to the bridal room to retrieve the nosegay Nan had carried during the ceremony. As they walked back down the corridor toward the social hall, ugly guttural sounds only Rebecca could make resounded off the walls. "*Schvanger? Vat vil everyone tink?*" Lena hoped Nan didn't know that *schvanger* meant pregnant. She wasn't ready to explain herself to a child. She told her to wait right there and hurried off to join Jack. More Yiddish words pierced the air. "*Zoy'neh. Kurva.*" Hurt mixed with fury and resentment boiled up inside her. Like hot magma, she was ready to erupt.

Ida ran up and caught Lena just before she reached the door to the social hall. "What's going on?" she asked, breathless. "Did Jack just tell her?"

"Yes, and I'm going to give her a piece of my mind. How dare she call me a whore?!"

"Wait," Ida said, placing a hand on her daughter's shoulder. She glanced around. No one was in sight. "You can't deal with Rebecca when she's like this. I know. I've been there." Lena shook her head no. "I'd like to scream at her myself–shake some sense into her," Ida said, "but she's out of control. Anything you say now will make it worse. Let Jack handle his mother."

Jack's voice, full of fury, came through, cutting off his mother's tirade. "Be quiet, Mama. Don't you **ever** call my wife those names. Never forget, she is *my* wife and she's having *my* baby . . ."

Lena stood still listening to her husband defend her honor. Yes, she thought, he's standing up to his mother. I knew he could do it. No matter what Rebecca might ever try, she will not come between us. Jack is stronger than that. We are strong together.

***

Lena had an easy pregnancy. Morning sickness didn't last long, and she loved waking up each day with Jack at her side kissing her growing belly, saying she was beautiful, even if they were in a bedroom next to her in-laws. She constantly reminded herself of her mother's words the morning after they spoke about her living with Jack's parents. "Let's not make waves," Ida had said. "Papa and I will visit, and when the baby gets older and easier to travel with, you'll come to us. I don't want to cause you any trouble."

Until December, when Lena was in her sixth month and had to give up her job at Abraham and Strauss, she and Jack took the hour-long subway ride together to downtown Brooklyn every morning. She wasn't thrilled when she had to go home to the Bronx by herself on the nights when Jack had school. Lena was allowed to help in the kitchen now, although the sting from her mother-in-law's slandering words after the wedding remained, and she was never allowed to cook dinner for her husband on the nights he was home, which annoyed her. The kitchen was Rebecca's domain.

"Put your feet up today, Mama," Lena told Rebecca one chilly Sunday morning a month after she moved into Jack's childhood home as the second Mrs. Roth. The endearing word for mother stuck in her throat. Even so, she purposely used it. "I'd like to make dinner for all of us. You shouldn't always have to do it."

"You know how to cook?"

"Of course I do. I'd like to make my mother's special beef stew."

Rebecca threw her hand in the air. "*Ech*. It was never as good as mine."

Lena bristled and tried again, in a sweet voice. "What about a meat loaf? Or anything else you might like."

Lena tried hard to win her over, to no avail. Rebecca remained cold. Jack was the only person who was afforded the warm side of her personality. And then in April, Sarah was born and Rebecca's warmth overflowed. She became a doting grandmother. Too much so for Lena's taste.

"Jack, please tell your mother I am perfectly able to bathe my own baby," she told him one day when he got home from work. "She either hovers over me telling me what I'm doing wrong or pushes me away and insists on doing it herself. I'd argue, but I don't want to upset Sarah."

"She wants to help, sweetheart. Let her."

"No, she wants to take over. She tells me to take a nap."

"And that's not a good thing? You need the sleep."

Lena was disgusted. Certainly she was tired. What new mother wasn't? Still, she refused to be shoved aside. Didn't he understand that was exactly what his mother was doing? "No," she said. "I'm the mother, not Rebecca. I will take care of my own daughter."

The tenuous relationship between Lena and Rebecca trod on more thin ground with the once-a-week visits by the Pearls. When she first came home from the hospital with her newborn, Lena wanted her mother to act as baby nurse, but she lived in Rebecca's apartment. It was clear to her that would never work. Two grandmothers vying for their granddaughter would only cause problems. Instead, Ida and Harry began their regular Sunday visits to the Roths. As Ida had said, it was easier for them to travel the subways to see their granddaughter than for Lena and Jack to pack up a newborn baby and go to them.

On a late spring morning, before her parents arrived, Lena was in her bedroom changing Sarah's wet diaper. Teckla and Rebecca were preparing blintzes. The thin pancakes, rolled with sugar and farmer cheese, sizzled on the stove, filling the apartment with their sweet scent. Through the open doorway, she heard her sister-in-law's voice.

"You see Sarah all the time," Teckla said. "Why don't you let Ida hold the baby today? They schlep all the way up from Brooklyn. It's the least you can do."

Lena was so glad Teckla brought up the subject. She and Jack had noticed how Rebecca only let Ida hold the baby when she was serving or cleaning up. Even during the meal, Rebecca kept the baby on her lap. It took an iron will for Lena not to scream at her mother-in-law, grab her daughter, and put her in Ida's arms. And Jack refused to address the issue. Other than defending Lena after the wedding when Rebecca called her those awful names, Jack avoided confronting his mother, and it irritated Lena. She wanted him to stand up for her. Whenever she mentioned this particular issue, Jack said, "Your mother gets to hold Sarah sometimes. She seems fine." Lena knew differently, and now that even Teckla had noticed it, she decided it was time to put a stop to her mother-in-law's selfish behavior.

Later, while seated at the table, Rebecca wrapped her arm around Sarah, pushing the infant's head into her chest as she maneuvered her knife and fork, cutting into the blintz. The baby wailed and Lena jumped up. "Give her to me," she said, reaching out her arms for her daughter. Then, as usual, she tempered her tone and told Rebecca to eat. "Enjoy the blintzes, they're delicious." Lena constantly bit her tongue, holding back how she really felt for Jack's sake. She knew that once Jack got his degree and found a good accounting job, they would move out. Maybe in a year–two at the most was their hope. So she promised herself she would not complain and she took her own mother's lead, swallowing her feelings and her own desires to keep peace in the family. Now it was time to stop that. Lena walked around the apartment to quiet the baby, then came back to the table, handed her daughter to Ida, and sat back down to finish her lunch.

Later that day when they were squirreled away in their own bedroom with Jack seated on the rocking chair putting Sarah to sleep, Lena said what had been on her mind all afternoon. She used her most assured voice to avoid an argument from her husband, who always seemed to protect his mother.

"From now on sweetheart, I think it's best if we visit my parents in their home on Sundays." Jack gave her a skeptical look, and Lena felt the cords twang in the back of her neck. "Your mother has Sarah all the time. My mother needs to have her granddaughter alone so she can dote on her all she wants with no interference. I don't think I'm asking for much."

"You can visit them anytime you want. You've got all day. You're not working yet."

Lena took a deep breath to calm herself. Sure, she was planning on going back to work when Sarah was three months old. The department store had said they would take her back. That wasn't the issue, though. "I know I can go whenever I want, and I probably will for now," she said, feeling her jaw clench. "But I'd like us to go together too. Once I'm back at work, we'll only have Sundays so I'd like to start that now. It's best this way. Your mother will have to get used to one day a week without Sarah."

Jack pinched his brow. Realizing he had not liked her words, Lena forced her chin to relax. "Please, don't get me wrong, honey. I want Sarah to be with both her grandmas. I want her to have that unconditional love that only a grandmother can give. It's a beautiful bond. I wish I'd had it. Sarah's fortunate to have both her grandmothers."

Family bonds meant a great deal to Lena. Being an only child was fine; however, she wanted her daughter to have siblings one day, to have a relationship as close as her daddy's with his sister. She and Jack dreamed of the day– "not too far in the future," they'd say with fingers crossed– when they'd be able to afford their own place. They would have another child then, maybe even two. Lena was aware of the attachment between Jack and his sister from the time at the automat when Jack told Teckla about his relationship with her before mentioning it to his parents. It was Teckla who had influenced him to bring them together, probably sooner than he would have otherwise. Lena adored her sister-in-law. As a little girl, she was in awe of Teckla, especially when Nan was born. Lena was eleven at the time and, watching Teckla feed the baby, she dreamed of the day when she'd be a mommy too. And now Teckla was more than a sister-in-law; she had become Lena's big sister–the one she could confide in.

One late winter afternoon, on her day off, Lena took Sarah up to Teckla's apartment, as she often did. This time, not wanting Rebecca to show up unannounced again, which annoyed the two women to no end, Lena told her in-laws she was going to a friend's. There was important information she wanted to share with her sister-in-law and did not want Rebecca around.

"Another baby! That's wonderful," Teckla said. Her smile quickly faded and she scooted to the edge of the sofa. "You are happy about it, aren't you? I'm sorry. I know this is a delicate subject. Maybe I'm overstepping my bounds."

Lena kissed her daughter's pudgy hand, then stood up from the floor where she'd been playing with her and took a seat on the sofa next to Teckla. "You are not overstepping your bounds," she said. "Don't even think that. It's a logical question, probably a lot of people will wonder why so soon and will Jack have to quit school and how will we manage. Although from you, it's perfectly all right."

Teckla let out a little laugh. "You mean my mother, don't you?"

Lena nodded. "But Jack and I don't care. Rebecca can think what she wants. I'm not her favorite person anyway, and yes, we are happy about the baby. Sure, it's a surprise, though a lovely one. And yes, Jack will have to leave school and get a second job, which will kill your mother, and we'll still be in their apartment. With two babies, I definitely won't be able to work. One is hard enough for your mother to take care of."

Nan dropped the rattle she'd been shaking for her baby cousin and ran over to Lena. She threw her arms around her aunt's thickened waist. "I'm so excited," she said. "When will it be born? Oh, I hope it's another girl."

Lena laughed and kissed her head. "Slow down, Nan. It's a long way off, six more months. I'm not due until September, but I am going to need your help when the baby is born. Will you do that, even if it's a boy?"

Nan was only too happy to help Lena. She adored her and baby Sarah, but just as Lena had heard Rebecca's hateful words after the wedding when she found out Lena was two months pregnant, Nan had heard them too. She released her grasp on Lena's expanding waist and stood up straight and tall with an air of authority well past her twelve years. "Are you going to tell Grandmother today?" she asked. "I'll come downstairs with you. That way, she might not yell too much."

Lena met Teckla's eye and the apologetic look on her face. She listened as Teckla tried to assure her daughter that Grandmother Rebecca would be happy with the new addition to the family. Lena wasn't so sure about that. Her dreams for her precious son would be shattered. And would she call her a *Zoy'neh* again?

Teckla turned her attention to Lena. "She may not show it," she said, "but my mother likes you, and you know she adores Sarah. You saw the change in her, from the moment she held the baby in her hands nothing else mattered. Don't worry. She'll be fine."

Rebecca's metamorphosis had been remarkable. Although she was possessive, she no longer called Lena ugly names or mentioned the disgrace she had brought on the family, though no one but Rebecca thought it had been a *shanda*. The baby was all that mattered to her. Rebecca bounced her on her lap and kissed her fingers and toes. She fed her and changed her, sang Yiddish lullabies and called her *ketzela*, an endearing pet name that she never used with Nan. Lena doubted that she had called her own daughter *ketzela* when she was a little girl. There wasn't a sweet bone in Rebecca's body. Yet with Sarah, she was different. She was Jack's child and anything of Jack's was perfect, except for his wife. This baby snuggled in Lena's womb was also Jack's child, Lena thought, but she could not quiet her anxiety. At some point, she was sure, Rebecca's true personality would blast forth, and Lena was afraid she would be the recipient again, especially when Rebecca learned her son was going to quit school. After all, it was Lena's fault. That's what Rebecca would say.

Lena bent down and lifted Sarah to her lap. She kissed the baby's tiny fingers and stared at the large area rug under her feet. Rebecca's slanderous accusations at the wedding still reverberated, as if spelled out in the blue and pink roses bordering the gold wool. Lena looked up and saw the words captured in the dust particles swarming around the room, caught in the sunlight streaming from the window, barely noticeable as they settled on table tops and bookshelves, lamp shades and drapes. Lena was frightened. She did not trust Rebecca's new persona.

***

Lena woke to a gush of warm water. "Jack, wake up." She shook her husband's shoulder. "My water just broke. It's time."

He shot out of bed. They dressed, reminding each other to keep quiet, not to wake Sarah who was sleeping in her crib against the opposite wall with her little tushy up in the air. After watching his wife breathe through two contractions, fifteen minutes apart, a nervous Jack called a cab, then banged on his parents' door to let them know; and then they were off to the hospital to have their baby.

The moment they walked in the door Jack shouted, "My wife's having a baby." He was already pacing the floor and they were only at the admission desk. "Go home, sweetheart. Do what the nurse says," Lena told him from the wheelchair. She felt safe with Jack and would have loved having him stay with her, though that wasn't done. And waiting in the lounge, traipsing back and forth with other expectant fathers, was just ridiculous. Labor could take hours. "I'll be fine," she said. "Just like with Sarah–wait at your mother's, and the hospital will call you when the baby's born."

Reluctantly, Jack kissed his wife goodbye and watched an aide wheel her through the double doors to the room where their baby would be born—a place fathers were not allowed.

Lena was given a bed with crisp white sheets and told to relax while a nurse listened to her heart and took her pulse. Her compassionate eyes and the gentleness of her touch made Lena feel safe. The pale green room smelled of ammonia, letting her know it was freshly cleaned. Even the nurse in her starched uniform looked as if she had just stepped out of the shower. The doctor walked in as she was taking Lena's blood pressure.

"I don't feel well," Lena told them. "My head hurts."

"How's the pressure?" he asked the nurse.

"One fifty over ninety."

"Is that bad?" Lena asked.

"No, honey, just a bit high. You'll be fine." Lena held her head in her hands moaning, then doubled over as a strong contraction hit. "Breathe," both medical professionals said at once. Lena groaned, trying her hardest to do as they said, then finally, as it subsided, she lay back against the soft pillow and the nurse wiped her brow. "I'm going to put you into twilight sleep," the doctor explained, "and you won't remember a thing. When you wake up, you'll have a beautiful bouncing baby."

Despite the risk of hemorrhage, which Jack had read something about in a newspaper article, Lena gratefully accepted the injection of morphine combined with the amnesiac scopolamine that so many women of the day were using during childbirth. Jack wasn't sure she should take it again. Lena had tossed his concerns aside. She came through Sarah's delivery with a healthy baby and no memory of pain, and she wanted the same outcome with this one. She also wanted her head to stop pounding.

Lena screamed from the pain as her contractions got stronger and closer together. It felt like someone was pummeling her brain. She thrashed around and the nurse held her arms down. "Shh. Shh. It'll be over soon," she told Lena. There were other voices in the room, though she couldn't see anyone. It was as if she was asleep and awake at the same time. "It's a good thing she won't remember this," she heard someone say. Sometime later–she had no idea how long–Lena felt a big ball push through her legs and a hot, burning sensation. She heard a woman's voice say, "The head's out." Then another warm gush, like the one earlier when her water broke, poured out of her and she sensed her body lifting, as if it was floating above and she was looking down at herself lying in the bed. She heard frantic voices. Someone said "We're going to lose her." There was a great deal of red on those clean white sheets. It was a mess and had a pungent odor. She saw an index finger on the neck of the Lena lying in the bed and heard a deep voice say, "Stay with me, Lena. Come on, breathe." People were moving every which way under her. Hovering above the confusion, she watched them scurry. Everyone seemed to be rushing around, yet she was peaceful. One person stood by the feet of the Lena in bed, one at her chest, and she told herself to listen to them, to breathe. That wasn't a problem. Her breaths were soft and slow. Shallow. Then all the voices stopped, and she felt herself float away.

***

Jack paced the floors of the apartment. "*Ess*, Jacky," Rebecca said, telling him to eat. Eleven-month-old Sarah napped in the baby buggy, having just finished her noon-time bottle, and Teckla, who'd come to keep her brother company, was seated with Rebecca at the table. Nan was in school, and Karl, as usual, had gone off to his club. "She'll have the baby. You'll tell me later," he'd said when his wife complained that he was leaving.

"It's been six hours," Jack said looking at his watch for the umpteenth time."

"Stop worrying," Teckla said. "Babies take a long time. I was in labor for ten . . ." The ringing phone cut her off. Jack ran to the kitchen and grabbed the receiver off the wall. Everyone hurried from the table and gathered around him, not a word uttered as they strained to hear the quiet voice on the other end of the line. Jack kept the phone tight to his ear. His eyes opened wider and wider as he listened, mute, until a scream rose from the deep depths of his gut. "No!" he cried and crumpled to the floor. Teckla caught the phone before it fell and told the doctor who she was and asked him to please tell her what had happened. "My brother can't speak now."

From the floor, with her hysterical son gathered in her arms, Rebecca looked up at Teckla. "The baby? *Toyd?*" Teckla listened to the doctor and turned back to her mother. She shook her head no. "So, *vat* happened?" Teckla placed the receiver on the hook and stood staring into space, not saying a word. "*Vat?*" Rebecca said again, not understanding why her son had collapsed in hysterics. Teckla's words confirmed what she feared. "Not the baby. It's Lena. She died." Then Teckla bent over and cried.

Rebecca glanced at an inconsolable Jack, whose tears poured like enormous globules, then back up at her daughter. Teckla would gather herself together, she was sure. It was Jack who needed her now. Rebecca rocked him like a baby as he blubbered Lena's name crying "no, no, no." Mucus filled his nostrils and drenched his lips. With the handkerchief from her pocket, Rebecca cleaned him up as she used to when he was a little boy.

A few minutes later, Teckla wiped her eyes and bent down next to her brother. "Get Papa's schnapps. Pour him a big shot," Rebecca told her daughter. "It's under the sink." Rebecca got Jack to sit up enough to sip the liquor. "Come on, Jacky," she said when he pushed the glass away. "Drink it all."

"No, Mama," he said. "I have to go to the hospital. I have to see her." Jack jumped up and raced to the door. "You can't stop me," he yelled and ran into the hall. He was pounding on the elevator button. Rebecca and Teckla reached him before it arrived.

"Come on, Jack," Teckla said. "This is no way to go to the hospital. Calm down. Let's get our coats and we'll go together."

"Not now," Rebecca yelled. Standing in front of the elevator, she assured Jack that he would see Lena after his sister took care of all the details. She looked at her daughter for confirmation and Teckla nodded okay. "You're in no condition," Rebecca told her son, and he fell to the floor again, bent over himself, and bawled.

Not wanting the neighbors to see, Rebecca pleaded with Jack to get up and go back inside. He rubbed his hands all over his face and head, caught his breath and then stood up, letting his mother lead him to bed–the one he'd slept in as a child and all through the years before he shared one with his wife. He gulped the alcohol she offered, then curled up in a fetal position. Rebecca kept repeating, "*Shluf mein kind*," as she stroked the blanket covering her bereft son. Her tender touch followed him as the alcohol did its job putting him to sleep, allowing Rebecca to put her plan into action, the one she'd concocted while she rocked Jack back and forth on the kitchen floor and watched him crumble in the corridor. This was how it had to be.

She closed the door behind her and found Teckla sitting on the club chair in the living room wiping her eyes. "You said the baby lived?" Rebecca asked her daughter. Teckla nodded yes, and Rebecca tightened her jaw and shook her head hard from side to side. With her brows knitted together, Teckla gave her mother a questioning look.

"No," Rebecca said. "The baby died."

"What do you mean? The doctor said she's fine."

"No. We must tell Jacky the baby died. He can't know."

Teckla argued but Rebecca insisted. "Did you see him? He was crazy. He couldn't even stand up. He didn't know what he was saying or what he was doing. If he sees that baby, a girl you say, he'll collapse completely. He'll become a *meshuganah*. Every time he'll look at her, he'll think of Lena. No, he must not know the baby lived."

"He's not going to go crazy, Mama. Give him time. He just found out his wife died. *Oy gevalt!* How could you do this?" Teckla shook her hands in the air – as if that would make her mother see how wrong she was. "This is terrible," she cried. "What happens to the baby? We just leave her at the hospital?"

"Tell Ida to take her. I have to help Jacky now. I can't have two babies to feed."

Teckla pleaded with her mother. She offered to help with the girls but Rebecca was adamant. "No. We do as I say."

"Well, let's see how Ida takes to your idea," Teckla said and went off to call Lena's parents, a call she never dreamt she'd have to make.

As per Jewish law, which Rebecca insisted they honor, Lena was buried the next day. Dark clouds threatened rain, yet the gravesite was filled with mourners. Rebecca looked around, surprised by the number of people who came to say goodbye to Lena. Jack, who could barely stand, was between his parents. They held tight to his elbows, keeping him erect while the prayers were said, but when he held the shovel in his hands preparing to toss the first shovelful of soil over the casket, Jack dropped to the ground and howled reaching for his wife in the ground below. Karl grabbed his son before he jumped in and joined Lena. Harry, who had stood stoic in his sorrow throughout the service, helped Karl drag Jack away. Teckla's husband hurried over and stayed by his brother-in-law's side, allowing both fathers to go back and join the rest of the mourners covering the plain pine box with earth. After the service was over and everyone dispersed, Ida and Harry hugged Jack then pulled Rebecca to the side.

"*Gey avek*," Rebecca said. "Leave me be."

"No. We will not go away," Harry said with authority. He looked over to where his son-in-law had been standing. "Jack can't hear me now. He's already at the car, so listen closely Rebecca. I do not like your idea. If it's money, Ida and I will gladly help support the two girls, but they should be kept together. Jack should know his daughter is alive."

"Oh, the *gonif.* I spit on your money." She let off with a slew of Yiddish terms all bringing up the fact that they were fancy-schmancy people who didn't mind kicking her Karl in the gutter when they took the butcher shop from him.

"How dare you talk to us this way!" Ida said, coming to her husband's defense. "We just lost our daughter. Jack is distraught, sure. You don't think we are?" She suggested they give the situation some time. "We'll take the baby home from the hospital, and when Jack is ready we'll bring her to him. That's how it should be."

"*Nein, nein*," Rebecca growled. She pushed her hands as if to shove them away and spat on the ground.

Harry took his wife's hand. "Come," he said. "I don't even want this woman near the baby. If it wasn't for Jack, I'd take Sarah too." He looked over at the woman who was once a good friend. "Just don't ever come crawling to see this new granddaughter. She's not yours anymore."

CHAPTER 19

Eighty-four Years Later

"I need to know about my grandmother Lena's death," I told Nan who was sitting across from me. It was a sunny summer day, just a week after my mother's funeral. Rather than a local restaurant as I had suggested, we were having lunch in the dining room at Elmwood on the Hudson, the independent senior living complex where she lived. Nan insisted, having no idea why I would take her out and have to pay for her lunch when she gets one meal a day free. I didn't care where we ate, as long as I got the truth about Kate and my mother.

China and silverware clinked in the background. With my elbows on the table, I leaned forward and looked her directly in the eye waiting for her to say something. Nan squinted giving me a skeptical look. Did she honestly have no idea why I was asking? I then told her about my genealogy search. I watched her eyes closely, and she seemed sincerely interested. There was nothing cagey about her look, nothing to make me feel that she was holding back on me. When I finished my discourse, I told her I'd discovered some disturbing facts pertaining to Lena. "Mainly about the baby she had."

"Her whole death was disturbing," Nan said. "I loved my Aunt Lena and was devastated when she died. It destroyed Uncle Jack."

"And what about the baby?" I was not going to let her sidestep me on this.

"There was no baby. It was awful. Lena died in childbirth and the baby died too."

Nan looked so innocent that I was stunned. Did she really not know the baby had lived or was she perpetuating a lie? I gathered my thoughts and told her of my discovery going back to how I found Kate with the cameo and the painting. She stared at me, her eyes growing wider and wider with each sentence I uttered. When I finished, she sat back, shaking her head. She pushed her plate away with such force I thought it would fly off the table. I couldn't eat a bite either. This unsettling story was enough to digest.

"Let's walk," Nan said and stood up, her hands shaking. "I need some fresh air."

Nan mumbled questions to herself as we left the dining room. I threw a few dollars on the table to cover my cost and followed her out. We walked along the brick path bordered by freshly planted summer flowers, the vanilla scent of heliotrope in the air, while Nan posed questions to which neither of us had answers: "Why did they say the baby died? Did my mother know?" I was sure she meant Teckla, not *my* mother who certainly never did. No one ever thought to tell her she had a sister? She definitely would have mentioned that to me at some point in my life. I couldn't help being sarcastic. This whole thing made my stomach turn. I was crazy with impatience, wanting answers. Nan kept walking and tossing out more questions as if she was cross-examining her dead relatives. She played judge and jury with her declaration. "It had to have been Grandmother Rebecca's idea. No one else had a mean streak like her."

We sat on red-painted Adirondack chairs under the copper beech tree. Its bounteous, leaf-filled branches created an umbrella effect, but this story was not going to be shaded anymore if I could help it. Nan asked again what I knew about Kate, and I told her everything I had learned. "So she was in Brooklyn all that time," she said making a statement, confirming the fact for herself. "This is so hard to fathom, Carolyn. I never imagined our family had secrets–at least none as big as this. The baby actually lived?" Her face contorted. If she'd been in physical pain, it couldn't have shown more. "I'm just sick over it," she said and buried her face in her hands.

"Kate has to know," I said.

Nan looked up at me, then at the blue sky. She seemed to chew on that thought for a moment. "No," she said, our eyes meeting again. "Don't tell Kate."

"What do you mean? Of course I'm going to. She'll be thrilled to find out there's some family she never knew of." As the words left my lips, I absolutely believed them, and then I remembered what Kate had said–that no one from her father's family ever contacted her. They'd moved away and had never even sent a birthday card. But I was from her mother's side. She would accept me.

"Carolyn, stop. Consider this. What good would it do now?"

"She'd know she had a sister. Wouldn't you want to know that? I sure would." My voice got louder with each word.

"Honestly, I don't know. Especially if I couldn't have a relationship with her."

Nan had a point. I thought about that for a moment and then said, "She'll have me. Her niece." I was heartsick that my mother would never know her sister, that her grandmother had perpetrated a disgusting lie. I agreed with

Nan that Rebecca had to be the guilty party. Who else would have come up with such a devious plan? Unfortunately, we'd never know if Teckla was in on it or anyone else. What did that matter anyhow? I had to believe Kate would be happy to find out we were related. I was all she had from her beloved grandmother Ida's side of the family. I would tell her stories about my mother, show her pictures. I'd make Sarah come alive for her sister, and I told that to Nan.

"That's all very nice, but you have to think about Kate. I can't imagine what I'd feel like if I learned my family had lied to me all my life. You say she has wonderful memories of her grandmother, unlike me. She must have loved her. And don't forget, Kate's not young anymore. You don't know everything about her and how she'd take this news. It's turning me inside out; imagine what it could do to her."

Kate was strong. I was sure she'd be able to handle the shock. I had to be. Not only was I the one person left from Ida's side of the family for Kate, she was the only one for me. Basically, she was the only family I had from both my parents' sides, aside from this ninety-five-year-old woman in front of me who I might have lunch with once in a while and nothing more. As to her daughter, well, she had dissed me. It was obvious she didn't want to be part of our family. Even when she was younger, after Nan had moved to Guam, she ignored us. I had to tell Kate she was my aunt. Deep in my bones, I believed she'd be happy with the news.

CHAPTER 20

Eighty-four Years Earlier

"Get up, Jacky." Rebecca stood at the side of her son's bed, shaking his shoulder. "What? You think they're going to hold your job for you? *Mach schnel*," she said telling him to hurry up. It was two weeks after Lena's funeral and she was frustrated. Jack had not gone back to work yet, and they depended on his earnings to help pay the rent.

"I'm going later, Mama. Let me sleep."

Rebecca walked out and closed the door softly, glad that he was going back to work. That was her Jacky, dependable and upstanding, not the man who'd been moping around the apartment all day, crying and sneaking gulps from his father's whiskey stash, or worse, spending hours at the pool hall with all those degenerates. She stuck her chest out with pride at his pulling himself together, and now, with only one baby to feed and one less adult in the apartment, they didn't need Jack to take on a second job. She stopped short with a guilty tightness clamping her chest and leaned against the bedroom door. She had never wanted Lena to die. She just didn't want her marrying Jack. Rebecca didn't want anything to do with the Pearl family anymore. Look at where it had taken them, she thought. Memories flashed through her mind as she stared at the blank white wall in front of her. They'd had happy times with Ida and Harry in the old country. She remembered all the plans they'd made for when they came to America. And then, she grimaced. When the Pearls got here and the money rolled in, they tossed their old friends aside. "Oh, my poor Jacky," she sighed. "Even Lena was poison."

Rebecca shook herself out of the painful reverie and walked down the hall to the kitchen thinking Jack could go back to school now and finish his accountancy degree. "He'll get past this," she mumbled to herself, "and go on with his life. Even find another bride–one that I'll like." She strutted off to prepare breakfast for her son.

Several hours later, the eggs gone cold, Jack emerged from his bedroom in slacks and a shirt. No tie, no jacket, as required for department store salesmen. "I thought you were going to work," Rebecca said. An upsetting mixture of anxiety and confusion coursed through her body.

Jack shook his head. "I can't. It reminds me too much of Lena. Every time I look across the aisle, I expect to see her."

"What are you talking about? Lena stopped working there two years ago. You're *meshuga*."

"Maybe I am a little crazy. I can't help it."

"So instead, you go off and shoot pool and come home stinking of gin. *Oy vey iz mear!*"

It took another week of Jack frequenting the pool hall during the day before he finally went back to A&S. He had taken advantage of the store's policy on bereavement time, and his manager had called to tell him if he didn't come back that week he'd lose his job. Rebecca wasn't making it easy either, constantly reminding Jack that they depended on him. Rent was high and diapers and formula expensive.

Over the next month, his paycheck, though less than it used to be, appeared as regularly as usual. Jack claimed his hours were cut, though Rebecca wasn't so sure. Christmas was approaching, and department stores were usually very busy in November. One night, when he crept into the apartment as silent as a burglar, Rebecca cornered her son.

"It's nine o'clock. Where've you been?" she said, surprising Jack as he slipped off his shoes by the door. He looked at her as if he had no idea who she was. "The store closed at six tonight so don't tell me you were at work."

"It was inventory. Then we went to eat." The stench of tobacco and gin spewed from his mouth. "I don't have to tell you where I am every night."

Rebecca bristled. "It would be nice if you were home sometimes to give your daughter a goodnight kiss," she said, then lowered her head and pressed her lips tightly together. "I'm so disappointed in you, Jacky."

On a snowy Sunday afternoon a few weeks later, Jack sat on the worn-out club chair with twenty-month-old Sarah on his lap, his face buried in her soft brown hair, his tears wetting her little head. His father walked into the living room with a half-empty bottle of booze swinging from his hand.

"Is this your doing?" Karl yelled. "I just got this bottle yesterday. You think it's easy to come by with all this prohibition crap?"

"What are you worried about?" Jack's voice was just as loud and bitter as his father's. "You can get more whenever you want."

"So you think your Papa's a bootlegger or a rum runner."

"No. Mr. Linsky from the deli is. He's a member of your club. He's got a stash in the back room and you know it."

"Sha sha," Rebecca said, coming in from the kitchen, rubbing her floured hands on her apron. "Be quiet. The baby."

"Right. The baby," Karl said. "Always the baby. I can't even talk in my own home." With his faced pinched in anger, he walked out. The sound of kitchen cabinets opening and closing reverberated through the apartment. Karl walked back in with a drink in hand, plopped himself down on the couch, and turned on the radio. The Breanna Jolley and Kyeree Williams talk show played in the background, their voices drowned out by his wife and son's heated conversation.

"What do you mean you're moving to Chicago?" Rebecca said, her voice alternating between anger and shock. Jack rocked back and forth with a whimpering Sarah against his chest. His mother pointed to the baby. "You see, you're upsetting her. She doesn't want you to leave."

"Mama, she's a baby. She doesn't understand what I'm saying. It's you who's scaring her with that tone."

"Me? Nah! And what about your job? You're just going to quit?"

Jack lowered his face and mumbled. "I don't have a job any longer."

Rebecca slumped down on the couch. Her fears had played out. "*Oy gevalt*," she said with a huge sigh. "That damn pool hall."

"Mama," Jack said taking a seat next to her, adjusting Sarah on his lap. "I can't stay around here any longer. Everywhere I go, everything I see reminds me of Lena. And it kills me to see Sarah, knowing she'll never have her mama."

"So you're just going to leave your daughter? Like that," she said, snapping her fingers. "Just pick up and go?"

"You take better care of her than I do, than I could ever do. Please, Mama, try to understand."

"And what about school?"

Jack shook his head and Rebecca's dreams crumbled. "If it hadn't been for Lena, everything would be fine," she said. "But no, you had to go get her pregnant. You're just like your father. You'll never amount to anything. You'll scrounge for every dollar . . ."

"Don't say that!" Jack shouted. "I loved Lena. I still do and always will. That's why I have to get out of here." Sarah cried louder and Jack rocked his daughter, tempering his anger. "I'll get a job, Mama, just not in a department store anymore. No matter where I'd be, I'd picture Lena at the notions counter."

Rebecca's anger switched to misery as the realization hit that she couldn't change Jack's mind. "I understand you hurt," she said. "Time will make it better. I promise it will. Don't leave, Jacky."

"*Les him allein*," Karl growled from his side of the room. "He can't take care of the baby anyway. Always coming home drunk. Never holding her or feeding her. Nothing. He leaves it all up to you. Let him go."

Filled with sadness, Rebecca stood and took Sarah from Jack's arms. Humming a Yiddish lullaby, she carried the baby back into the kitchen and placed her on the floor with a set of measuring cups to play with while Grandmother finished her baking. This is how it had been since Lena's death three months before, and how it would be for years to come. As miserable as Rebecca was at the thought of Jack moving far away, she felt a great deal of satisfaction knowing she was right in her decision. If, as he claimed, Jack saw Lena everywhere he went, so much so that he couldn't even take a job in a department store hundreds of miles away, how could he have ever looked at the baby that caused Lena's death? And she was sure Jack would not stay away long. He was her boy. He wouldn't leave his mama for too long. No, she told herself, once he gets himself together, he'll be back. His room will be waiting.

Three months later, a letter arrived from Chicago. Rebecca recognized the town in the return address from Jack's two previous letters where he'd written he'd finally found a job in the rail yard as a switchman. That made Rebecca upset. Manual labor was not what she'd dreamt of for her son, yet she was happy he'd gotten a job and would now be able to send them some money for Sarah's care, which was stretching their budget. In both letters, Jack told her that he was glad Rebecca was raising his daughter. He knew she'd be loved, which made Rebecca pat her chest. Yes, she thought, as she read them, I do love her, but Sarah needs her papa. Rebecca was waiting for the day Jack would come to his senses and return home. This letter, though, the one clutched in her hand, wasn't in Jack's script, and since Rebecca was not able to read English, she hurried upstairs to Teckla's apartment.

"Read this," she said thrusting the letter at Teckla, who was sitting at the kitchen table with Nan, teaching the almost-two-year-old Sarah her colors. Teckla laid down the red crayon she'd been using and took the paper from her mother. Rebecca stood, shifting her weight from one foot to the other, impatient to hear what was written and why it wasn't in Jack's hand. Teckla read a few words silently then sucked in a loud breath.

"What?" Rebecca said, her voice full of anxiety. "What's it say?"

Teckla stood up, shaking her head from side to side with the letter dangling from her fingers, as if she didn't have the strength to hold it. "Mama, come," she said slowly and led Rebecca away from the girls.

"What is it?" Nan asked as her mother and grandmother walked out of the room. Teckla waved her off saying she'd tell her later, that she should continue coloring with Sarah.

Seated together on the sofa, with the letter in her lap, Teckla held her mother's hands together in hers. "It's not good, Mama" she said, tears filling her eyes. "Jacky died."

Rebecca ripped her hands away. She clasped them to her breasts and swayed back and forth absorbing Teckla's words and wanting to blot them out at the same time. "*Mein* Jacky," she cried, tears pooling her eyes. "How? What happened?"

Teckla began to explain and Rebecca grabbed the letter and shook it. "Read it to me! I need to hear it."

Teckla took the letter back and read the words written in script on the plain white paper.

"Dear Mr. and Mrs. Roth,

"I am filled with sadness as I write these words to you. Your son, Jack, and I worked together in the rail yards these past two months and became friends. He always said if anything happened to him, I should write to you. Unfortunately, that time has come. Jack died on Thursday, March 7th, in his sleep. I'm sorry it has taken me a few days to write this. I was waiting until the police report came back so I'd be able to tell you everything. Sadly, there was a faulty heater in the motel room he was renting, and it was the escaping gas that caused Jack's death. Please accept my deepest condolences . . ."

Rebecca's sobs forced Teckla to stop reading and hold her mother. She shooed Nan and Sarah away when they came in to see what the matter was and again, as with Lena's death, Teckla took charge of all the arrangements. This time it was her mother, Rebecca, who took to her bed.

Jack's body was shipped back to New York, and the Roth family found themselves at the cemetery in Long Island again, burying Jack next to his beloved wife. "Two young people in the prime of their lives, with a beautiful daughter who is too young to remember her parents," the rabbi said in his eulogy, "is sad beyond words." He continued with all the appropriate prayers and Shiva was held, again, at the Roth's apartment. Despite her bereavement, Rebecca found the strength to force herself out of bed each day. She had to take care of Sarah. She never forgot that, at Lena's funeral, the Pearls said that if it wasn't for Jack, they would have also taken Sarah to live with them. Rebecca would never allow that.

On the fifth day of Jack's Shiva, the Roths' living room was filled with neighbors and friends. Conversation flowed around Rebecca who was in the corner of the room, sitting on the low box provided by the funeral parlor, wiping the wetness from her eyes as she'd been constantly doing since learning of Jack's death. Karl's sister sat beside her, the two speaking in Yiddish about Sarah who was playing with Nan in the bedroom.

"So sad she'll never remember her mama or papa," Jack's aunt said. She touched her hand to her heart. "And that poor other baby. I said a *brocha* for her. Tsk tsk tsk. Such a shame she didn't live. You'd have two little ones running around here."

"It's better this way," Rebecca said, then turned at the sound of the door opening. She took one look at the woman who walked in wearing a knee length coat trimmed in fur and shot up from her seat. "*Gey avek*," she yelled. "Get out. You don't come here."

All talking stopped. Everyone looked toward the door to see Ida Pearl standing by herself, her leather handbag at her side clutched tight in her hand.

"Mama, how could you?" Teckla said throwing her mother a look of horror. "I'm so sorry," she told Ida as she stood up. "My mother is just so distraught."

Ida nodded her thanks to Teckla and looked directly at Rebecca. "In spite of all the bad blood between us, I hoped you would allow me to pay my respects. Jack was my son-in-law, after all."

Teckla gave her mother a pleading look, then walked over to Ida who was still focused on Rebecca. "I'm so sorry for your loss," Ida said. "I know what it is to lose a child. I thought . . ."

"It's your child that caused this," Rebecca said, and an audible intake of breath filled the apartment. "If it wasn't for Lena, my Jacky would still be alive."

Nan came running from the bedroom and stopped short hearing her grandmother's poisonous words. She looked from Rebecca to her mother to Ida, then back to Rebecca who screamed at her to stay with the baby. "You can't have Sarah," she told Ida. "Get out."

With an arm around Ida, Teckla led her out the door. "I'm so sorry," she said. "I don't know what to say." The two women continued their conversation as the door closed behind them and Rebecca, shaking with fear and anger, got up from the uncomfortable box and shoved it away. She heard voices buzzing as she went down the hall. Someone said the name Ida, another mentioned Lena's name. Rebecca heard the words old friends and Russia, argument and pinochle. She didn't care that they were talking about her or what she'd done. She stepped into Sarah's room, bent and kissed her little head, then walked into her own bedroom vowing never to let Ida near Sarah. Not ever.

A little while later, Teckla came back into the apartment looking for her mother. She found her sitting on the edge of the bed picking her cuticles, looking at Jack's picture on the night stand, mumbling to it in Yiddish. Teckla sat next to her.

"Your words were cruel, Mama," she said as if she was talking to a child. "Uncalled for. You are not the only one with *tsoriss*. Ida is suffering too, and she only wanted to give you her condolences. Why do you hate her so much? You used to be such good friends."

"She's no friend. Not after what they did to Papa."

"Well, you've got a great deal connecting the two of you, and not only years and history. There are two little girls," she said softly, "and I hate to be blunt, Mama, but Jacky's not here anymore. He'll never find out about Kate."

Rebecca's head retracted. "Who's Kate?"

"Jack's other daughter," Teckla whispered as she emphasized each word. "The one you said died."

"Sha sha!" Rebecca wiped the air fast, erasing Teckla's words, as if she could erase the baby herself. She shook with nerves. Her eyes shot left and right in fear.

"Nobody's here, Mama. Just listen to me. Ida and Harry should be able to see Sarah. I honored your wishes because Jack was alive. Now, these two little girls who are sisters," she emphasized, "should know each other, even if they don't live together. And you should have the pleasure of another granddaughter."

"Never!" Rebecca yelled, slapping her daughter's face. Teckla reared back, her eyes open wide. Rebecca hadn't hit her daughter since she was a little girl. She was sorry, but she refused to hear another word about any of this. "You know they want Sarah," she said, her eyes getting moist. "They said so at Lena's funeral." Rebecca blinked but the tears fell. Like a deluge, they flowed and she blubbered the rest of her words. "I will *not* let them take her. I can't. It's all I have left of Jacky."

Teckla drew her mother into her arms. When the crying slowed, she spoke softly and tried to make Rebecca understand that the Pearls would not take Sarah. "Ida didn't even say anything about seeing her. I just know it's not right to keep this secret going."

Rebecca pulled away. She would have none of it. As she wiped her eyes, she took command again, insisting that Teckla obey her wishes. From slaps to hugs, anger to comfort, mother and daughter crossed swords again while Rebecca turned pale and sweaty with every angry discourse. Finally, Teckla threw her hands in the air.

"Okay. I don't like it, but I won't go against you. I don't want you getting sick over this. We've lost too many people in our family and I don't want to lose you, too."

Rebecca fell back against the pillows and closed her eyes. She'd won. Relieved, her breathing slowed. Teckla stayed to make sure her mother was all right. In the quiet of the bedroom, they heard muffled voices coming from the living room, the scraping of chairs and the door opening and closing. Rebecca wanted to stay in her room with the lights off and remember her son. She opened her eyes and told her daughter so. Then she reached out and touched the cameo brooch on Teckla's blue cardigan.

"What's this?" she asked running her finger over the silver flower in the woman's hair, as if their disagreement had never happened. "When did you get it? It's pretty."

Teckla sighed. "It's Ida's," she said. "Don't get upset, please. She just gave it to me. She wants her granddaughter to have something of hers, even if Sarah never gets to really know her. I'm to give it to Sarah on her sixteenth birthday unless . . ." Rebecca's breathing accelerated again, and Teckla laid her palm on her mother's arm. "Don't worry, Mama. When it's time, I will tell Sarah it's a family heirloom. That's all. I promise."

CHAPTER 21

Eighty-four Years Later

Driving up the Saw Mill Parkway, having just left Nan's, I wanted to kick myself. How could I have forgotten to ask her about the cameo brooch? Most likely she wouldn't have any idea why my mother had the exact same pin as the one Kate had painted from her grandmother's description. Obviously, Nan knew Ida Pearl; they'd have to have met at some point, even if it was just at the wedding. But would she know if the cameo my mother was given for her Sweet Sixteen was really Ida's? Maybe the family heirloom was from the Pearl side of the family and not the Roths. Nan was my last chance at solving this mystery. I pressed on the gas to kick up my speed. The minute I get home, I told myself, I'm going to call her. I'm not waiting for another visit.

"The same exact cameo brooch?" Nan asked when I explained why I was calling. I reminded her of how I had found Kate after noticing the brooch in the painting. "I was already living in Israel when your mother turned sixteen," Nan said. "I moved there in '36 when it was still called Palestine. Sorry, I have no memory of . . . oh wait . . . yes."

I could almost hear Nan's thoughts scrambling in her head. "Yes, what?" I prodded, scooting to the edge of the kitchen chair where I'd plopped myself to make the call.

"It was after Uncle Jack died. At Shiva one day. My mother was wearing a cameo that I'd never seen before. I can picture her coming into Sarah's room. We were building with her Tinker Toys. You know, they were made of wood back then, not like the plastic ones today. Oh, they were so much better. Anyway, I asked her where she got the brooch. I didn't remember her putting it on that morning, and I was always aware of my mother's jewelry. She liked wearing earrings and pins, bracelets and beads. Nothing expensive, mind you; we couldn't afford that. And whenever she got dressed, she asked me if they went together or matched her outfit, and I remember that brooch didn't look good with blue. It would have been prettier on any of the brown tones or cream."

This story was taking so damn long. I wanted her to get to the point already. Nan could ramble on forever if I let her. I understood she was old and memories were precious, but enough was enough. "So who owned the cameo originally? Whose was it?"

"That's the interesting part," Nan said. She sounded like she was so pleased with her memory. "My mother told me it was Ida Pearl's and she was supposed to give it to Sarah when she turned sixteen. I remember how confused I was, and it must have shown on my face because my mother said she'd explain it to me later."

Nan was probably playing the scene in her head. I needed it on her lips. Each time she took a breath, it seemed like forever before she exhaled, and I was on edge waiting for her to finish.

"So when we were back upstairs in our own apartment," Nan finally continued, "I asked her why Ida couldn't give the pin to Sarah herself. Mama reminded me that Grandmother Rebecca wouldn't let Mrs. Pearl ever see Sarah. They'd had some horrible argument and that was just the way it had to be. I thought it was cruel and now that you tell me the baby lived, I suppose that had something to do with it. All I know is, my mother said that if Grandmother died before Sarah's sixteenth birthday, Ida would take the brooch back and give it to Sarah herself. It seemed strange to me to talk about someone's possible death when they were in perfect health. But they were all a little nuts. Grandmother was nasty. Papa Karl didn't appear to be happy ever. My mother was okay. I used to hear her argue with Rebecca, although mainly she was a very good daughter and let her mother rule the roost. That's why I got married so young. I wasn't even eighteen. I had to get out of there."

We finished our conversation realizing that if Grandmother Rebecca had died before Sarah turned sixteen, Ida probably would have told Kate about her having a sister and everything would have been different. "I wouldn't be going through this now," I said. "My mother would have always known."

Just before we said goodbye, Nan reminded me of how she felt. "It's what Kate will go through if you tell her. I'm totally against it, Carolyn."

So, I thought, Nan is just as demanding as she claims Rebecca was, and she doesn't even realize it. I put up a pot of water for tea meditating on what my life might have been like if Rebecca had died before my mother's sixteenth birthday. Mom would have known her sister and maybe when Kate moved to California, we'd have moved too. I would have liked growing up where the temperature never dipped below fifty degrees, and that was in the middle of the night. I opened the wrapping on the tea bag and inhaled the aromatic mixture of blackberries and sage. Though I never wished anyone dead, it was a shame that Rebecca had outlived Ida.

CHAPTER 22

It was a cloudy morning, the type of day that made one want to stay inside and curl up with a good novel. My life right then was a story in itself. I didn't need another author. One thing that would brighten the day for me would be telling Anita I was right about the cameos. Not only was there a connection between the two, the one in the painting was actually my mother's!

As I walked across the parking lot after teaching my exercise class, I played with words in my head making up imaginary conversations I'd have with Kate. I opened my door and the phone was ringing.

"First, I'll apologize for going behind her back," I told Anita. She had called to see if I wanted to have lunch that afternoon. "Then I'll tell Kate how thrilled I am that we're related, and I'll tell her about the cameo being my mother's."

"What do you mean?" Anita was totally confused, and I wanted to fluff my feathers. I told her all I'd learned.

"I was right all along," I said. "I sensed there was something more than just a coincidence. It was that silver flower."

"So the brooch was from Lena's family, not Jack's. Wow. What an incredible story! It's like out of a movie."

I agreed and wondered who would play the evil Rebecca. Anita and I tossed around names and then I said, "So now I can tell Kate what her grandmother meant when she said she lost the cameo."

"Christ, Carolyn, you're being selfish." As quick as a bee sting, the light touch with all the kidding was gone. I paced the floor with the phone pressed to my ear, sweaty in my workout clothes. "She's not young, you know." Anita kept talking, barely taking a breath. "She could have a stroke. Forget about it. Let's have lunch and go to the outlets. You need a fun day."

I stopped in front of Kate's painting, the one of her front door. No matter what my reprimanding friend said, I wanted to open that door, so to speak.

"And don't go imagining you can all of a sudden be her loving niece. She barely knows you. Remember Bill's story? He and his brother aren't exactly buddies. They've only seen each other once since their discovery."

"She liked me," I answered, emphasizing the like to get it through Anita's thick skull.

"Sure, she liked you, but, most likely, she'll be furious and take it out on you–not want to see you ever again. Or is it that you think you can take her daughter's place? Or that she . . ." Anita stopped talking for a moment, then her irritated voice changed to one of compassion. "Car, I'm sorry. I have to say this." I stared at the blue painted door on the canvas. "She might really be your aunt, but she can't fill the void. No one can take your mother's place."

"I know that! That's not what I want." Fuming, I said a quick goodbye making up some excuse that I had to get off the phone and telling her I needed a day to myself. I could not listen to her anymore.

That afternoon I took myself to a little town just a few miles up the Hudson. I enjoyed the quiet ride along the river and browsing the antique shops and art galleries by myself. Whether it was a coincidence or some karma connecting me to Kate, on view that day in one of the galleries was a collection of paintings by several artists of all different kinds of doors. I thought of Kate's painting hanging in my condo and as soon as I got home, I called her. I needed to forge a closer connection with her so when I finally revealed the deeply held family secret, she'd already feel close to me. She seemed pleased to hear from me.

"There was an entire collection of paintings of doors," I told her. "The ones from Italy were the most colorful, though none as beautiful as that painting of yours. It's right here in front of me, hanging on the wall between my dining room and kitchen." She teased that I shouldn't spill anything on it when carrying dirty dishes, and we hung up with me saying I'd be in touch.

That phone call went well, so I came up with another plausible reason to reach out to her a week later after viewing portraits of women painted in the late nineteenth century in the Neue Galerie in Manhattan. "I stood there looking at these lovely women, all in ornate gold frames," I said, "and it made me wonder if you found the perfect place to hang the portrait of your grandmother."

Kate said she had, that it was in her dining room, and she reminded me her grandmother's painting was from the mid-twentieth century. "I wasn't even alive in the nineteenth," she laughed, "but I always did love the high-necked Victorian dress. That's why I chose that old one of Grandma's for the painting. I'll text you a picture of it. Oh, and Carolyn, Ben, my grandson, is coming to spend a few weeks with me, and I'm going to take your suggestion and speak to him about his weight."

That was the connection I needed. I'd be able to ask her about Ben in future conversations and offer suggestions, though that wasn't going to give me a reason to get back to LA. And then, a few days later, I received an email giving me the perfect opportunity. It was from the American Academy of Health and Fitness Professionals announcing an upcoming seminar in San Diego, which was less than two hours from Los Angeles on the five, as they say out west. The academy was offering a course to become certified as a Medical Exercise Specialist, and since I had time on my hands, I could expand my little fitness business and take on private clients. People who really needed personal training from injuries or loss of ability due to aging or illness. With that certification, I'd learn more about diabetes and exercise. Another way to bring me to Kate. I called her and told her I'd be "on the coast." I do love the lingo–so Hollywood–and that I'd be driving up to LA for a few days.

"That's lovely, dear. Please do come and see me when you're in town."

Those were the sweetest words I'd heard in weeks. A month later, I arrived in Los Angeles. It was too late in the evening to call so first thing the next morning, before she'd start painting and not answer, I grabbed my phone and punched in her number.

"Hi, Kate. I'm back in town." I was sitting on my hotel bed, my legs tangled in the covers. "Yes, the conference was wonderful. I feel rejuvenated, ready to get back to my classes and start a new business. I'll tell you all about it when I see you. That's actually why I'm calling this early. I'd like to take a ride to Malibu this afternoon and have lunch on the water. I'd love it if you'd join me."

"I used to go to the Sand Castle there," Kate said. "It's been such a long time. I thought it got wiped out in one of the mudslides, or maybe an earthquake."

"Oh no, the restaurant is up and running–just under a different name." My concierge had told me about the destruction and that the owners rebuilt making the pilings higher and sturdier. These Angelinos didn't seem to let Mother Nature's wrath stop them, and as long as they figured the restaurant would hold, I was willing to go. Besides, it was a gorgeous August day. What could happen other than Kate having her own personal earthquake when I told her she was my aunt? "So how about it, Kate? Come with me. I'd love to spend some time with you."

"That's a lovely invitation, dear, but I'm not sure. I'm kind of busy . . ."

Her words drifted off. Maybe she was figuring out how she could rearrange her day. "And I really don't each lunch," she added.

"Let's make it later then, for dinner." I wouldn't let anything stop me now, when I'd finally gotten back here.

"I'd really like to, but I don't want to hold you up, ruin your day. Plus, I eat dinner on the early side, and I wouldn't want you to have to change your plans."

I assured Kate that I didn't have any specific plans other than seeing her, and I had to convince her I didn't mind waiting until later to eat. She finally agreed. "I'm glad. I'll pick you up at three and we'll have a lovely drive on the Pacific Coast Highway."

***

"I know I've said it before–ever since you brought me the painting," Kate said, "my head has been all a-jumble with memories–new ones popping up every day." We were seated at a table for two, along a totally open wall, looking out at the Pacific Ocean, the sound of the waves our background music. A wrought iron railing was all that separated us from a long drop to the sand. "And I had a dream the other night. When I was younger, I had it a lot, one of those recurring dreams. In it, I'm walking across a street holding my mother's hand. I can't see her face, but her hand is soft and she's wearing gloves. Then, in the middle of the road, her hand is gone. She's not there anymore. I run to the sidewalk crying and some lady comes by and hugs me." Kate looked up at me and shrugged her shoulders. "And then I'd wake up. I never understood that dream. Irv used to say it's because I wanted my mother."

I didn't have to be Freud to understand that dream, and she had just given me an opening to bring up the subject of Lena Pearl being the mother of two girls, not one. We'd finished our dinner. I had a delicious lobster Cobb salad, just the way I like it with the ingredients all in their own sections, and Kate had devoured a cheeseburger with sautéed onions. She said it was her favorite meal and she never made it at home. "Beth's husband used to grill the best burgers," she said. Her eyes took a downward turn. The air stilled for a moment. The breeze off the ocean stopped. Then, as if nothing had happened, Kate looked up and smiled. "But this place has the best burgers on the entire coast."

Instead of mothers, Kate turned the conversation to our favorite foods and asked me what I would order for my last meal if I was on death row. I laughed because Stan and I used to have the same discussion and I told her that. "Is he your husband?" Kate asked.

"No, just a man I dated for a long time. He died about five years ago."

After offering her condolences, she told me she'd wondered if I was married since I never mentioned a husband. "I see you don't wear a ring, so I assumed you were either divorced or widowed, and then when you said his name, I figured I was wrong."

"Well, actually, I *am* divorced. But that was so long ago, just a little blip of time in my life right after college." I told Kate the whole story and was exhausted from going over the details, digging deep and bringing up all that anger and sorrow again. It did make me wonder why people lied. Doing so by omission was different, to my way of thinking. Sometimes there were reasons to keep a secret, but not in Alan's case. Not telling hurt more than if he had fessed up. And I could not figure out the upside to concealing the story of Kate and my mother. Not now, and certainly not back then when it originated.

"Did Alan want the divorce?" Kate asked when I finished.

"No. He called the next day and begged me to let him come home. He said he'd go back to school and would stop playing the horses, that he was afraid his gambling was becoming an addiction. It frightened him and it scared the hell out of me. I wanted my marriage to work so I gave him a second chance. He sounded so sincere."

"I imagine he was disappointed in himself."

"Yes, and he claimed he was even more so for hurting me. For a few weeks everything seemed fine. Alan came home every night after work. Then one day he told me the book store changed his hours and he had to work an extra shift a few nights a week. I wanted so much to believe him, to trust him. Anyway, I went to the store one night just to make sure. He wasn't there. I asked someone, who didn't know I was his wife, if Alan was on a break. The guy shook his head and told me he only worked days. I asked if he might be working a double, and the man said Alan had left at five, to come back the next day if I wanted to see him. I sure did want to see him. To tell him we were done."

The breeze off the Pacific was exactly what I needed to cool me down after relating that story. With every word, I felt myself as Carolyn Lesser again. I shook my head to erase that name, that woman whose husband had destroyed her ability to trust men.

I had gotten so far from the subject of Kate and my mother, the Pearls and the Roths, and I had to find my way back, but Kate was fascinated with my Alan story. I realized this was bringing us closer and that's what I wanted, what I needed. She asked some more questions and her sympathy touched me. "That must have been very difficult for you," she said, "to have your love destroyed like that. I'm so sorry you had to go through that, dear."

While waiting for the valet to bring the car around, she asked if I gave him another chance. "We separated that night," I told her. "Baseball offers three strikes; I only gave two. Alan swore he'd never lie to me again, but how could I believe him? After the divorce, I took my maiden name back. I didn't want anything to do with him ever again."

We headed south with the blue Pacific way down below on our right. It was time for me to introduce another maiden name. Once, when I was about twelve, my parents and I took a trip out west and drove this same road from Santa Barbara to Los Angeles when there was barely anything on the side to keep us from tumbling over the embankment into the waves. I was petrified. Now, with Kate in the passenger seat, my only fear, if you could call it that, was how she would react to the true story of her birth. Yes, I was a little concerned. I figured she'd be upset and confused, but she wasn't going to keel over like Anita had said. With my eyes focused on the curvy road, I asked Kate if she was ever upset about being an only child?

"That's a strange question, dear." She looked over her shoulder at me. I glanced quickly in her direction. "No. I don't think so," she said. "Why? Are you?" Her expression was full of compassion. "I'm sure it was difficult taking care of your mother all by yourself."

I admitted it was, yet refused to let her get me off topic. Searching for the right words to bring up to the Roth/Pearl story, I asked, "Wasn't it difficult for you, when your grandmother died? You didn't have any siblings to help?"

"That's true. Although I was married. I had Irv."

There it was again. Marriage. After Alan, I never wanted to marry again. That's why it was so good with Stan. He was safe.

Kate was very quiet, looking out the window at the ocean. I assumed she was reminiscing about her husband and maybe her grandmother when she surprised me.

"You know, Carolyn, I never minded not having a sister or brother. I had a very close friend who lived in my building. We were best friends for many years, even after I was married and moved out here. I suppose you could say she was my sister."

I told Kate about Anita then asked if her friend still lived in New York. "Do you ever see her?"

"No. Unfortunately, Anna died about twenty years ago." She chuckled, like she'd just remembered something funny. "You asked if I wanted a sister or brother. That wasn't what I missed. You know, my grandmother was the only mother I ever knew."

I nodded and kept my eyes on the road. She'd given me my entrée. All I had to do was give her time and Kate would tell me how she missed having a mother and then I could tell her the truth. We had about fifteen minutes left of the drive.

"Well, there was one time I wished I had a real mother," she said. "Don't get me wrong, Grandma was like a real mother, no one could have been better, but you know what I mean."

I didn't answer, just nodded again. It wasn't the time.

"Anna scared me one time and that's the only time I remember wishing I had my real mother."

"What happened?"

Kate began the story staring straight ahead at the windshield. "It was in the afternoon one day after school. I had been playing upstairs in Anna's apartment. I remember running down the stairs all out of breath and shoving the door open." She turned towards me. "You know," she said, "we never had to lock our doors in those days." Kate draped her arm over the back of the seat and shifted her weight in my direction. "Anyway, Grandma was in the kitchen washing dishes, and I remember feeling like tears were going to burst out of me from all over. They filled my belly, my nose, my ears. 'Anna told me she was lucky,' that's what I told my grandmother, 'because she had a mommy and I didn't.' I asked her if that meant bad things were going to happen to me because I wasn't lucky?

"Grandma wiped her hands on a towel and tossed it over her shoulder, like she always did, then bent down and hugged me. 'No sweetheart,' she said. 'Nothing bad is going to happen to you. You are a very lucky little girl, Kate. You have me and Grandpa, and we love you so much.' She was always telling me that."

I glanced at Kate as she smiled, obviously from a sweet memory. My story could wait. I would let her give me the perfect opening. All I had to do was listen for it so I peeled my eyes to the road and let her continue.

"'But I don't have a mommy,'" I said, and Grandma sat and held me on her lap. I remember it clearly. She said, 'Your mommy loved you very much, but she got sick and God took her to heaven.' She kissed my *keppie*; she always kissed my head, like it was her favorite place. 'And,' she said, 'I know she still loves you.' I don't remember her exact words. You see, my grandmother let me believe my mother was watching me from heaven. At the time, it was a little creepy, thinking my dead mother saw everything I did; however, it was also very comforting."

Kate turned back to face the front and settled into the seat. "I suppose that was all I needed to hear," she said, "because the next thing I remember is asking if I could go back upstairs to play with Anna and her sister and then stopping when I realized Anna had another reason she was lucky and I wasn't. She had a sister."

It took a moment for me to form the words in my mind, I was so stunned she'd brought up the word sister. Before I could say anything, though, Kate went on with her story.

"Grandma pulled me close and kissed my *keppie* again. 'Come. I'll take you upstairs,' she said. We went into the hall and climbed up the two flights to Anna's apartment.

"Grandma and Anna's mother sat at the kitchen table with glasses of tea in front of them while we girls played in the living room. I knew my grandmother preferred a pretty cup, but I guess she didn't care because she looked really serious talking to Mrs. Newman. I have no idea what my grandmother said or what she and Anna's mother talked about. All I know is, Anna never teased me again, and if she were alive today, we'd still be best friends."

We were almost at the exit for Venice and I still hadn't mentioned my mother. I was about to, when Kate lay her head back against the seat and asked if I minded if she closed her eyes for a bit. How could I slam her with my story–or I should say the true story of Kate and Sarah–when she looked exhausted? Relating those memories must have taken a great toll on her. I clicked on the left turn signal and took the ramp to Lincoln Boulevard, letting Kate rest. In a few short blocks, we'd be in front of her house, and my opportunity would be gone. Another half hour was all I needed.

"Would you like to stop for a cup of tea?" I asked.

CHAPTER 23

Kate left me in her kitchen slicing bagels while she went to see what Ben wanted. He was in the dining room and had called to her, saying he had a question. It was the Saturday after our dinner in Malibu. Kate had called me the next day to apologize for not wanting to go for tea. "I'm glad you got me out," she'd said. "I needed that. I used to go out every afternoon, but ever since Beth died, I just haven't had the *koiech*." I understood the Yiddish expression; she hadn't had the strength or the desire. "You made me realize I could still have fun," she said and then invited me to brunch on this Saturday to meet her grandson. Over the phone she told me that he had gotten heavier and she was very worried. "His neck seems to have grown bigger and bigger," she said and asked if I'd work with him. "You've got that new certification. He could be your first client. I don't think he lives too far from you in New York, and I'll pay for all the sessions."

Needless to say, I was thrilled by the prospect. I'd hoped Ben would be a vehicle to bring us closer and give me the opportunity to speak to her more often, and here she was offering it to me like a beautifully wrapped gift on Christmas morning. I told her I'd do what I could and realized I would have to win him over. What nineteen-year-old wanted a trainer old enough to be his mother?

"I don't want to lose him," she said, as if I hadn't responded at all. "Please, dear, help him get this weight off. You're the professional." She sniffed back tears. "I couldn't help my daughter. I never thought she was sick. She didn't look it. Didn't act it. It was always just about her weight. But now, if I can do something to help Ben . . ."

I assured her I would and that I'd be happy to come for brunch. I even picked up a chocolate babka on my way over. My mother taught me well; never show up empty handed, she'd always said. I cut through a sesame bagel and listened to Kate and Ben's conversation through the open passageway. They were standing in front of the painting of her grandmother. Ben's voice came through as sharp as the knife in my hand.

"Carolyn gave you this? I don't understand. How did she have a picture of your grandmother?"

Listening to Kate explain, I pulled a wicker basket from the soffit where many hung above the wood cabinets and draped it with the yellow linen napkin she had laid out. Ben's next question made me stop midstream.

"She flew all the way here to give it to you? Three thousand miles? Isn't that a little weird?"

Kate told him that at first she thought it was, but then her words filled me with a warmth I hadn't felt in a very long time. "In a way," she said, "I've got my grandmother back, plus I believe I have a new friend."

"Friend?" Ben said. "She's so much younger than you."

Ben's confusion was palpable. His mother probably never had friends as old as her own mother, plus the whole concept of returning a painting to the artist wasn't exactly logical. But Kate's sweet laugh told me all I needed to know. To her, we were friends despite the age difference, and I was comforted hearing the joy in her laughter. Soon, she'd find out we were more than friends, and I decided to use Ben to get me to that point. Kate had said Ben was the one interested in genealogy, so while training him, I'd tell him about my research, leaving out the Roth/Pearl story. I'd offer to help him with his search since he was busy studying. It would be Ben who would find out Lena's name, and after we compared our findings during our training sessions the rest would follow easily. He certainly would want to tell Kate she had a sister. It was a stunning discovery. I had to admit, it might be a bit dishonest on my part, but with all the dishonesty my family had created, what was wrong with a bit of avoidance? I wouldn't have to lie. I'd just never reveal that I knew it all along.

I placed the bagels in the basket while listening to Kate explain about the time she had painted the picture and how glad she was to have it back. When he started questioning my motives for returning the oil, I picked up the basket and, with a bounce in my step, joined them.

We sat around Kate's mahogany table. The portrait was on the wall, directly opposite me. I wished I could have spoken to my lady, like I used to as a child. I'd have asked her opinion. Kate said Ida was going to tell her how she lost the cameo. Perhaps that was how she planned to tell her she had a sister. Unfortunately, we'd never know. Now I had to ask Ben a few questions.

"What kind of work are you doing this summer?" I asked as I spread cream cheese on the other half of my bagel. Ben had already consumed one bagel, half loaded with cream cheese and lox and the other with a heaping portion of egg salad, and now he was spreading another half of an onion bagel with butter. I was trying to steer the conversation to exercise. "Your grandmother told me you've got a great internship with the Dodgers. Do you get to play ball with any of them? You know, just throw it around for fun?"

"I wish," he said. "My friend's father is the team photographer, and he's got me cataloging pictures and doing all kinds of office stuff."

Computer work and filing was not going to burn many calories, so I asked Ben if he played the game with his friends.

"I did as a kid, but not anymore. But I love baseball. I've got tickets for tomorrow's game."

"So, what sports do you play? Tennis, golf?" I thought I was on comfortable turf with my questions. Boys like to talk sports, but Ben didn't seem to participate in any. "I'll bet you surf," I said. "Growing up out here, isn't that what all the kids do?"

"Yeah, I used to surf, but now I don't have any time. Besides, I'm in New York. Where can you surf in the city?"

I told him about the beaches on Long Island and surfing segued into swimming and that was a positive. Ben said he swam when he got the chance, but with school and working he didn't have much time. "You can swim at the Marriott if you want. I do laps every day. Want to join me later?"

A smile spread across Kate's cheeks and her eyes lit up. She had been quiet up until then. "What a great idea, Benny," she said. "I'd like to come, too, if you don't mind."

I was sure Ben felt trapped. "You swim at the Y, Grandma. What do you need a hotel for?"

"A change of pace. Besides, the Marriott has a beautiful pool, and we could have one of those fancy drinks that come with paper umbrellas. I'd like that. I haven't been swimming with you since you were a little boy."

Ben shook his head. "I don't have time."

I doubted that was the real reason. I had to try something else, some way to get Ben to feel comfortable with me so he'd accept my help. Kate was depending on it–and I only had two more days.

CHAPTER 24

"Watch the guy on second," Ben said. "He's going to steal."

We were seated in the first row, field level seats, right behind home plate. Ben certainly had connections. Our swimming date never occurred, but I had called Kate and invited them to join me for a baseball game. The Dodgers were playing the Mets. Ben accepted immediately and said he could get us great seats and that I shouldn't go online to buy them. I let him take the reins as long as we'd have another afternoon together. Kate hadn't said a word yet about me training him. She was smart, waiting for him to get comfortable with me.

Ben and Kate had their eyes peeled on the runner. She looked so happy sitting in the sun staring out at the brown baseball diamond with its emerald green outfield, her grandson at her side. "There he goes. See, I told you, Grandma."

"You do know your baseball, Benny," Kate said. "Remember the first game Grandpa and I took you to?" He nodded and Kate turned to me. "Irv had to explain to Ben why we weren't Dodger fans. He told him when the Dodgers played in Brooklyn they were neighborhood guys. They were our heroes and they just lived down the street, around the town. They ate in the same Chinese restaurants and delis we did. Ben couldn't imagine eating a pastrami sandwich with his idols at the next booth." She turned back to Ben. Seated in the middle, between Ben and me, Kate kept us both in the conversation. "And Grandpa told you how he cried when the team left Brooklyn, even though we were already out here." It was like she was watching a tennis match shifting her head side to side. I should have sat next to Ben. "We came a year before the Dodgers and still we felt betrayed. Once a Brooklynite, always a Brooklynite." She laughed. "It was a conundrum. We wondered could we root for the LA Dodgers, but decided, nah!" She swiped her hand in the air. "They'd always be the Brooklyn Bums to us."

"So, who you rooting for today, Grandma?"

Kate and I looked at each other. "The Mets," we said, in unison.

The snap of the hot dog as my teeth bit the skin, the vendors hawking beer and peanuts, the crunch of shells under my feet were all beautiful music that day.

"You know, Benny, Grandpa used to take me on dates to Ebbets Field."

"I know. I've heard all about it. And Mom told me she learned her numbers sitting next to Grandpa at games here staring up at the scoreboard."

"Right. And didn't Grandpa teach you how to figure out the stats?"

"Yup. It was the best math lesson I ever had."

"Same for me." I said. "Except it was my father who taught me, and I still don't really understand it. Math was never my forte."

Ben took out his scorecard and showed me how to mark strikes and balls, at-bats and runs, and everything else that goes on in a game, all with their proper abbreviations. I pretended to be fascinated. My head was swarming with numbers and symbols that I didn't care about, but we were making a connection and that's what was important.

Kate sat back, her head facing the field as if she was concentrating, but I had a feeling her mind wasn't on the game. Her eyes looked far away and I wondered where her thoughts took her, where she'd gone. She had a bit of a smile as she reached over and gave her grandson a gentle pat on the shoulder. All of a sudden Ben was on his feet and the crowd was cheering. Music blared through Chavez Ravine. The scoreboard flashed. "What happened?" Kate asked. "I missed it."

"Ramirez hit a home run," Ben said. "You didn't see it?"

Kate leaned over and whispered in my ear. "I was thinking about Beth. And Irv."

I nodded. It was my turn to give her shoulder a loving pat.

"We used to have such wonderful times here," she said. "Me and Irv, Beth and Jonathan and the boys . . . my whole family up in the bleachers watching Gary Sheffield and Cruz and Beltrie." She sat back and I'm sure she didn't see a thing that was going on in the game.

I left Kate to her memories and watched the pitcher throw balls and strikes. It was an unusually warm day for Los Angeles, and the sun was smack over our seats. I was glad I wore a baseball hat, though mine didn't have a team logo on it. It had an embroidered picture of a pair of flip-flops with "Simplify" written underneath–what I thought was going to be my motto until I found out my mother had a sister she never knew about. Kate was decked out in her Dodger regalia, the T-shirt and hat that Ben had given her for a belated Mother's Day gift. She might not have been a fan of the team, but she sure was a fan of her grandson.

"I'm going to get a bottle of water," I told Kate. "Do you want one?" I didn't ask Ben since he was constantly slurping his oversized Coke.

Kate looked up at me making a visor with her hand to shade her eyes from the afternoon glare. "No thanks. I'm fine."

"You really should have something to drink," I said. "It's awfully hot out."

"You know, you're right, Carolyn. Would you mind getting me a beer?"

"Beer?"

"Sure, why not? It's a ball game."

Ben chimed in. "Go for it, Grandma. I'll have one too."

She reached for her pocketbook. I waved her off and headed up the steps thinking they really should have some water, but I didn't say anything.

The next morning, as I was packing up my toiletries, my cell phone rang. I didn't recognize the number so I let it go figuring it was a telemarketer. I'd just zipped up the quart-sized plastic bag that held the gels and liquids I was allowed to take on the plane when the phone rang a second time. Again, it was a New York area code, but I still didn't recognize the number and didn't want to bother with whoever it was. Even though I'd put my number on the Do Not Call list, I received lots of calls from charity organizations and it was hard getting them off the phone. I was about to contact the valet service to bring my car around when the phone in my room rang. That was strange. No one had my room number and, anyway, my friends would use my cell phone. No one called hotel rooms anymore. I figured there was a problem with my bill since I'd just paid it on the television. I picked up the receiver and said, "Hello."

"I've been trying to get you on your cell," a male voice said. "This is Ben. Grandma wanted me to call."

I couldn't believe it. Kate must have pestered the hell out of him. "You're calling about exercise, aren't you?"

"What? No! Grandma's in the hospital."

CHAPTER 25

I sped down Lincoln Boulevard looking for cops out of the corner of my eye. Because I'd spoken to Ben for so long, I only had an hour to drop off my car at Hertz and get through airport security in time to board my flight. Ben had explained that Kate fainted shortly after they got home from the game yesterday. She'd refused to go to the hospital, no matter how much he pleaded, saying she'd be fine. She claimed it was just that she wasn't used to sitting in the hot sun for so long. Later that night, he said he woke to sounds coming from the bathroom, that he wanted to go in but didn't want to embarrass his grandmother. Instead, he stood outside the door calling to her, listening to her groaning and vomiting, flushing the toilet several times. She kept saying, "Leave me alone, Benny. I'll be fine." But he didn't budge, and as she walked out to go back to her bedroom, she fainted again. He called an ambulance then.

I rushed through the airport pulling my wheeled carry-on bag behind me, phone in hand, waiting for a text from Ben. He'd promised to be in touch when he knew something more. At the gate, I checked my email and voice mail, in case I hadn't heard the bing. Still nothing. Why the hell hadn't I canceled my flight? Kate was in the hospital, she might be dying, and here I was getting on a plane and no way to be in touch for six long hours. No Wi-Fi, no service. Shit. I didn't want to lose her. Not now when I'd just found her. She was my only link to my mother, to a real family. I couldn't wait anymore. Making my way down the Jetway, I called Ben. Damn, it went directly to voicemail.

During the flight, I read my book–or tried to–and leafed through *SkyMall*. Nothing helped my anxiety, not even the glass of wine I'd sprung for. Again, I berated myself for not going to the hospital instead of flying home, though Ben had insisted Kate would be okay; it was only dehydration and the fluids and anti-nausea meds would help. I wasn't so sure. Couldn't dehydration lead to death? I didn't want her to die. I choked up just thinking about it. It felt as if I'd swallowed a tightly wound ball of barbed wire. And then the tears flowed. I couldn't hold them back as I pictured my mother's last moments, and I wasn't with her. I should have been holding her hand. I should have been holding Kate's.

The second the plane touched down, I grabbed the phone from my bag and turned it on. Ben's text flashed on the screen. I was flushed with overwhelming relief. Kate was fine.

Anita was waiting outside baggage claim. "So, did you tell her?" she asked, before I even had a chance to click the seat belt around me.

I shook my head no and a smug smile crept up Anita's face. She looked up, like she was praising the stars.

"Don't look so pleased with yourself," I said, giving her a cunning grin. "It's not what you're thinking." As she drove onto the Van Wyck Expressway, I told her about Ben and my plan to get him to do his genealogy. "That way, he'll discover the secret and tell Kate."

"Clever. Then you won't have to lie."

"I'm not lying." Boy, she pisses me off. "If it all comes from Ben, then how can it be that I'm lying? Kate will never know that I started the research myself."

"Well, you know how I feel about this. There's no upside to Kate knowing. She'll never be able to meet her sister, and you just might destroy her memories of a loving grandmother."

I stared out at the darkening clouds. I might not only destroy those memories for her. I might destroy my one chance at having a family, if Kate ever found out I went behind her back. But with Ben revealing the secret, that wouldn't be an issue, I told myself. I'll have to get him to find Lena's death certificate, and then pretend to be shocked when he tells me her name and all the details. And when I tell him why I'm so shocked, he'll certainly want to tell Kate we're related. Or I hoped he would. If he didn't want to, or didn't want to do his genealogy, I'd have to take my chances and tell Kate myself, as much as it worried me. I didn't want to lose her. I shook those thoughts out of my head. For the last six or seven hours, I was afraid she was dying. I could *not* lose her now.

We were crossing the Whitestone Bridge. Anita looked like she expected me to say something more about not lying. Instead, I told her about the baseball game and Ben's phone call. "I was so worried," I said, "and there was nothing I could do." I tapped the message icon on the phone. "Here's what he said: 'Grandma's home. Tests came back negative. Docs wanted to keep her another night cause of her age. She refused.'"

"She sounds like a tough old broad," Anita said. "I like that woman."

"A tough old broad," I repeated silently. Those words made me wonder. If Kate was a tough old broad, then what was wrong with me telling her about my mother, if I couldn't get Ben to do it? "I'm going to call her now," I told Anita. I needed to hear Kate's voice. "I'll put it on speaker." I wanted Anita to hear how incredible Kate really is.

"I'm sorry," Kate said when I told her she'd given me a scare. "It seems I did that to everyone, even me. You see, I didn't want to drink too much, not being a fan of public bathrooms. At my age, the bladder doesn't hold too much." Her cheerful voice turned melancholy when she added, "And the beer tasted so good." She quickly switched to upbeat again saying, "Ben is getting tickets for a Mets game sometime in mid-September when it won't be so hot. I want you to join us. I'm ready to live again. I told you, having the painting of my grandmother somehow kicked me back into life and I'm going to grab all I can. One little emergency room visit isn't going to stop me."

I loved how she kidded and was so happy she wanted to go anywhere with me. I said, "Sure, I'll fly out to California when the Mets play the Dodgers." Anita shot me a look that made my toes curl.

"No, I'm coming to New York." She sounded like a little girl planning her first big trip. "And you've got to remind me to stay away from beer and hot dogs. Obviously, they don't agree with me anymore. Boy, it sure stinks getting old."

I laughed and Anita got a look on her face saying "What's with you? You're such good buddies?"

"Ben's staying with me for a few days," Kate said. "He insisted. And I'm going to talk to him about his weight. I'm really worried about him. And I'm going to suggest he talk to you about an exercise program. You can discuss it with him when we see you next month. I'll call you with the date as soon as I know it."

Anita's stare penetrated my skin like a blazing hot sun. "What? What's the matter?" I asked.

"So she's coming to New York and you're going to another baseball game together? That doesn't seem strange to you?"

"No, why?" I kept up my false bravado, not wanting Anita to know how insecure I felt about this. I reminded her that it was Kate who'd suggested I work with Ben. "He goes to school here," I said matter-of-factly. "She's coming to visit him, not me."

We drove on in a compatible silence. My mind was playing its own movie with Kate and Ben the stars. There was the grandson bringing his grandmother a cup of tea while she recuperated in bed. He handed it to her and climbed on top of the covers and settled in. They watched a movie together, an old movie on TCM that she suggested. The soup he'd prepared, knowing she should be eating a light diet after her recent illness, simmered on the stove, its savory scent perfuming the air.

"You know, Kate's a lucky woman," I said looking straight out the windshield as if it were my movie screen. "Her daughter's gone, but she's not alone. She's got Ben." I wondered who'd be making me soup when I was eighty-four and not feeling well.

"I'm sure she'd rather have her daughter," Anita said. "It's nice that Ben's good to her. But I still don't understand why she's inviting you to the game. Just to give Ben a workout plan? Nah, it's got to be something else."

"Maybe she just likes me." Though I suspected it wasn't that simple. "She is very worried about Ben and . . ." A thought occurred to me. "Or maybe I remind her of her daughter?" Anita lifted her brow. "No." I was very emphatic. "I am not trying to take her place."

CHAPTER 26

Kate stood in my entranceway wearing a brown leather jacket and a bright blue pashmina. "This really is so much nicer than a hotel," she said.

"Come, I'll show you your room." I led the way pulling her suitcase behind me over the wood planked floors to my office where I kept a day bed for guests. It worked as a couch at all other times. "Then we'll have a glass of wine. I'm sure you could use one after the long flight." I felt a huge grin plastered across my face.

Kate smiled. "I'd prefer vodka, or anything hard, if you have it." She laughed. "I already had a martini somewhere over the Rockies, but I can always have another."

I fixed her drink the way she instructed– "Shaken, not stirred. Just like James Bond." –and told her my plan for the next day. "We can take the train into the city and go to the Met. You said you wanted to see it again. So, how about we make the ten-thirty? That way we don't have to rush." I had no idea how long it took her to get ready. As my mother aged, she got slower and slower.

"You don't have to come with me," she said. "It would be lovely, but you've probably got plans for the day."

I was not about to let her go into Manhattan alone. Plus, I wanted to spend as much time together as possible and figured, at some point, probably one night over a glass of wine, I'd broach the subject of genealogy again, just in case I couldn't convince Ben. It would be like two girlfriends at a sleepover. We'd be in our pajamas curled up on the sofa talking about all kinds of stuff, and I'd steer the conversation to family and get her to agree to my researching hers.

***

"Let's walk," Kate said exiting the museum and stepping out into a radiant autumn afternoon. "I never get to do that in LA."

A soft breeze blew golden leaves across the sidewalk as we walked up Fifth Avenue while Kate reminisced about her days as a young woman in the city. "Irv and I used to take long walks in Central Park. We walked everywhere," she said. "Always hand in hand." There was a glow emanating from her smile. "If I'm right, Carolyn, the lake isn't far from here. That's where we had our first date. He took me rowing. My grandmother told me that my parents used to go ice skating on that same lake. Funny, isn't it? I wonder if couples still do that."

I thought they probably did, although no one had ever taken me skating or rowing. But Kate didn't need an answer. She was deep in memories, and I loved that she was sharing them with me. It reminded me of being with my mother. We'd go shopping or to a show or museum and she'd tell me stories of her childhood and the school holidays when her Aunt Teckla would take her to the city. Whatever they did, they always stopped at the automat for lunch. Kate had her memories, but she should have had these memories too.

There was such an ache in my gut over what could have been.

Kate pointed to the buildings as we turned east on Ninetieth Street. "I used to paint portraits of ladies who lived in buildings like these," she said. "I think one of them actually was on this block." She looked around as if trying to find the exact building. "That woman had the largest foyer I'd ever seen, complete with an enormous crystal chandelier and marble floor." She let out a little laugh. "They were all nice ladies, but give me a landscape any day."

Ben was standing under the awning of Pascalou Café. Like all kids today, his eyes were fixed on his phone, but as soon as he spotted us coming up the block, he slipped it into his pocket and ran over. It was sweet how he hugged his grandma and led her into the restaurant.

We sat at the window I'd specifically asked for when I made the reservation. Kate looked out at the hustle and bustle of New York City and rubbed her hands together. "This is so wonderful," she said. "And Benny, you look terrific." She was right. His face and neck looked thinner than the last time I'd seen him. He still had many pounds to shed, but he'd made progress. "Have you been jogging or something?" she asked.

"Nope. Haven't done a thing. There's no time."

Perhaps it was running all over campus, I thought, getting to class on time, racing between the frat house and school. Otherwise, there was no way he could have lost that much weight in six weeks.

We ordered lunch and were sipping mimosas and Ben was telling us about his classes when Kate leaned over and pulled his shirt collar down. "What's this?" she asked tapping at a spot on his neck.

Ben reached his hand behind his head, and in an instant his bright eyes turned dark. "Oh no, not again." He dropped his head in his hands and sighed.

"What's the matter, Benny?" Kate asked. "What's wrong?"

It must be wonderful being wrapped up in a grandma's love and I say grandma, not grandmother, on purpose. My mother had a grandmother. There's a big difference. I never had either and couldn't help feeling a little jealous as Kate leaned over and rubbed Ben's back.

Ben sat up straight. "I had a growth there removed a few months ago. Dad came up 'cause it was real surgery."

"What type of growth?"

"Don't worry, Grandma. It was just a sebaceous cyst, but it took a long time to heal." He rubbed the back of his neck again. "I didn't know it came back."

"Well, I think you need to go to the doctor again," Kate said.

"It's probably no big deal. Just a zit," and he carried on regaling us with stories about his one-handed biology professor. I couldn't help laughing a little even though Kate gave him a look only a grandma could give. But she chuckled too. We were back being a happy little threesome. Anyone would have thought we were a family having a lovely outing. Actually, we were, though I was the only one who knew it, for now. And when Ben's dessert came Kate didn't seem upset. Obviously her talk with him had made an impression, which must have made her happy, though he still hadn't said a word to me about exercise. I was getting worried. Training him was the only way I saw for us to connect. I needed him to feel comfortable with me, to accept my help with his genealogy. It was the best way to reveal the secret, the safest. Kate would have no reason to be angry with me.

Ben wolfed down his crème brulée, while Kate and I sipped our tea. Three waiters came to our table singing "Happy Birthday," carrying a candle-lit piece of cake.

"How did you know?" Kate asked me. "Or did you tell her, Benny?"

"No," I said. "It was all me." I had to fudge the truth–fudge, not lie–or how else would I have known her birthday? "Remember, I looked you up when I first saw your signature on the back of the painting?" I hoped she wouldn't realize I'd only learned the year of her birth from the website, not the date.

"Oh, yes. I forgot about that."

Ben thrust his fork into the carrot cake and scooped up a piece, uninterested in our conversation. I wondered how he lost weight if he was still eating like it was his last meal. None of this seemed to register with Kate, or she just wasn't saying anything. If he were my kid, I wouldn't have been able to hold my tongue. Crème brulée and cake? Too much.

After a polite argument over the bill when I wound up only paying for the birthday cake, we left the restaurant. On the sidewalk, Kate kissed her grandson goodbye, and I gave him a peck on the cheek too. We turned right heading to the corner to catch a cab to Grand Central Station. Kate called over her shoulder, "Don't forget to call the doctor, Benny. We'll see you Sunday and I want to know you have an appointment scheduled." Ben waved and headed north to Columbia.

CHAPTER 27

My plan of our spending the waning afternoon hours on my balcony, with freshly brewed tea leaves I'd bought especially for the occasion and talking about families, was debunked the minute I unlocked the front door and Kate announced, "It's been a magnificent day, dear, but I desperately need a nap." I grabbed my book and settled in the chaise lounge, the balcony all to myself as usual, while she slept. The novel remained unopened on my lap while a soliloquy played in my head. As the late afternoon sun dipped down over the Palisades across the river, I imagined Kate hugging me when she learned, from Ben's research I hoped, that she was really my aunt. "I'm so sorry you never had the chance to know my mother," I'd say. "It wasn't right to keep you girls apart." And Kate would cry a little, then say she's glad she knows the truth now. "My grandsons are wonderful. I love them to death," I imagined her saying, "but they're young and so involved in their own lives, as they should be." She'd smile and tell me she was happy I was part of her life. "How wonderful it'll be to have you by my side as I grow even older," she'd say, and we would talk about seeing each other more often.

Kate and I didn't have any dinner plans. We were going to be in all evening, maybe order a pizza or just have cheese on toast as she had suggested. "With a lunch like that, I cannot possibly eat dinner," she told me on the train. I picked up my novel and laid back. Maybe my imagined dialogue would turn into conversation over toasted multi-grain with cheddar. Maybe I wouldn't wait for Ben. It didn't seem like we were getting any closer to my training him, or that he and I were getting any closer either, although he didn't pull away when I kissed him goodbye after lunch.

The next day was filled with events. Kate and I started our day over breakfast at my dining room table. The painting of her blue door greeted us each time we passed it going back and forth from dining room to kitchen. I noticed Kate glance at it as she carried the dirty plates and silverware when we were finished. She took a step toward the kitchen, then stopped and stood in front of the painting. Her chin was raised a bit higher, like a peacock showing off its colorful feathers, though I wasn't able to read the expression on her face.

"The painting is perfect," I said standing a few steps behind her, my arms laden with jam jars and butter balanced on a basket of left over muffins. "Because I feel like a door opened for me when I met you."

Kate's voice was a bit pensive and very soft. "It did for me too," she said, and continued to stare at the painting. I moved up next to her, my eyes also on the oil. Her fingertips touched my shoulder and rested there. I felt loved. I could tell her now, I thought. It was the perfect time. And after her initial shock, we'd hug. I licked my lips, readying the words and then, with a quick nod, Kate stepped back and walked into the kitchen. The moment was gone. She placed the dishes in the sink, pulled her shoulders back, and announced, all bright and cheery, "Speaking of doors, I'm going to get dressed. Wouldn't want to walk through Roosevelt's front door in my bathrobe."

Kate and I left forty-five minutes later to visit FDR's home in Hyde Park, and after a full day of Franklin and Eleanor, we drove to Anita's house.

"Come for dinner," Anita had said last week, when I told her Kate was going to be staying with me. "Bill and I want to meet her."

"Okay, but I don't want him bringing up the story about his finding his half brother." We were on the phone, so I couldn't see her reaction but I heard the tsk of her tongue meeting her teeth. She was pissed. Honestly, I was afraid Kate might offer sympathies to Bill if he told her that it hurt terribly knowing his father had lied to him. I worried Kate would say she understood and that she wouldn't want to know if her grandparents had kept such a secret from her.

"I'll tell him not to say anything, but you know how I feel." Anita sounded exasperated, annoyed. "Therapy has helped Bill, and at least his brother is alive," she'd said. "They've seen each other again and talked about their father and how they're dealing with his lying. For Kate, there's no sense in it. Maybe if your mother were still alive . . ." The hum from my refrigerator broke the silence coming from the other end of the line. Of course, if my mother was living, things would be different. I didn't need Anita to remind me of that. "No, probably not even then," she added, as if she'd thought long and hard about this. "Kate is too old to deal with it. It'll crush her beautiful memories. Don't do that to her, Car."

I was breathing hard when we said goodbye. Anita might tell Bill to keep quiet, but I wasn't so sure about her. She just might mention Bill's story to get Kate's reaction, to prove to me that she's right.

Bill and Kate were in the dining room, sitting around the table talking about places they'd like to visit while Anita and I got dinner ready. Everything seemed to be going perfectly. Still, I was on edge, waiting for the cat to pounce.

"Kate looks nothing like your mother," Anita said, standing at the kitchen counter placing aromatic sprigs of fresh dill on top of the poached salmon. "You gotta admit that."

My skin prickled. I continued tossing the salad. "So what are you saying?"

"If it wasn't for Nan's story, I'd never believe they were sisters." She walked over to the stove and sprinkled sea salt on the little red potatoes in the frying pan. "Your mother was short and plump. Kate's long and lean with freckles sprinkling her nose. Not an ounce of family resemblance."

"Well, they were. And I've got freckles."

"Yeah, yeah, I know. So do a lot of people." She tossed the salted potatoes in olive oil.

"So you doubt Nan's story? You doubt the birth certificates?"

"No. I wish I could, but no." She swirled the potatoes around the sizzling pan.

I let out a frustrated breath and picked up the salad bowl. Tired of hearing all the negatives, I looked at my friend and merely said, "Let's bring the food out."

The glass table was set with Anita's Dansk dishes. I placed the teak salad bowl in the center. Anita walked in and put the salmon platter next to it and looked up at Bill. "Did I hear you two talking about cruises?"

"Yeah. Kate and I were discussing places she should go. She wants to do more travelling."

"But I want to stay on dry land," Kate said. "Bill's idea of a river cruise is enticing, but not good if I plan on painting the cities I visit. I'd need more time than the cruise ships give you." I slid the salad bowl across the table and motioned for Kate to start. She lifted the mixed greens onto her plate while explaining her plan. "It seems I've caught the travel bug. It's been a long time since I felt like going anywhere other than my studio." She looked across at me. "I want to get back to painting outdoors."

"En plein air," Bill said.

"Yes. I used to do it. I like painting from the actual visual conditions, the way the sun glistens off the water or the breeze moves the grass. It's so much more exciting than having to imagine it all in a studio." I watched her eyes sparkle with each word she spoke. Her voice changed from a mere conversational tone to exuberance. "I want to feel that breeze," she said, making a fist as if she could grab it. "And actually see the colors in the sky, the purples and oranges in sunset, the bright yellows of morning, the grays on a cloudy day. I want to watch a bird go from tree to tree and observe his wings in flight, and I want to bring that movement right onto the canvas."

I envied Kate's enthusiasm. It was intoxicating. I wished I could be there with her, see what she saw and how she brought it onto the canvas. "So you're going to travel?" I said. "Will you go alone?"

Once again, Anita shot me a look of disapproval. What did she think I was going to do?

"I'm not sure," Kate said. "I might find a group, or maybe invite Ben. We could go on his spring break."

Bill chuckled. "I doubt a college kid of nineteen wants to go on spring break with his grandma," he said. "No matter how cool Grandma is."

"You've got a point," Kate said. "I'll have to think about it."

We chatted about college kids on spring break as we ate our dinner. The fish was perfect, savory with hints of shallots, white wine, and dill. I chewed and swallowed, mulling over ways to get invited on Kate's painting vacation while Bill and Anita reminisced about their exploits in Fort Lauderdale on spring break in the '60s.

"I totally understand what you mean about painting outdoors," I said, resting my fork on the plate. "Though it must be more difficult than photography. It takes a moment to take a shot, once I've got my settings, and if the weather changes, I can take another one, but you've already painted what you see and feel. What happens if a cloud comes over and changes everything?"

"That's what I love about it," Kate said. "The picture is alive, constantly changing. Years ago, when I was out at Joshua Tree painting the rugged rock formations, dark clouds suddenly filled the sky. I put the bright yellows away and squeezed out ochre, one of my favorite colors, then mixed it with shades of brown and black and added a little gray. Lucky for me, the rain stayed away and the painting turned out magnificent. Robert sold it for a bundle."

I wondered what a bundle was but didn't dare ask. "I've never been to Joshua Tree," I said. "I hear the scenery is magnificent. I'd love to shoot pictures there." Anita's bright eyes and nod let me know she thought it was a great idea. But when I asked Kate how far the national park was from her home, Anita's expression darkened. She'd read my mind. Deal with it, I told her—under my breath.

CHAPTER 28

The Mets took the field. It was Kate's last day in New York, and we were seated behind home plate with me next to Ben and Kate on my other side. The blazing sun made me glad I'd slathered sunscreen on my face.

"We'll come back this inning," Ben said, his eyes glued to the field. "Dickey's got a good arm. He can do it." The count was three and two. "No! Don't walk him," he yelled as the pitcher threw the ball high and outside. Ben threw up his arms and turned to me. "What's he gonna do? Walk 'em all?"

Baseball banter was something I always did with my father, and I was having a great time playing commentator with Ben, so relieved we'd finally seemed to connect. Getting him to be my client was another matter. Nothing had been said yet, and I wasn't the one to open that discussion. It had to come from his grandmother, and I didn't want it to seem as if I was pushing for it. If I had to, I'd ask her why she hadn't mentioned it to him. I needed more time with Ben, to see him more often so we could get into his genealogy.

The next batter stepped up to the plate, slammed a line drive to right field, and Pagan bobbled the ball. Now Atlanta had runners on first and second, and Benny bent forward, the pain of another loss just too much for him. I patted his back. "Come on, Ben, don't give up yet." He grabbed his soda–his second–and took a long drink.

Kate stood up. "Come on, Dickey, strike him out," she yelled. Well, not quite yelled; that wasn't her style. She sort of sang the words along with the hundreds of other screaming Mets fans. We all joined in. "Let's go Mets! Let's go Mets!" The music blared. The jumbotron flashed pictures. The stadium erupted. Dickey peered in at the sign, nodded his head, brought his glove down from his chest to his belt, kicked his leg up, and floated in a knuckle ball. Strike three!

"Yes!" cried Ben, high-fiving me, then excused himself to go to the bathroom. That must have been his third trip.

We sat through four more excruciating innings then gathered up our garbage, tossed it in the can, and walked out of the stadium swallowing a 6-3 loss. While we walked to the car, Ben and I debated the call at third when Wright was out. His face was lit up, and I felt great as, like two old friends, we took apart the last inning when Dickey gave up two runs. Kate remained quiet and slipped into the back seat after I clicked the doors open. Ben grabbed the door before it closed. "No, Grandma," he said. "You sit up front."

"No, I'm going to lay back and probably fall asleep, Benny. You sit up there."

I had a feeling I knew what was on Kate's mind. She wanted to keep Ben with me, chatting about the game and anything else that came up so when she brought up the subject of exercise, he'd easily accept my training him. I didn't think it would be a problem, not after today. I just needed her to finally say something. And if she didn't, as scared as I was of her not wanting anything to do with me once she realized I'd gone behind her back, I had decided I'd tell her myself. I couldn't hold this in. It meant too much to me, and I had to believe she'd be fine. Angry at first, yes, but eventually she'd get over it. Kate didn't seem the type to hold a grudge.

Traffic was backed up as usual, and Ben kept his eyes open, helping me meander around cars backing out of parking spots. I assumed Kate had fallen asleep and decided to take the opportunity.

"I don't know if your grandmother told you," I said while we waited in the long line of cars creeping our way to the exit. "I've been researching my genealogy and it's fascinating. She said you'd probably be interested in doing yours."

"My mom started it, but . . ." He shrugged a shoulder. Obviously, he didn't want to talk about his mother. I saw a very well-brought-up boy when he politely asked about my research.

"Yes, I did find something interesting." I felt my fingers twitch on the steering wheel. I could have revealed the whole story right then, but I didn't. I still wanted Ben to be the one to do it. As much as I told myself Kate would be fine with the news, I had to admit I was afraid. I couldn't lose her now when she seemed to honestly care for me. That moment in front of the painting of the blue door, when she touched my shoulder, I felt warmed with love, like a little girl again having her mother tuck her in at night.

I glanced in the rearview mirror. Kate's eyes were closed. I couldn't tell if she was sleeping. It didn't matter, she obviously wasn't the least bit interested in my genealogy. Ben was, so I went on. "I found my grandfather Jack's shipping record," I said. "It was incredible with all kinds of information, the year and names of everyone he traveled with and . . .

"Hey, Grandma," Ben turned to look over the seat back. "You should do yours. Maybe you'll find some relatives you never knew about."

"I doubt they're alive," Kate said. She sounded like she was talking in her sleep.

Ben laughed. "Yeah. Probably right. One of these days, when I don't have so much school work, I might do it."

Another look in the rearview mirror told me Kate would not be saying another word for a while, and Ben seemed to let his thoughts drift away. I picked up the thread before they were all gone.

"If you want to do your genealogy, I can help. I've learned a lot since starting mine."

"Nah, not right now. I don't have the time. Thanks anyway."

I'd hit a wall with him, for the moment. I wasn't going to give up that easily.

CHAPTER 29

Two weeks after the Mets game, Kate called to tell me about Ben's doctor appointment. It had taken her prodding and calling his father for Ben to even bother making it.

"Oh, Carolyn, it's what I feared. The dermatologist was concerned that the cyst had come back. He sent Ben for blood work." Kate let out a huge sad sigh. "He's got diabetes. I'm so frightened. I can't lose him too."

I knew exactly what Kate meant. She was so sure her daughter had died from undiagnosed diabetes, how could she not be petrified? I felt awful for her and wanted to allay her fears. "As upsetting as it is, diabetes can be controlled," I said. "Let's be thankful he's under a doctor's care. You did the right thing, pushing him for that appointment."

"It's hard to get through to kids. They think they're indestructible, and I'm afraid he won't do what he's supposed to. The doctor told him he has to exercise in addition to taking insulin. Please, Carolyn, help him."

I didn't know much about blood sugar levels, other than that there's an appropriate one to safely exercise. I had one woman in my class with the disease, and she accepted full responsibility for her exercise sessions, always carrying lifesavers or glucose tablets in case she felt weak. I, too, was afraid Ben might not be that responsible, being only nineteen. As much as I wanted to work with him to accomplish my genealogy goal, I was very concerned that now it was out of my realm. Until he got himself stable, I'd be very uncomfortable. "I can give him exercise tips," I said. "I'm happy to help, but there's got to be someone better equipped than I am."

"Ben knows what he has to do. He tests his sugar level several times a day, and he's learning how to adjust his insulin and what to eat and not eat. No, Carolyn. I'd feel better if you were the one working with him. That way, I could keep an eye on him so to speak. Besides, I've already talked to Ben and he's willing to work with you. He said he thinks you're cool."

That made me smile. It felt pretty great just having a kid his age thinking someone my age could be cool. And I was glad he was willing to take exercise tips from me, not only for my sake, but for his, even though I was anxious about it. If he was a healthy guy, I'd have no problem–even if he had a knee or back issue–but this was different. I truly felt bad for Ben and decided I would make it my business to learn more about the relationship between diabetes and exercise. Kate was bent on my being the one to train him, and I certainly didn't want to disappoint her. "I want to be in touch with his doctor," I said, and Kate agreed that would be a good idea. Even though diabetes was controllable, it wasn't an easy diagnosis to deal with, especially at Ben's age and being away from family. He didn't have a mother to hug him and help him through it. I missed my mom so much and I wasn't even sick. I could only imagine what it was like for him. Plus, living in a fraternity house with all the late night snacks, pizza, and beer that flowed like a river made this disease even more difficult to deal with. He'd have trouble keeping his sugar down. How could he ignore all those influences?

"He's scared," Kate said. "The doctor actually told him he could have died. He said Ben had lost so much weight because his sugar levels were so high. And I thought he looked great." She sniffed back tears. "I honestly never thought of this. Thank God I got him to the doctor. I couldn't go through it again."

I wanted to hug Kate, to hold her tight and tell her that I'd do everything in my power to help Ben. "You're not going to lose him," I said. "I'll make sure he's diligent. We'll get this under control. We will get through this, and Ben will be fine." Oh, how I hoped I was right. Ben was not just another client, he was family. Failure was never an option for me, and even less so now.

I called Ben as soon as we hung up and let him know what his grandmother had said. Through his bravado, when he quipped, "It's just diabetes. I can deal with it," I heard a little boy trying to sound brave. I wished I could have embraced him, too, and told him everything would be okay. But it wouldn't, unless he was steadfast in his care of himself. We talked about exercising, and I explained how cardio workouts helped lower sugar levels.

"You can go to the gym at school," I suggested. "Three, four times a week. Walk on the treadmill. Ride the bike. Do anything that gets your heart pumping. You want to kick up those endorphins and drop those A1C levels."

"I walk nine blocks to school and back. That's good, isn't it?"

"Yes." I didn't want him to feel like a failure, like this was entirely his fault. Unfortunately, diabetes ran in his family. I wondered if it was from Kate's side or her husband's. I wasn't aware of anyone else in the family having it. "The more you walk the better," I explained. "Even tossing a ball around with your friends, playing football or soccer is good, but you need to set aside some time for a real workout." I wanted to make it seem easy. If Ben saw it as a burden, he'd never do it. Then a thought came to me.

"I'm coming into the city on Thursday. I've been wanting to shoot pictures at the Central Park Zoo."

"I didn't know you were a photographer too."

"An amateur," I said with a laugh. "You could meet me and after I'm done, we'll take a good walk through the park, cover some miles. It'd be your workout for the day."

"Do you have one of those manual cameras, an SLR? I wanted one for my birthday, but Dad just got me a point-and-shoot."

"I do. You can play around with mine, if you want. How about it, Benny? Does Thursday work for you?"

I was surprised and comforted he'd accepted my invitation so readily. Kate would be relieved, too, which made me even happier. With all that, I still was anxious. Would Ben take this seriously? Would I be effective?

***

"Hey, Ben, over here," I called, spotting his light-blue Columbia windbreaker. He stood at the edge of Central Park among throngs of tourists fascinated by the horse drawn carriages lining Fifty-Ninth Street. The scent of horse dung permeated the air. I waved my arm. My camera, hanging on my shoulder, banged my side.

Ben and I walked through the park's gates leaving the concrete world of New York City behind and entering a wonderland of orange, gold, and crimson. Central Park was alive with autumn color. The sounds of the street, horns honking, bus doors whooshing as they closed, brakes screeching, all evaporated as Ben and I made our way along the path. We avoided the topic of diabetes and focused on photography.

"I don't know how to use one of those," he said pointing to my Nikon with its zoom lens. "I've just got this little thing."

I assured him he could get great pictures with a point-and-shoot.

"Yeah, but you'll get great close-ups."

I paid the twenty-four dollars and we headed directly to the large mammals. Seriously, twenty-four dollars! Not even a student rate for Ben. For a moment, I thought we could have skipped the zoo and just walked the park taking pictures at the lake and the Bow Bridge and along the reservoir, but the poster propped up on an easel by the ticket booth changed all that. "Can I use your camera to get close to him?" Ben asked pointing to the photo of the snow leopard.

We walked in and followed the map to find the spotted animal. "Turn the lens 'til you see exactly what you want," I said, handing Ben my camera. "And bend down. You'll get a better shot of her face." We were directly in front of the real live leopard, and she was gorgeous. Her pale green eyes stared at Ben as if she were posing. He clicked off two shots and stood up.

"Look at her tail," he said. "It's almost as long as her whole body."

"It's three feet long." I read the words on the sign hinged to the fence. "She uses it for balance." I turned to him and said, "I've got some great exercises to challenge your balance and work your core at the same time using a stability ball. We'll do it sometime."

Ben was having a good time with my camera. I kept the setting on "Animals" rather than using "Manual." Stan once said that if the camera geniuses figured out how to make these settings, why stress over F-stops and shutter speeds? I agreed, but had wanted to try. He had been teaching me, but since his death I'd lost interest. Now with Ben, I was going to kick it up again. An extra benefit to my connection with him. I prayed I'd be a good influence and get him to exercise regularly.

Focusing on the snow leopard's huge paws, Ben stood on the bench. A half-empty bottle of water was shoved in his windbreaker pocket. "Where do these guys come from?" he asked.

"Central Asia, it says. And they're an endangered species." I read on and told him that their bones are used in Chinese medicine, the perfect segue into the conversation we needed to have.

Ben hopped off the bench and gulped some water as we walked over to the polar bears. "Speaking of medicine," I said, "I'm sorry about your diagnosis. It's not an easy one to deal with."

"It's okay." Ben shrugged it off, as I was afraid he'd do.

"Are you on medication or do you just have to change your diet?" I knew he was on insulin, but didn't want him to know Kate had told me everything. Here I was again, being deceptive. It's fine, I told myself–again. I'm not lying. Sometimes a little deception is needed. Ben could be sensitive about Kate discussing him with me, and I wanted to respect his privacy–let the information come from him.

"I've got some pills to take," he said, "and I'm supposed to take insulin twice a day."

"Supposed to?"

"Well, yeah. I've got these little needles I have to stick myself with. Guess I'll get used to it."

From the way he looked everywhere but my face, I could tell he didn't want to talk about that. Too bad, I thought. "Taking insulin is really important. Without it, your sugar levels will be out of whack and you'll get really sick. So get used to those little needles, Benny." He nodded, his eyes peeled on his toes. "And if there's any way I can help, let me know. I'm not a nutritionist–as a matter of fact, you should see one–but I do know a little about diabetes."

"Thanks," he said, our eyes finally meeting. "I've seen a nutritionist." Ben then asked if there was a bathroom nearby. We walked back to the same restroom he'd visited when we first entered. Afterward, we took pictures of the polar bears and the red panda and moved on to the sea lions. I was taking shots of them being fed while Ben looked for a water fountain. He'd already finished his sports bottle.

"That's gonna be a great one," Ben said. He returned just as I clicked off a shot of a two-year-old catching a fish on the fly. "It's feeding time for sea lions," he said, "and feeding time for Ben. Can we get some lunch now?"

I told him that I had planned to walk north in the park, to the lake, then cut across and exit and go to a restaurant on Columbus Avenue. It would give us more exercise. "After all, that's why we're here. Taking pictures just makes it more fun. You don't always have to go to a gym."

"Is there anything closer? I'm not feeling great."

"What's the matter? Did you have breakfast?"

"Yeah. I had a bagel and orange juice. I'll be fine. This happened the other day too. I just feel tired–like weak. I need to eat something."

Frustrated, the words flew from my mouth. "Ben, you should not be drinking orange juice. It's got a high sugar content. If you really want it, cut it with lots of water."

"That's nuts. It's OJ. It's supposed to be good for you."

"Not if you have diabetes." I briefly explained about foods with a high glycemic index. "Your nutritionist probably told you all about that, so just take it as a reminder." And, I thought, pay attention. Please.

The Dancing Crane Café right there in the zoo was the closest place I could think of to eat. It should have only taken us a few minutes to walk over, but Ben stopped twice to sit. I found some loose peanuts in the bottom of my pocketbook and made him eat them. I thought of running over and getting him a hot dog, or anything, but I was afraid of leaving him alone. He didn't look good, but he insisted on getting to the café.

The outdoor seating area was open. Ben sat at a round table and I rushed in to get us some lunch. There wasn't much in the way of healthy options to choose from other than turkey sandwiches. Balancing them on a tray with two bottles of water, I stepped out into the sunshine and walked to our table. Ben wasn't there.

Off to the left of the dining patio, somewhat hidden by a clump of trees, I noticed a figure lying under an elm. He was wearing a light-blue windbreaker. I grabbed my camera, left the lunch on the table, and ran over.

"What happened?" I bent down and gently touched his shoulder.

Ben mumbled, "I'm so tired. I can't move."

"You can't stay here like this. Come on, Benny, sit up. Do you have your insulin?" I remembered that high sugar levels made you very lethargic, and assumed his was since he probably hadn't taken his insulin that morning. Thank goodness I'd read up on this stuff. Ben shook his head no. Shit. Insulin would get his sugar down. Plus, he needed to carry it with him anyway, if he planned on eating. What was I going to do? I was terrified. His skin was the color of paste–the kind kids use in elementary school–a grayish white.

"OK. Stay here. I'll be back in a sec." I ran to the table, grabbed the water bottle and sandwiches and flew back. "Here, have a sip," I said, propping up his head. He barely moved. With my free hand, I tore a piece of turkey from the sandwich and told him to eat. He didn't want to but I insisted. I wasn't sure I was doing the right thing, but knew turkey was better than the carbs in the bread. I should have realized something wasn't right the minute we said hello that morning. Ben's breath had smelled like Juicy Fruit yet he never looked like he was chewing gum. Sweet smelling breath is another sign of high sugar levels, and I was afraid Ben's was hitting the sky. After he swallowed a few bites and some water, I said, "This isn't right. You've got to get up." He shook his head. "Okay, then I'm calling an ambulance. We've got to get you to the ER."

"No. No ambulance." Ben pushed his way up to a seated position and rested his head against the tree. "Give me a minute," he said. "Just wait . . . I'm . . . I'm better."

The color was coming back to Ben's face. He didn't look great, but I wasn't anxious to call an ambulance. I wasn't anxious to have him pass out on me either. I gave him a little more time keeping my eyes on him. I barely blinked. Only two minutes later, I'd had enough silence. "Okay. Can you stand?"

Ben nodded, showed me he could. "Wow. That was something." He was trying to sound macho, but I could tell he was frightened.

"Yeah, it was. You scared the hell out of me." I didn't want to sound like his mother, but I was the grown-up here, and he needed to see a doctor. He argued when I suggested it. "No, Ben, you've been thirsty all morning, and you peed at least three times in the past hour. Those are all signs of high sugar levels. Plus, you're more tired than you should be, unless you're hung over." He shook his head. "Okay then. Be honest. Have you been taking your insulin? Because if not, you could be seriously ill."

Ben held onto the tree trunk and picked at its bark. "It's embarrassing," he said. "The guys'll think I'm shooting up, and I don't carry it around with me, so how am I supposed to take it before I eat?"

I wanted to shake him. What the hell was he thinking? But who was I to get angry? Just some friend of his grandmother's?

"Jeez, Ben, don't you know how serious this can be?" His shrug reminded me of students who frustrated me to no end when they didn't work up to their potential. "You've got to take your meds."

I recognized the look on his face. It's the same one I used to give my mother when I didn't want to hear whatever she had to say.

CHAPTER 30

I bit my lip 'til it almost bled worrying Ben would collapse again, but we made it out of the park with him on his two feet, and I hailed a taxi. Fifth Avenue goes downtown–the opposite of where we had to go–and traffic was fierce. The driver pushed his way across the road and made it to the next corner, cutting off a long row of cars. Horns honked, drivers shouted, thrusting their middle fingers out their windows at the cabby, and we turned left. I sat on the edge of my seat willing him to go faster, but when you're stuck behind a garbage truck in Manhattan, there isn't much you can do. I looked at my watch. What good was that? The taxi edged its way around the truck. I was sure we'd hit the cars double-parked and never get off this damn street. We crept forward and navigated around a cab dropping off a fare. I rocked forward and back in my seat. I'd read what could happen with uncontrolled diabetes, and it scared the hell out of me having his life in my hands. If anything happened to him, Kate would be inconsolable. She'd fall back into her depression, probably worse than ever. And she was depending on me! Oh, why did this have to happen just when I found my family? I couldn't lose them now. I looked over at Ben who was staring out the window and wished he knew we were cousins. I wanted so much to tell him right then and make him understand why I cared so much–why I was sounding like a mother.

Finally, we reached the corner and turned. The street was clear and the driver sailed up the avenue dodging buses. As we crossed Ninety-First Street everything changed.

"Where are we going?" Ben asked. His eyes were glassy.

"What do you mean, where're we going? We're going to your doctor."

"I thought we were getting lunch."

Oh boy! That was it. I leaned forward and told the driver to take us to the emergency room. "Mount Sinai. On a hundred and fifth. Hurry!" I wanted to shake Ben. What the hell was he thinking, not taking his meds?

It must have been a slow day at the ER. Ben was taken in immediately. The nurse let me follow even though I had to say I wasn't a blood relative. I listened to the intake interview and couldn't hold back. "He's diabetic," I said. "Let's cut to the chase. He hasn't been taking his insulin . . ." The nurse looked at me, then Ben. He nodded in agreement, and I told her the rest of the story.

While Ben was out having more tests, I went to the waiting room and used his cell phone to call his father. Ben had given me permission, after I convinced him his father had to know. Mr. Moss answered on the first ring.

"Hi!" He sounded thrilled, probably assuming it was Ben on the other end. I was sorry to disappoint him.

"Mr. Moss, this is Carolyn Lee. You don't know me, but I'm a friend of your mother-in-law."

"What happened to Kate?"

"Nothing. She's fine. I'm calling about Ben." I gave him a brief rundown. I assumed he would come. What parent wouldn't rush to help their child?

"Is it serious?" He asked. "Ben's got class tonight."

With my hand in a tight fist, I explained the dangers of high sugar levels, leaving out the word death, which I refused to consider now that Ben was in the hospital. The doctors would get him stable. I told that to Mr. Moss, hoping I was correct.

"Between getting to the airport and waiting on the tarmac, taking a cab from La Guardia, I don't know . . ." His hesitation pissed me off. "Do I really need to be there?"

Seriously, he wasn't rushing right to his kid's side? My mother would have dropped everything if I was in the hospital. I imagine Ben's mother would have too. "Yes," I said not able to keep the irritation out of my voice. "Ben needs you."

"Okay, but I'm not taking a plane. It's faster for me to drive. I've got to get home, get a few things. I'll call you when I'm on my way."

As expected, Ben was hyperglycemic. His sugar levels were out of whack. Those were the exact words the doctor used when he came in the room almost an hour after Ben got back from having an EKG and other tests. Ben was in bed texting with some friends, and I was seated next to him checking email. It wasn't as if we hadn't talked. We'd covered our favorite television shows and the books on the syllabus for his English Lit class–even places we'd go together for more photo shoots. And then he got a text. It took him into another world. Thankfully, he put the phone down when the doctor came in.

"You are one lucky guy," he said. "If it weren't for Miss Lee here, you might be lying on a slab in the morgue. Maybe not today, but one day soon." I couldn't believe a doctor would speak that way. He scared the shit out of me; I could only imagine how Ben felt, if he took it seriously. "We've got you stabilized now, Benjamin, but you *must* take your medication. I can't be more emphatic about it. You can live a normal life with diabetes, you can play sports, you can bungee jump off the Great Barrier Reef if you want, but you *must* keep your sugar levels in check."

I told the doctor Ben's father was on his way and that if there was anything specific about medications or protocol, "anything at all, his father should hear it. I'm sure he's going to want to see you."

"Good. When he gets here, have me paged. Until then, we'll get the paperwork ready to have Ben admitted."

"I have to stay here?" Ben sounded like a kid given a time-out in pre-school. "I'm okay now. I've got a class tonight."

"As I said, this was serious." The doctor kept his eye on Ben the whole time he spoke. "I want to monitor your sugar levels and make sure we've got you on the correct dose. And, obviously, you need to be educated. Like I said, you can lead a normal life, if you understand what you have to do and why. You can control this disease."

Ben turned to me. "Will you stay here? At least 'til my father comes?"

A warm sensation enveloped me. It was more a feeling of belonging than of need, though being needed was nice too. I hadn't felt that since my mother died. I reached over and placed my hand on his arm. "I'm not going anywhere, Benny. Don't worry."

Ben's father arrived just as the patients were being served dinner. He had the same brown eyes as his son with thick lashes a woman would envy. After introductions and a thank you from Mr. Moss for staying with Ben all day, I walked to the door. "You need to spend some time with your dad," I said when Ben asked me to stay. "I'll be back in a little while. I'm not going home yet."

Although, I certainly could have, with his dad there, I had this deep desire to stay and not just because Ben wanted me to. I had a feeling Kate would have also, or maybe it's what I wanted to believe. Yet I didn't want to be in the way. At first, Mr. Moss seemed like a nice man, but when he uttered a quick second thank you, I felt he was shoving me out the door.

"I'll be in the lounge," I said, refusing the shove.

"Tell me again how you know my mother-in-law," Mr. Moss said as he walked into the hospital lounge later. I was seated in one of the vinyl-covered chairs sipping a cup of tea from the vending machine. I began the story of the painting from the beginning.

"I get it," he said. "You felt a real kinship to that painting. So why'd you want to get rid of it? Did you imagine she'd pay you? Refund your money?"

"No." I explained about not having a place for it in my condo and how it didn't match my decor, which I realized sounded pretentious. The skepticism on his face made me omit the cameo part of the equation. I pushed that out of my head and tried to tell Mr. Moss how much I wanted Kate to have it once I learned the woman was her grandmother. He wasn't making this easy and the more I said, the deeper I dug myself into fiction I couldn't climb out of.

"You do see how strange this all sounds. If you loved it so much, you would have kept the painting. What are you really after? Did you expect some priceless piece of art in exchange? Because, if that's it, you can drop your so called friendship with Kate right now. My mother-in-law's paintings sell for a nice price, but she's no Picasso."

"That's not it at all. I didn't expect anything from her." As the words poured out of me, I was ashamed. Of course I expected something–to know why the cameos were exactly the same. And now, I still wanted something. Family. Even if he had to be part of it. I was stunned by the change in him. "Becoming friendly with Kate was a bonus," I said, trying to steer him away from attacking me any further–and to get back to the truth. "And then . . ."

"And then you met Ben and it's like you're one little happy family, the three of you going to baseball games and having lunch together. I don't buy it."

The man with the warm, friendly eyes so appreciative of my taking care of his son was totally gone. He'd turned into a prosecutor. I wouldn't have been surprised if he'd asked me to put my hand on a Bible and take an oath.

"Ben likes you," he said. "He's too young and gullible to be wary of your motives. And as far as Kate's concerned, she's just happy to have her painting back." He looked utterly disgusted. "I called her on my drive up, and she gave me an earful all about you, her new friend."

"You told her Ben was in the hospital?"

"No! That would be stupid. She'd get sick worrying about him, and then I'd have to fly out there to take care of her–maybe have to put her in a nursing home."

"Why would you say that? Kate's fine."

"Sure, now she is, but if she gets . . ." He slapped the air, as if slapping my face. "Forget it. It's none of your concern."

Yes, it was, and I needed to know what he meant. I pressed for an answer and he shut me down saying, "You're not family. Remember that. And you barely know her, so don't get involved." My blood was on a slow boil. I despised his ugly tone and hated the accusations he'd thrown at me. And on top of that, I couldn't tell him we were related. Not now, after fudging why I'd given Kate the painting. I was sinking deeper into the quicksand of lies, and it felt like a vise was clamped tight on my chest. I forced a congenial tone, deflecting my anguish, and told him I agreed. "If you're worried about Kate, there really is no need for her to know Ben's in the hospital. She's been very worried about him."

"Yeah. I hear you and Kate speak quite often." His brow raised. "I don't get it. You have a painting, you give it back to the artist, and all of a sudden you're great friends."

His suspicion was palpable and I worried he might infect Kate with the same. I gave him the most charming smile I could muster and said, "I know. It is an odd story." I was not going to let him put me on the witness stand and perjure myself anymore. Even if I deserved to be.

"Well. Be careful," he said as he turned to walk out. "You can never take her daughter's place."

Whoa. I didn't expect that. Of course I couldn't, and Kate would never take my mother's. Anita once said the same thing. It aggravated me then and made me bristle even more now. Those were special bonds that could never be severed. Kate was my aunt and I truly liked her and I was worried. What did he mean about her getting sick? Was it a pattern of hers after hearing disturbing news? Did she actually get physically ill? I needed answers. I'd ask Ben, once his father was back in Virginia.

CHAPTER 31

When I called Ben the next morning, he told me he was being released and that his dad was staying a few days. "I'll call you next week," I said. "And when you see your doctor, ask him for an exercise prescription." As much as I had learned about it, I felt better having a plan from a medical professional.

"You'll help me with it?" Ben asked.

I knew if he was saying that, he was really scared. I was happy he felt he could depend on me and not only so I could put my plan in place. I liked the feeling of helping someone in need of exercise, not only wanting to have a svelte figure. I assured Ben I would do what I could to make it easy for him to incorporate exercise in his busy day and keep his blood sugar levels where they should be. We said goodbye and I slipped on my jacket and locked the door behind me.

Anita lived about a mile from me in Tarrytown. With my window wide open, I drove north on Route 9 enjoying the crisp autumn air, passing Main Street with all its stores and restaurants, then turning right up the hill to Pine Street. Other than the enormous white pine on the corner shaped like a pyramid, I never understood the name of this street. It was filled with red maples, their bounteous leaves a brilliant crimson. Soon those leaves would carpet lawns and in another month or so the trees would be bare. Snow would fall, the first one always beautiful, but after that it would get icy and slushy, and I didn't want to be here for that. I didn't have to anymore. I was retired and I didn't have to take care of Mom. I could get subs for my exercise classes, so why stay in the cold northeast? An idea began to sprout.

I pulled up alongside the curb in front of Anita's white painted-brick house with its black shutters and honked, letting her know I'd arrived. A terra cotta pot full of fat yellow mums sat on her front steps, the kind of flowers girls used to wear to their high school's Thanksgiving Day football game.

Thanksgiving, I sighed as I thought about the holiday just five weeks away. I wondered where Kate would be spending it, whose table she'd be sitting at. Without her daughter and grandkids, it would be a very sad day for her as it would be for me. I wished we could be together, but that was out of the question. Unless . . . No, my idea–the one that came to me in the car–was for the winter. But maybe . . . It sure would make the holiday better. It had always been my favorite. No religion. No gifts. And the food was good. Chestnut stuffing, corn soufflé, sweet cranberries, and moist turkey. Anita had always included Mom and me; there was never a question. But this year, she was going to her son's in Boston to see her new grandchild, and I didn't know what I was doing. I felt so alone.

Anita got in the car and we drove to the park a mile away. As we crossed the wobbly bridge leading to the parking lot, I looked out at the river below. The water made lovely music as it trickled over rocks traveling downstream. It was as clear as fine crystal–just as my mind was with my latest idea.

"I'm going out to California for the holidays," I announced as I locked the car. "And I'm seriously considering renting a place, staying there for the winter."

Anita gave me that astounded look of hers. "Since when?"

"The idea came to me this morning, driving over to your house." We walked along the macadam path dotted with early fallen leaves in reds and gold. An earthy, woodsy scent filled the late October air. "Why should I stay here?" I said. "I don't have anything keeping me in New York, and who needs snow and ice?"

"And when you're in sunny California, you'll tell Kate she's your aunt."

I nodded. Bicycle tires hummed as three riders passed by.

"Not a good idea," Anita said. Again.

"I know how you feel, and I don't agree."

Anita drew a deep breath and released it soft and slow. "Oh, Car," she said in a calm pleading tone. "Think about it. Please."

We continued walking, in silence. I remembered another time Anita pleaded with me to think about something. It was a few years ago when I was planning to fail a student. Anita, in the same frustrated tone she'd just used said, "Give him a D, Car, not an F. Think about it. His parents were just in a horrendous car accident. He doesn't know if they're going to make it or not. Have a little compassion." She reminded me that if I failed him he wouldn't be able to graduate. I argued about sticking to the rules. It was the principle of it, a moral principle. There were good reasons for rules. But after a few days of considering what she'd said, I did give him the D. His parents survived, though not without a hard fight, and I was glad to see him in cap and gown at graduation with them sitting in their seats applauding. I remember Anita looking at me as he walked off the stage with his diploma. She gave me a thumbs-up and later said she was proud of me. I had thought about what she'd said then and had seen her point. But not this time.

We walked three miles, sidestepping around little dogs on long leads and piles of goose poop. By the time we reached the lake, we were chatting like the good friends we were. We'd agreed to disagree before, so there was no need to voice it now. We circled the lake, adding another half mile to the walk and enjoying the children's happy squeals. "Remember when we used to take the boys here?" she said, pointing to the playground with its new orange-and-red jungle gym. "I can't believe that was so many years ago."

"And now one of them has his own son," I reminded her, the new grandma. "Makes you feel a little old, doesn't it?"

I had spent many weekend afternoons here with Anita pushing her kids on the swings while Bill was off golfing. Yes, I was part of her family, like she always said. But Kate was my real family. My blood.

On my way home, I clipped the Bluetooth to my ear and, while at a red light, dialed Kate's number. It rang several times. My dashboard clock read eleven thirty. Just as she answered, after five rings, I realized I'd forgotten the three-hour time difference. I hoped she wouldn't be annoyed getting such an early call.

"Yes, dear, that does sound lovely," she said when I told her my plan. "I'm sure you could find something to rent."

I told her that's what I planned to do, that there were sites specifically for short term rentals. "Of course, I want to find something close to you. If not Venice Beach then Santa Monica or Marina Del Rey."

"Oh. Of course you'd want to be in this area. I suppose you'll find people to be with. You could join the Y. That's a good place to make friends. But you see, I'm not going to be around very much."

"Why? Where are you going?"

Kate told me she would be at a friend's home in Palm Desert from Christmas through New Year's. "I used to go every year after Irv died and my grandsons were old enough not to need a babysitter on New Year's Eve. It was all us widows and we had so much fun. We hiked at Joshua Tree. Remember, I told you about the painting I did there?" I answered with an mmm- hmmm. "And we browsed through the shops in Palm Springs and probably imbibed a bit too much. The San Jacinto Mountains were the perfect backdrop for cocktails on the patio in the late afternoon." She stopped abruptly and I wondered if we'd gotten cut off. Then she said, "And, then Beth died. After that, I didn't go anymore. I didn't go anywhere."

I heard her swallow. It seemed every time she mentioned her daughter, her throat filled with tears. God, she must be hurting so.

"And when I get back from the desert, I'm going to be busy painting."

Kate told me about the show her gallerist wanted her to be in. "I've got to come up with five new pieces of work by the end of June and let me tell you, that's no easy task anymore. The painting I did of Washington Square will be in it. Robert wants cheerful pieces, paintings that evoke a love of life–embracing life–nothing dark and depressing. I think he's trying to be my therapist."

"Can you do it? Do you have it in you?" I wished I was sitting with Kate rather than talking over the phone three thousand miles away.

"Yes, I believe I do. Even with that hole in my heart–and it'll never go away–I'm smiling again. I love the flowers, the sun on the water, those little bubbles the tide forms along the shoreline as it goes in and out, and the way the seagulls hop through them. All the beautiful things in life."

I told her those were gorgeous images. "I'm looking forward to putting my toes in those little bubbles all winter long."

"You know, Carolyn, at first I felt guilty when I smiled or laughed or had a positive thought, but I gave myself a good talking-to, looked at my grandmother in the painting, and decided it was time to grab whatever life I have left. That's what she would have told me to do."

I didn't want to think about whatever life she had left. Kate was eighty-five now. I wanted to spend as much time with her as I could, and this winter would be my opportunity.

"So you see, dear, I'm going to be very busy this winter. Remember the conversation at Anita and Bill's about my travelling and painting en plein air? Well, I've decided to go to Key West. I've always wanted to paint in a tropical setting, and now I'm going to do it. So, why don't you come out in June for the show?"

Like a punctured balloon, I deflated.

CHAPTER 32

Whether it was serendipitous or coincidence, I wasn't sure, but I had an appointment with a new client Tuesday morning who had a lower back problem and diabetes. Now, I'd have the whole winter to work with her as well as Ben. My mother used to say everything happened for the best. I wondered, would my staying here this winter prove her right?

"Stand with your back against the wall," I said, pointing to a narrow space on her family room wall free of paintings and framed photos. "Place your feet about twelve inches in front of you and separate them just about hip width, and keep your head as close to the wall as possible, nose facing front." As most people do, she lifted her chin so the back of her head would touch the wall. "It's okay if your head doesn't touch," I said correcting her posture. "Just retract it and get it as close as you can. It strengthens your neck muscles." Reminding her to keep her shoulders and lower back as close to the wall as possible as she slid down, I watched her perform my favorite core exercise. I gave her my spiel about needing strong thighs and buttocks to be independent as she aged. She was younger than me by a few years and already losing abilities, and I thought of Kate, so much older, and how independent she was, going off alone on a painting adventure. Then an image of my mother appeared in my mind's eye, and I realized how things could change in an instant. It pained me that I wasn't able to get Mom to walk again, that I threw up my hands too easily when she refused to try. I left her, the mother I dearly loved, in the hands of physical therapists, strangers who didn't know the woman she was before pneumonia stole her spirit. It had happened so fast. If only . . . No, I couldn't go down that road, it was much too upsetting. All I know is, I should have tried harder. And then Ben crept into my thoughts. No matter what I did, my mother, Kate, and Ben had their feet planted in my mind, twisting my guts with insecurity and guilt.

"Did you check your sugar before I came this morning?" I asked my client. Even though we weren't doing an intense workout and getting her heart rate up, I needed to be careful. I didn't want a repeat of Central Park.

"Absolutely," she said. "I'm nuts about taking my sugar levels. I had a scare one time and I'll never do that again."

She told me the story of when she was at a restaurant with a bunch of friends. Everyone around her seemed to be cooled by the air conditioning, but sweat was pouring down her face. "I knew something was wrong," she said. "I went outside to get some fresh air and called one of the women, asked her to get me some orange juice from the kitchen or a piece of candy. By the time she came out, I was pretty sick. I'd vomited and she said I looked spaced-out, like I had no idea where I was. She called an ambulance. It didn't take them long, but by the time they got there I was feeling better. The juice helped."

"So your sugar was low." The opposite of Ben's, that's why the orange juice helped. I'd make sure he understood the difference.

"Real low, and I was dehydrated. I'd had a busy day, tennis and swimming, and thought I'd be eating more carbs, but I was wrong." The wall slides seemed to be going easy. I kept watch on her form reminding her to keep her belly button pressed to the wall while she went on with her explanation. "You have to know your body. You have to know how much insulin you need for what you're going to eat."

"I know a kid, he's about twenty, in college." I told her what happened to Ben.

"You can go into a diabetic coma if your levels are constantly high," she said, confirming my fear. "He's got to take his meds."

I hoped Ben's doctor and the dietician he was scheduled to see would lay it all out for him. I would do my part, too and keep this all from Kate, which didn't sit well with me. If she found out about his hospital stay, she'd be angry I hadn't told her right away, though how could I, when her son-in-law made it sound like she'd get sick? Until I knew his concerns were legitimate, I'd keep quiet. It worried me that shocking news would actually do that to her. Were Anita and Nan right? I didn't want to believe it.

CHAPTER 33

It was late in the afternoon. The rain still couldn't decide if it wanted to soak the grass or just give it a sprinkle. Figuring Ben would be home in the fraternity house and his father, who I didn't care if I ever spoke to again, was back in Virginia, I called.

"Does Kate really get so anxious that she could wind up in the hospital?" I asked, after checking on Ben's progress. "Your father seems to think so."

"Yeah, she can," he said sounding very serious. "She did."

"After the Mets game? That wasn't from anxiety; it was dehydration."

"No. It happened a few years ago. She got really sick."

It felt like ice-cold water poured down my spine. "What happened?"

Ben let out a huge sigh, as if he didn't want to talk about it. "Grandma almost had a stroke."

"What? When?"

He took another deep breath and let it out slowly. The hairs on the back of my neck stood at attention. Whatever happened must have been really bad. It frightened me. What if my news did the same thing?

"It was right after Dad told Grandma we were moving to Virginia."

Yes, that was disturbing news, I thought. She'd just lost her daughter and now she'd be losing her grandchildren. Her whole family was being wrenched from her. I heard a scraping noise, like a chair being dragged across the floor. If Ben was going to sit, maybe I needed to do the same.

The next night–I was doing homework and Dad was watching baseball–Grandma called from the hospital. She said she'd been having trouble catching her breath–that it felt like a marching band was pounding drums in her chest– like her heart was about to fly right out. We jumped in the car and raced over."

"Did she have a heart attack?"

"No, she thought it might be, but it was A-fib and her blood pressure was sky high. It was really scary."

"I'm sure it was. An irregular heartbeat is very scary. I know someone who has Atrial Fibrillation and it's controlled with medication."

"Yeah, well Grandma's wasn't. Every pill she took got her sick. She was back and forth to the hospital for about two weeks. They'd keep her a couple of days, let her go, and then she'd be back again. One medication was so bad, her whole body trembled. She couldn't stop it. We were afraid she would have a stroke. Finally, the doctor said she needed an ablation."

I'd never heard the word and it didn't sound good. Ben explained it to me as best he could, which was fine with me. Fancy medical terms were not what I needed right then.

"It has to do with the electrical impulses to your heart," he said. "It makes it beat normally and, like Grandma said, stops the drums and tubas. It's not open heart surgery, but it's still dangerous. They stick a catheter in your heart and you could get an infection or it could puncture and bleed. You could even die."

"Thank goodness that didn't happen." I felt my own heartbeat slow. "Obviously, it worked."

Another deep sigh escaped Ben's lips. This time it sounded like relief. "Yes. If she hadn't had the ablation, she eventually would have had a stroke. Now, her heart is good, beating like it's supposed to, but she's not allowed to have wine . . ."

"What about vodka?" I thought of how she loved her Stoli.

Ben laughed. "That's fine, which is a good thing for Grandma. But no caffeine or chocolate either, so make sure she doesn't have any when you're with her again."

Which I hoped would be soon, though I was not about to be the food police, other than making sure I never offered her anything forbidden. Why ask for trouble? Then I got scared–really frightened this time because I'd never expected Ben's answer. It felt like a huge rock set itself deep in my stomach. Would Kate's finding out she had a sister she never met and never could meet land her in the hospital again? And if Mr. Moss was worried about her having another attack over anxiety, stress, fear, whatever, maybe he wasn't so bad. Was my need for family making me read everything all wrong? Oh, this was so irksome. I didn't want to think about it. All I wanted was for Ben to do his genealogy and break the story to Kate.

After hanging up the phone, I cuddled up on my couch with the crimson-and-white afghan on my lap, a novel in my hands. The rain lulled me to sleep. A little while later, my cell woke me.

"Hello, Carolyn," Kate said. "I hope I'm not disturbing you."

"Oh no, not at all. It's great to hear from you." I stretched, then scooted to a sitting position, thrilled to hear her voice. The living room was so dark. I reached over to the ceramic lamp on the end table and turned it on. The light emanating through the linen shade was exactly how I felt. Luminescent. Kate had called me. Then, in an instant, I was queasy all over. Why was she calling me? Other than when she phoned about Ben's diagnosis, I'd been the one to initiate our telephone conversations. Was it merely a coincidence or had Ben called her? What did he tell her?

"I've been worried about Ben," she said. "Have you seen him? How's he doing?"

Whew! Yet now, I was going to have to make up a story . . . again.

"As far as I know, he's fine," I said. That was honest. He was fine now. I told her about Central Park, leaving out his collapse.

"Yes, he told me he was meeting you. I was glad he'd agreed to go."

"Well, you know the intention was to get him walking."

"I figured that out. Very clever of you and I really do appreciate it. So how'd he do?"

Shit, now I had to lie. But this one was considered a white lie. For Kate's benefit. That's okay to do, isn't it, when you think the truth might hurt someone? "He was great," I said, crossing my fingers as if that ever made a difference. Then it hit me. I was doing exactly what Anita was suggesting I do–not tell Kate–and for the same reasons. I shook that off, telling myself this was different. Keeping the story of Ben's collapse a secret was not the same as keeping the Roth-Pearl family story secret. I trusted, or maybe it was hoped–I was so torn up, I couldn't figure myself out anymore–that if we broke the story to her slowly and showed how excited Ben and I both were with the news, that

Kate would be fine. She wouldn't have a stroke. She would benefit from that truth being revealed. So would I. But knowing about Ben getting sick, well, how was that to benefit her? "We had a good time," I said, which I believed was true, "and we walked quite a bit. I think he's going to be okay." That was true, too, as long as he listened to his doctor and took his insulin. If Ben didn't listen, I didn't know how I could ever tell Kate that I knew he was ill all along. And that I wasn't able to help him. I'd gotten myself into such a complicated situation not wanting to lie, yet not being able to tell her the truth either. Oh, this was all so vexing! Why did I ever find that cameo? My life would be so much simpler now–and, I realized, so much emptier. Like Scarlett O'Hara, I didn't want to think about that. Instead, I asked when was the last time she spoke with Ben.

"Last week sometime. Before you went to the park. But that's not unusual. It's not as if we speak every week. And the other day when you and I talked, we never mentioned him. And, concerning that phone call the other day, I'm sorry if I sounded like I was pushing you aside. Even though I'm looking forward to Key West, I'm so consumed with having to produce five more paintings by June that. . ."

"Don't worry about it. I understand."

Kate sighed. "Well, that's a relief. So I'll see you in June for the show?"

"Absolutely, I wouldn't miss it."

"And you'll keep training Benny?"

Oh, to be loved like that. Her voice was soft and pleading, with a tinge of desperation. I blinked back misty tears, assuring her I would, and I knew getting him to do his genealogy was not the only reason.

CHAPTER 34

"You've got to keep your spine neutral," I told Ben who was attempting to do bridges on a stability ball in my living room. I stood next to him watching as his head rested on the huge green ball. His feet were planted on the floor, but his butt kept sagging. "Squeeze your seat. Don't let your tush sag. This is great core work."

Along with walking New York City's streets on brisk autumn days, on my recommendation Ben had been working out on the treadmill and StairMaster for the past two months in Columbia's gym. He often called to tell me how many miles he'd covered, proud of himself as they increased and as the pounds decreased. To help him kick it up a notch, I had suggested he do some strength training to boost his metabolism and offered to come into the city to teach him some effective exercises. He said he'd rather come up to Tarrytown, after finals, that he'd have plenty of time on his hands.

"How come you didn't go home for the holidays?" I asked as Ben lifted and lowered his pelvis. I thought it was sad that he was alone, even though Christmas wasn't actually his holiday. He had two weeks off, and I couldn't understand why he wanted to stay in the city.

"Virginia doesn't feel like home," he said keeping his eyes front, avoiding mine. "I don't have any friends there. Remember, we moved right after high school. I was only there a month before I left for school."

"I imagine your dad misses you. He'd probably like you home for awhile."

"I doubt it. He's always with his girlfriend." Oh, how I ached for him. I wanted to shake his father, knock some sense into him. Ben might be a young man, but I was sure he missed his mother and from his melancholy tone, he obviously missed his father too. It didn't matter how old one was, no one should feel abandoned. Even at my age, I felt the utter aloneness of not having any real family. Friends were wonderful, just not the same, especially at holiday time. "Anyway," he said, "I am going down in a couple of days, once my brother gets there."

I was glad of that. Glad they had each other. I wanted to help Ben feel good about himself, and he seemed to after completing sixteen reps of bridges. "Great," I said. "How about a bigger challenge? You're up to it." I had him turn over with his hands on the floor in front of him and knees on the ball. "This one's really good for your abs. Just don't go flying off like one of my clients did." I explained how to pull the ball to his chest and then straighten his legs. "See how many you can do. It takes a lot of control. Keep your abs tight."

Ben struggled pulling the ball forward, grunting with each breath, though he managed to complete eight repetitions. On the ninth, the ball slipped from under him and he dropped to the floor. "Enough!" He rolled onto his back. "I'm done." He put his hands behind his head, cushioning it like a pillow, and I sat on the floor next to him watching his breathing slow as he perused the photography on the walls.

"These are terrific," he said. "Grandma sent me a camera like yours for Chanukah, since Dad never got the message or thought an SLR was too expensive. His head's not screwed on right anymore."

"What do you mean?"

"It's not like he listens when I talk to him." Ben's mouth turned downward, as if he'd tasted something awful. "His girlfriend's got him wrapped around her finger. It seems like he does whatever she wants and I'm a second thought."

"Oh, I doubt that. You know, it hasn't been easy for him either, losing your mother and moving across the country." Oh my God, was I actually defending his father? "Even if he doesn't seem to be, I'm sure he's still mourning your mom and this woman isn't taking her place, or your place either." I knew the feeling of losing the one you loved. After Stan died, I couldn't find my footing, and we weren't even married. Ben was young, only considering himself like Stan's sons only thought of themselves, never what their father needed. "Maybe you could try to cut him some slack."

Ben grunted a yeah. "You know, he's still not sure why you went to all that trouble to give the painting to Grandma. And he doesn't like your being friends."

My back straightened. Mr. Moss's skepticism wasn't a surprise, but I didn't expect him to be so opposed to my friendship with Kate or to be so vocal about it that he actually told Ben. Oh, that pissed me off to no end and made me uneasy. Would he try to come between us, to influence Kate–and Ben too? I stood up to shake the anger off and was acutely aware I'd have to step lightly around Mr. Moss. I'd have to watch my mouth, not antagonize him, and that wasn't easy for me when I was so aggravated.

"No. I'm sorry," Ben continued turning his head, looking up at me. "Dad didn't say he didn't like it. He said he wasn't comfortable with it."

I wasn't sure if being uncomfortable was any better. "He can't control her friendships," I said, holding back my anger, making it sound so logical, how could anyone think differently?

"Right. Grandma let him have it."

"What do you mean, she let him have it?"

"When Dad called her from the hospital . . ."

My brow shot up. Oh God, did he tell Kate? She knew all along? My stomach tied in knots.

"No, he didn't tell her we were at the hospital or that he'd met you."

Relief poured over me like a summer rain washing away thick humidity. Before my knees gave way, I plopped onto the floor and continued listening to Ben's explanation.

"Anyway, Dad kept saying, 'Don't get so riled up, Kate' and 'I'm only looking out for you. You know how people take advantage of seniors.' I could tell from his side of the conversation that she was pissed. He was shaking his head and saying 'no, no' and 'I'm sorry.' When he hung up, he looked really sad."

"Did he say anything to you about it?"

"Yeah. He said, 'I guess Grandma doesn't want me taking care of her. She told me not to butt in.' I felt a little bad for him, but he was wrong." Ben sat up and faced me. "For whatever it's worth, I'm glad you met Grandma. She's got friends. She's always had friends, but she seems different with you. Happier. After Mom died, she kind of went into a cocoon. And now it's like she's back to herself."

My smile met his and a very pleasant quiet filled the room. "Come here," I said standing up. I led Ben through the kitchen toward the dining room. "See that painting of a door?" I pointed to Kate's oil.

"That looks like Grandma's front door."

"It is. Kate gave it to me when I returned the painting of her grandmother. You said you're glad she and I are friends. Well, this door represents what that friendship means to me." We stood together staring at the blue door with the orange-and-purple birds of paradise framing the brick steps. "It's not just her front door, Ben. It's like a door opening to something new. A new experience. A new relationship."

Ben seemed to contemplate the metaphor. "That's kind of cool. Doors. I wonder what Grandma was thinking when she painted it?"

"She probably wasn't thinking anything other than planning out a bigger work. Her gallerist showed me the finished painting. This was just a section of it."

"She does that a lot. She gave me one of a baseball when I was kid. My brother has one of a guy at bat and they're both from the same painting." Ben looked up at the ceiling, as if for answers. "I wonder what happened to it? Grandpa used to have it in his office."

"What kind of work did your grandfather do?"

"Retail. He was some kind of manager in a department store."

"Like Jack," I said.

"Who's Jack?"

Right. Who is Jack? What made me say that now? Just that I'm so utterly consumed with telling Kate we're related. Everyone in that damn family is constantly on my mind. I can't shake them even when I should. "Jack was my grandfather," I explained. That was all that was needed right now. "My mother's father. I mentioned him to you when we talked about doing your genealogy."

"I remember. Did you find out any more stuff?"

"Lots. It's really fascinating. You should do yours. What about over your school break? You don't have any studying to do. I'll help you." And, I silently said, I'll make sure you think it's your own discovery. I couldn't let Ben find out I knew everything all along or he'd never trust me. I was on shaky ground, but I was going to take control. It would all work out. If only my heart would stop pounding so hard.

"No. It all sounds interesting, but I'm not into doing it now." Ben stepped back into the kitchen and asked for a glass of water. "Okay, I'm ready," he said, putting the glass in the sink. "You got anymore torture for me?"

No, kiddo, I thought. You're torturing me. What was I going to do now?

CHAPTER 35

"Step right in," Ben said as he answered my knock. "At your own risk."

Risk was right. I handed him the stability ball I'd ordered for him and made my way past a pile of dirty cleats, the putrid odor of sweaty, smelly feet emanating from the footwear, and a ping pong table laden with empty beer cans. Garbage bags stuffed to bursting were scattered across the floor. At least they had the decency to put the garbage in plastic. Taking it out to the street was obviously another matter, though I didn't say anything, not wanting to sound like a criticizing old fuddy-duddy, which I suppose I was.

"Did you ever play beer pong?" Ben asked.

"No. And I don't want to learn." My memories of fraternity houses weren't warm and fuzzy. I met Alan at one and look where that landed me. "Show me where you work out. It doesn't look like there's much room here."

Ben led me down the hall to an empty bedroom. "The guy who lived here dropped out at the end of the semester, so we use his room as our gym."

I wondered why someone would willingly leave an Ivy League school and asked Ben.

"His Mom's sick and he wanted to transfer closer to home." He gave a little shrug. "I get it."

With a sympathetic smile, I let him know I did too. "So how was Virginia?" Ben had returned just a few days ago.

"Virginia's Virginia. Cold, snowy. We went to DC a few times. It was great being with my brother . . . and my dad, when *she* wasn't around." It was interesting how Ben rarely mentioned his father's girlfriend and when he did, it was never by name. "Dad said I was looking good and asked if I had a personal trainer. I told him it was you."

"And?"

"He didn't look pleased but said that whatever I was doing, I should keep at it."

"Good." I figured Mr. Moss probably asked Kate about it and let her know how he felt. I sure hope he didn't put any bug in her head to doubt me or my intentions, and even if she put him in his place again, I had to be careful. Since it was obvious now that I'd have to be the one to reveal the secret and when I did, I'd have to make it sound as if I'd just recently uncovered it. If she or Ben–or his father–ever thought differently or learned I'd gone behind her back, Mr. Moss would be proved right. Then for sure, he'd be more likely to influence Kate, and I could lose the family I so desperately wanted. Shit, I always prided myself on being honest and truthful and here I was getting deeper and deeper into a lie. Then the realization hit me. I was doing exactly what Alan had done to me. Lied and kept secrets. And look where that led me. I didn't want Kate to throw me out of her life, as I'd done to Alan.

Ben showed me around the rest of the house, and I pretended all was fine, even though I couldn't stop the guilt from twisting my stomach into knots. I led Ben through his workout, then we went to get lunch at the diner around the corner.

"Grandma called last night," Ben said, holding his grilled cheese in midair ready to take a bite. "She's always so happy when I tell her I'm going to see you."

Ben looked happy too. His eyes were bright; his face lit up like everything was right with the world. I knew he was feeling good about himself, and I believed he credited me with some of that. So maybe he wouldn't get mad if I told him the truth. "I spoke to her too," I said, still contemplating how I'd tell him about my mother and Kate being sisters. He might be able to give me some pointers on how to let Kate know so she wouldn't get sick again. I let him carry on the conversation while thoughts scrambled in my head.

"Grandma finished the painting of Washington Square. The one she was working on last summer when I met you." Ben wiped his greasy fingers on a napkin. "That painting is so different from what she's done the past two years. It's bright and sunshiny." I smiled at his description. "The whole time she's been painting it, she's been cheerful," he said. "Just like she used to be, before . . ." Ben turned his face to the window, and I watched his Adam's apple go up and down as he swallowed hard. In an instant, his entire expression changed, and I doubted he even noticed the passersby or the cars stopped at the red light on the corner. I knew that feeling, when words got caught in your throat and your mind wandered to memories. It was bittersweet. A tear formed in the corner of Ben's eye. I reached out and touched his hand. "I know, Benny. It's hard. I still tear up when I think of my mother." He turned back to me and took a sip of his Diet Coke.

"Her grandmother was really her mother, you know. Or *like* a real mother." His voice was quiet with contemplation. I nodded. "I can't imagine never knowing your own mother." His eyes closed as he slowly shook his head.

Now was a good time. He was quiet and the atmosphere seemed perfect for a serious discussion. I spoke slowly. "Ben, I've got something to tell you." He opened his eyes and cocked his head like a puppy, giving me a quizzical look. "And I need your help." I leaned in and began.

"When I met Kate, I thought I was merely meeting the artist who painted the oil that hung in my parents' living room my whole life." I spoke in a matter of fact tone. Nothing titillating. Just the facts. "And during our conversation that day, Kate mentioned your mother had been planning on researching their genealogy."

Ben nodded as he ate. I wasn't sure if he was letting me know he was aware of his mother's plan or telling me to go on. I reminded him that I'd offered to do Kate's family history while I did my own and that she didn't want it.

"Yeah, 'cause Grandma probably didn't want you to do very much. She wasn't very excited about my mom doing it."

"Why not?" I was so certain that Kate should know about my mother that I couldn't imagine why she wouldn't want to. I was looking forward to telling her stories about the sister she never knew and about her grandparents, Karl the presser, who I barely remembered, and Rebecca the . . . well, maybe I wouldn't tell her what a miserable woman she was. And maybe she'd come to New York again and meet Nan this time. These people were her story. Didn't we all want our stories?

"Grandma said she never knew anyone from her father's family and that it hurt. She'd heard tales about her parents and that was enough. 'Leave it alone' is what she told my mom."

"Well, I'm afraid I did do the research that your mother had started. In fact, I'm still doing it." I knew I was fudging the truth. I wasn't deceiving myself, or hoped I wasn't. If I told this tale enough, I might start believing it myself and that wouldn't be good. "And I found some of Kate's relatives."

"Live ones?"

"Some."

Ben's eyes opened wide. "Cool," he said putting his sandwich down. He looked eager to hear more.

"I'm really glad you think it's cool, though when I made these discoveries, I was quite stunned. Remember that night after the Mets game when you turned to your grandmother and said she should do her genealogy, that she might find some live ones and she said they were probably dead?"

Ben nodded. He took a bite of his sandwich. I guess he thought this was all stuff he already knew. "Well, Ben," I continued, Kate has a cousin living in Riverdale, not far from here. She's ninety-five years old."

"Wow."

"And she's also my cousin."

"What?" Ben had the most incredulous look on his face. "I don't get it." His eyes couldn't have gotten any narrower.

I told him the entire story. At points, Ben stared at me, eyes wide open in wonderment, other times he looked down at the ground. When I finally came to the end and told him that Kate and my mother were sisters, his mouth hung open. It took a few moments for him to close it and speak.

"I don't get it. They never knew? How the fuck could that be?"

I told Ben the story that Nan had told me and how she was sure it was all Rebecca's doing.

"That's sick! The whole thing is . . . it's . . . it's insane. Who does that?"

He dropped his head in his hands and rested his elbows on the table, then looked up wide-eyed. "I can't believe it. No. It can't be."

I took his hand in mine and assured him I was as stunned and just as furious when I heard the story. Then I told him my plan. "That's why I need your help. I don't want Kate to get so anxious over this that she'll get sick. If you think the information is pretty cool you could say that and get her really interested."

"Absolutely not! No way. You *cannot* tell Grandma."

"Ben, wait. Think about it. This is good news. Kate is my aunt. With me, she'll have a connection to the family she never knew."

He jumped up almost knocking over his chair. "No, Carolyn. Do **not** tell her." He slapped the table. The glasses shook. "If our moving to Virginia almost killed her . . ." He shook his head with such ferocity it scared me. "No way," he said and looked at me with disgust. His upper lip curled and he recoiled as if I were poison. Then he turned and rushed out the door.

I threw down some money and hurried out after him. The wind kicked up as I turned the corner; a blast of cold air hit my face. "Wait up," I shouted, getting closer. "Please, Ben, stop."

He looked back over his shoulder and shook his head.

"Come on. Let's talk."

Ben stopped short, turned, and stood in the middle of the block clenching his fists tight. "Talk? Okay, you tell me. Is that why you've been so friendly? Why you say you want to help me? All to get to Grandma?"

"No, please. That's not it at all. Can't we go inside? I'll explain." Though I didn't know what I was going to explain. I just had to make him understand he was all wrong.

"Say whatever it is here. Make it fast."

"Come on, Ben. It's freezing out. And I can't make it fast. I need to talk to you."

He blew out a loud breath. "Okay. Come in, but I don't know if I can believe anything you say. You lied. You didn't want to train me. You just wanted to get closer to Grandma." His anger was tangible, and I was so sorry he thought I'd used him. It might have started out that way, but I really liked Ben and wanted to help him. I was glad he was my family. I didn't want to lose him. Damn. Why'd I have to open my mouth? I should have left him out of this.

I hurried to follow him up the steps. He didn't bother to hold the door open for me. Once inside, he stood with one hand on the ping pong table, the other on his hip. "All right," he said. "Talk."

"Not here. Anyone can walk through, and I don't think you want an audience." I was the adult here. Ben was angry, I got that, but I wasn't going to be bullied by an irate kid; plus, I had a feeling he was covering up for being hurt. And there it was again, that word–trust–knocking me in the head–and I was afraid I'd just lost Ben's. I followed him into his room and sat on his desk chair when he flopped onto his bed. I had to gain it back.

"Ben, look at me, not the ceiling. It's really important to me that you understand I was not using you. I sincerely care about you." He glanced my way and I continued. "You probably think it doesn't matter at my age, but I need a connection to family just as much as you do. I know you're hurting from the loss of your mother, and I don't mean to make this sound like my loss is worse because it definitely is not, but Ben I don't have my parents any longer, and I don't have any brothers or sisters. I'm not married and I don't have kids." He turned on his side and seemed to be listening though he still had that hard look on his face. "Sure, I have friends, but basically, I'm alone. When I learned Kate was my aunt, and that you were my cousin, I was so happy. I felt connected again, grounded. When I lost my mother I felt like I was floating in space. There was nothing and no one to anchor me. Of course, I have my memories, and if I hadn't found you and Kate, they would have had to be enough, but now they don't. Everyone needs family, at least I think so, whether it's one person or forty. That's why I need to tell Kate and why I think she should know we're related. It's all about feeling connected. In a sense, we're a tribe and the tribe should stay together."

I wasn't sure I was getting through to him. He moved his head a little from side to side as if he was contemplating what I'd said. His face softened a bit. Then he sat up.

"Okay, so you care about me, or you say you do. And I get it, you don't have any family. That's gotta suck. But telling Grandma is not an option. You once asked me if she could really get sick from anxiety. Hell, yes. And knowing she had a sister who lived in the same damn city, and she never knew it. It's fucked up, Carolyn. She cannot know. You're not the one who almost lost her. I am and I need her. So don't say a word. Ever."

Like a naughty child being reprimanded by an adult, I felt awful. But damn it, I wanted Kate to know. I needed her to. Yet if I told Kate the truth and she got sick, that would be the end of my relationship with Ben. He'd be so angry with me. Even though I didn't believe she'd die from the news—people didn't die from A-fib, though you could have a stroke from it and I surely didn't want that to happen. I didn't even want to think about it. So I reached over and placed what I hoped was a comforting hand on Ben's arm and told him I understood how he felt. "Please, believe me," I said. "I don't want to do anything that will hurt Kate. Or you either. You both mean too much to me."

Ben seemed to accept what I was saying. He gave me a little nod and I watched the hurt and anger dissipate from his face. Shit, what a mess I was in. I couldn't even bring myself to promise him I wouldn't say anything and, honestly, I couldn't make up my mind what I was going to do. Thankfully, Ben didn't press me on it. Maybe he thought my saying I wouldn't do anything to hurt either of them meant I'd keep quiet. Everything was so jumbled up in my head. I wished I could erase it all and start fresh, but what good would that do? I'd probably be in this same predicament because I wanted a family so badly now that it was at my fingertips. And on top of all that, I realized, though I didn't like to think about it, given their ages, Ben would be in my life much longer than Kate. I wanted to keep the relationship we'd formed and have it grow. He might marry one day and have kids, and I could be that older cousin they saw on holidays. I could be like a grandma to his children–babysit, have them for weekends. That would be so nice. And if I kept quiet and never told Kate, there'd be no issues. They'd both be in my life. Oh, I didn't know what to do anymore.

CHAPTER 36

The winter sun peered through my bedroom blinds, waking me. I looked at the clock. It was eight-thirty. Adrenaline rushed through my veins. I threw off the covers and slid out of bed. The alarm hadn't woken me, not even John Gambling on the radio. No surprise since I'd only fallen asleep four hours ago having tossed and turned all night mulling over everyone and their opinions–Nan, Ben, and Anita–and about Alan too. I understood him better, now that I was fudging the truth, and actually felt a little sorry for him. He didn't know how to handle his situation back then, just like I didn't know how to handle mine now. I hoped things worked out for him, that he found his way and that he was happy.

I had a half hour to dress, gobble down some yogurt, and get to class on time. In the bathroom while brushing my teeth and examining the dark circles under my eyes, I thought about Kate. Every time I thought I'd let it go, that I'd keep the long-held secret and accept only her friendship, the idea of family tugged at me like a lifeline thrown to a drowning woman, and I played with scenarios of how I'd tell her, after her show in June. Dressed in my workout clothes,

I went into the kitchen and grabbed a yogurt from the fridge just as the phone rang.

"Hello, Carolyn. This is Jonathan Moss, Kate's son-in-law."

I let out a sigh. I wasn't in any mood for his opinions. Then, in an instant, my pulse spiked. Kate, I thought, and shouted, "What happened?"

"What happened is you."

"Me?" My stomach felt rock hard, petrified that Ben had told him. "What do you mean?"

"My mother-in-law is nuts." I swear he growled like Clint Eastwood. "She was always such an even-keeled woman. Talented. Bright. And now she's doing things that are so out of character."

I chose my words carefully. "Why is it my fault? What's she doing that's so unlike her?"

"Kate Hemple barely ever cooked," he said. "She certainly never had the family for holiday dinners. They were always at our house. And now, I have no idea what's gotten into her. She's planning a seder, in the middle of working on a show, and expects the whole family to fly out to LA. And," he paused, "she's inviting you."

My head dropped back. I blew out a deep breath of relief. He still had Eastwood's "make my day" tone, and I wasn't sure if he was astonished or angry. Whatever it was, I was thrilled. With only five minutes to make nice, I spoke in my most friendly, charming voice and said, "I think that's wonderful. Kate wants her family together, and I'm honored she's including me." Actually, I was thrilled. Over the moon.

"Honored or not, you are not family. I don't understand how you've bewitched her. Out of nowhere, you show up, and now you're best of friends, being invited to a family event. It doesn't make sense. What did you do?"

"Mr. Moss," I said, swallowing my guilt and using my most diplomatic yet emphatic tone, the same one I used to use when I spoke to a father of one of my high school students who refused to accept his son's failing grade. "Kate and I somehow bonded over a painting. If my coming into her life has given her a lift, I'm glad. Maybe the time was right. Maybe she needed something new. I don't know what it is or was, but if my becoming friendly with her brought her spark back, as Ben says, that makes me happy." I glanced at the clock and continued before he could comment. "And I am not after anything, as I said before." I felt my stomach cringe with that lie. "It's true, we came together under odd circumstances . . ."

"That's for sure. I just want you to know, I'll be watching you. I can't control Kate's friendships, but I will not let anyone take advantage of her."

Watch all you want, I said to myself, and wait 'til you hear the best part. Sure, he frightened me–I have to admit that–but he got me riled up, too, and for a moment I wanted to blurt out the truth and see how he'd deal with that. With my hands shaking, I ended the call as graciously as possible then slipped on my coat, grabbed my bags, and with my pulse already in my target zone–probably higher–I ran across the parking lot to the clubhouse.

CHAPTER 37

Wedgewood china and freshly polished silver shone on Kate's holiday table. I never imagined she would set such a formal one. She seemed more casual to me, the pottery type, though I remembered she did serve me tea in bone china cups when we first met. Jonathan was seated across from me, and the air between us felt as cold as a Minnesota winter. Ben, next to me, wasn't as icy, though the greeting he'd given me when I walked in earlier was accompanied by a wide-eyed, lifted brow. I read it as a reminder and didn't react. I just said, "It's so good to see you again and be here with everyone." My sincerity couldn't have been more honest and I sensed he knew that. What he wasn't sure of was what I was going to do with the secret. Neither was I.

"I didn't know you had sterling," Jonathan said, turning a fork over in his hand.

"Read it." The irritation in Kate's voice rang through the room. I felt vindicated, not being the only one he seemed to annoy.

Jonathan looked at the tiny print. So did I. Rogers Brothers 1847 was engraved on the spoon and in tiny print, silver-plate. That didn't change anything. Jonathan still had that haughty look in his eye.

"Well, it's beautiful," he said. "I don't remember you ever using it. Why didn't you give it to Beth?"

"Because my daughter didn't want it. It was my grandmother's, and she thought it was old-fashioned and too formal."

I ran my fingers along the knife's smooth handle and wondered why Kate decided to use Ida's things now. Did it have something to do with the crystal bowl centered on the lace tablecloth, the same one from the painting? The same bowl I saw in Kate's sunroom the day I met her. The only difference was that floating rose petals had replaced the seashells. My hand went to the cameo resting against my chest, the ivory warm to the touch, and I ran my thumb over the tiny raised flower holding back a strand of the woman's hair.

Jonathan led the seder and we all sang the Four Questions in Hebrew, in unison: Kate, Jonathan, Ben, his brother, and me. It reminded me of the seders of my childhood, when I had a family and my father's voice boomed through *Dayenu* and when my grandpa, his father, zoomed through *Chad Gadya*, me stumbling over the words the longer the song became. Kate's eyes were a bit misty as she passed around the hard-boiled eggs, just like the salty tears represented by our dipping the yolks in salt water. Not every family used hard boiled eggs. Some only dipped parsley, but mine did both. I thought perhaps this was a custom both Rebecca and Ida had brought with them from Russia and passed on to their granddaughters. Kate cut into her egg and asked, "Anyone want the other half?" A jolt shot through me. My mother used to do the same. Despite Jonathan's iciness, Kate, and even Ben and his brother, made me feel as if I belonged. We chatted easily together and belted out the songs as if we'd been doing this for years. Just like a real family. I assumed Ben was comfortable with that, as long as I kept the reality hidden. Every once in a while, I felt his eyes on me and on the cameo then they'd quickly go back to the Haggadah.

"This is my favorite part," Ben said when we reached the portion of the service discussing the Jews in slavery building the pyramids. We all put our books down and passed around the glass bowl filled with the fragrant *charoset*. Ben scooped some up and spread it on a piece of matzo. "I love this. Walnuts, wine, and cinnamon all chopped up together."

"And apples," Kate reminded him. "You can't leave them out."

"Yeah, right. I always helped Mom make it."

I also helped my mother make *charoset* with its woodsy yet sweet scent all mixed up together representing the mortar the slaves used when building the pyramids. I always asked why we never ate it any other time of year. Like Ben, I thought it was the best food of the holiday. When the seder was over, I cleared the table of all the ritual foods to make room for the actual dinner. Kate went to the kitchen to get the *knaidlach* soup. Hearing her say the Yiddish word instead of matzo ball, hearing it roll off her tongue so easily, brought me back to my mother's *Pesach* table when I was growing up. The succulent braised brisket and roast chicken, the scents that infused our home, and the songs. Oh, how I missed it and how I was filled with joy and love sitting here with my newfound family, as long as I didn't focus on Jonathan. Didn't that man know how to smile? If not at me, how about his kids and his mother-in-law? Was my presence so distasteful to him?

Kate seemed younger than her eighty-five years with her bright smile, pastel-pink linen blouse, and tan capris. Even through her now-and-then misty tears, I knew this evening meant a great deal to her, too, which, again, made me feel that no matter how confused or upset my news might make her at first, she'd be very pleased with it. And Ben would come around once he saw that.

"So, Carolyn," Jonathan said as I picked up the plate in front of him dotted with egg yolk crumbs. "Kate told me you were going to see what you could find out about her family."

"I didn't say that, Jonathan," Kate said coming back into the room, a bowl of soup in each hand. "I said she was doing her own genealogy and offered to do mine, like Beth wanted to do."

Whenever Kate spoke to her son-in-law, she sounded pissed. I wondered if it was because he'd moved the boys away from her or because he tried to control her. Both would have upset me, if I were in her shoes.

Kate placed the soup on the table, one in front of Ben and the other on my place setting. "And," she looked at me for confirmation, "I said I wasn't interested."

I picked up two more messy dishes, held them in my fingers, and walked casually toward the kitchen, as if we were chatting about the weather. "That's right," I said. "You did." At the kitchen door, I stopped and faced Kate who was standing next to Ben's chair. "I did look up mine, though, and found some interesting stuff."

"Grandma's not interested," Ben said, cutting me off. His anger ripped through me like a knife. His voice, loud enough to shake the shingles on the house, made me shudder. "In hers, I mean. One of these days, I'll do our genealogy. I told you that, Carolyn. Just not now." He shot me a look that said cease and desist. Jonathan ran away with the subject talking about how much Beth wanted to do the research, and I, still shaky, slipped into the kitchen to get the rest of the soup.

I listened to their banter through the open door and made myself busy spooning matzo balls into soup bowls. I heard Jonathan ask Kate why she wouldn't want to know her history and she answered, "It's not important anymore." I wanted to know why it wasn't. But when Kate walked into the kitchen muttering, in a very definitive and pissed-off tone, "Just leave it alone already," I didn't ask.

In the dining room, Jonathan continued on the subject, talking to his sons about finding relatives they'd never known about. "Maybe I'd find one in some cool place I could visit," he said, and it made me think that I might have been wrong about him. Maybe he would be fine with my announcement. Or, my stomach roiled, did he know? Did Ben tell him? Was Jonathan fooling with me? Ben cut him off, bringing up Kate's show at the gallery in June, and I started to relax. Okay, so even if he did tell his father, Ben still didn't want Kate to know. Then I thought better of it. No, Ben would never have told him. He wanted this secret to stay buried. He was changing the subject so ancestors and unknown relatives would not be discussed, and I couldn't shake the torment it was causing me.

"Here, let me," Kate said reaching for the soup ladle. "I'll fill and you carry." She didn't utter a word about the genealogy discussion. I handed her the ladle and waited while she spooned the clear soup into the bowls then plopped two *knaidlach* in and a few sliced carrots. "Give that to Jonathan," she said. I saw her glance at the cameo. "He always wants two. And wait, here's another bowl." She handed it to me and I walked to the dining room with them. "I'll bring mine," she said. "Start. Don't let the soup get cold."

The soup looked and smelled delicious. The tone in her voice was anything but.

Kate took her seat at the table. Conversation stopped. Everyone except Kate focused on the first course. I caught her eyes on my jewelry.

"Delicious, Kate," Jonathan said. He lifted his wine glass in a toast. "Here's to the best matzo balls anywhere and the lady who made them."

He surprised me. I didn't think that man had a nice bone in his body. Kate tilted her head. Her thank you was compromised by the squint in her eye.

"Really, Kate. These are the best," he said. "I've tasted lots of others, but no one makes them like you. They've got *tam* and just the right density. Fluffy yet not too hard."

"So does that mean you'll have holidays with me? You haven't been back here since you moved east."

Like a sudden storm approaching, the air in the room shifted. You know the feeling when the wind picks up and the tree branches sway, when a cooling breeze cuts through a warm summer day? Anyone listening would have heard thunder rolling in. Kate must have felt it too.

"That wasn't fair of me," she said. "I know you have your life in Virginia now." Then, just like the weather–you can't stop it no matter how much you wish you could–Kate let one of her quips fly again. "I can't expect you to fly out here just for my *knaidles*, can I?"

Soup spoons stopped in midair. Jonathan lowered his and seemed to be entranced by the flexibility of his thumb. Ben shot a glance at his father, then his grandmother. His brother let his spoon drop, spilling soup over the rim, and I kept quiet. The silence seemed to go on for hours though it was just a few seconds later that Kate apologized.

"I'm sorry, everybody." She smiled at her son-in-law. "Forgive me, Jonathan. Honestly, I do understand why you don't come home. It's just, having all of you around my table, my whole family here with me . . ." She must have seen the pill of a look Jonathan threw me because she paused and looked directly at him. "Yes, you *are* all my family," she said. "It's not just blood, or marrying blood for that matter, that makes people a family."

Jonathan's eyes actually filled up. The word family must have affected him. It certainly did me. A smile crept up my cheeks as I replayed Kate's words– "My whole family . . ."

"You all know I've had profound losses in my life," Kate said. She sat in her chair remaining straight up, in command, like the CEO at a company board meeting. "I've lost so many in my life: my parents who I never knew, my grandparents who raised me, friends, especially Anna who was like the sister I never had, and my wonderful husband." She paused and her lips closed tight against her teeth. No one moved. We all knew what she was thinking. I could almost taste the tears she was trying, unsuccessfully, to hold back. She swallowed hard and continued. "And worst of all," she said, "my beautiful daughter." Kate gave her grandsons a bittersweet smile. "Not a day goes by without me thinking of your mother." Then she looked all around the table. She seemed to sit taller. "It's not only death that took those I love away. It's geography, too. I miss all of you. I miss the life I had, that we had. And for too long I was miserable. Then Carolyn found me." The air lifted with her light tone. "When she brought me the painting of my grandmother, she brought light back into my life. Even my paintings changed. And then, when I went to New York, I realized I still had my family even if miles separated us. I could still travel. I could go to New York or Chicago." She looked at her other grandson, Ben's brother, and then at Jonathan. "I could even go to Virginia, if I was invited. I flew to Florida, didn't I? And I don't have any family there." I snuck a look at Jonathan. He was engrossed in his mother-in-law's speech. "I'm too old to be alone," Kate said. "I need you all in my life, no matter how far away you live. And, whenever I can, I want my family around my table. When Beth died, I was in so much pain. I wanted to die. And now, this is what I want, what I need." She pointed to the crystal bowl and silverware. "And look at my beautiful things. Even though she's been gone for so many years, my grandmother is with us too." She turned her face to the portrait on the wall and let her eyes rest on Ida. Then she turned directly to me. "And Carolyn, that cameo you're wearing. It is such a coincidence. It looks just like the one I painted from my grandmother's description." I held my breath. "That must be the one you said your mother had. The one that brought you to me."

I couldn't find words so I just nodded.

"If it wasn't for Carolyn," she said, looking at her son-in-law and grandsons, "so much of my grandmother would have remained buried. I wouldn't have sat in my sun room reminiscing about my childhood, remembering beautiful times. I wouldn't have gone to a ball game with Ben or to New York. And my canvases would still be dark."

I felt nuzzled in a warm embrace.

"So you see," Kate continued, "when you talk about all that genealogy stuff, I really don't care. I don't need to research my family." She thrust her hands across the table. "You are all my family. I never knew my father or my mother, only their names, Lena and Jack, and I treasure the beautiful stories my grandparents told me about them. And those grandparents, the ones who raised me, were the most loving parents a girl could ask for. As to my father's family, where were they all those years? Where were Jack's parents, my other grandparents? Grandma Ida said they moved away. They never kept in touch, and she tried to make excuses, explaining they'd had an argument many years before. But they never reached out to me and that was very painful. They never even sent a birthday card." Kate's voice caught in her throat, as if she were still that child desperate for her absent family. I wanted to cry for that little girl. She collected herself and continued with more force and more sorrow. "So, why would I want to know about them or some aunt or cousin or anyone else in that family who was never in my life? They could have been, even if they lived far away. I never knew them. I never saw them. It hurt terribly, and I don't want to go down that road again. So please, don't press me on genealogy. I have no desire to know about them."

As everyone around the table murmured their understanding, I felt Ben's eyes rest on me as if he was saying, "See, I told you." I responded with a tiny nod, then looked up at the framed lady in the peach dress with a cameo pinned to the bodice. I spoke to her again, as I had as a child, though this time my words were silent. I thought about the secret she was forced to keep and how it must have pained her. And how it would crush Kate's cherished memories when she realized this grandmother, who she still adored, had lied. Could I allow that? I looked over at Kate and Ben, at the family around the holiday table, and my eyes misted over. This was my family. Kate had embraced me. Did I really need more? I thought about Teckla and how she was also forced to keep a secret and about Rebecca and Karl. I wondered if they were ever sorry. If any of them were. And I thought about my mother. My heart broke for her never to have known she had a sister. It shattered like pottery on stone, bits and pieces I could never repair. I smoothed my hand over the cameo pinned to my blouse, and a slight sigh escaped my lips.

END

ACKNOWLEDGMENTS

Numerous people, who gave their time and talents in making my dream come true, deserve an enormous thanks. It's a cliché, but true. I couldn't have done this without you.

First, a huge thank you to the team at Black Rose Writing for their faith in this story and for transforming a Word document into a beautifully bound book.

To Pamela Taylor, your brilliant editing made this a much better novel. Thank you for all the extra phone calls, suggestions, advice–and pen! I've enjoyed our journey together immensely and look forward to more.

Kathleen Furin, my book coach, your probing questions made me dig into my characters and find themes that surprised me. I'm so grateful.

Susan Breen, your classes at Gotham Writers Workshop helped bring out phrases and sentences I didn't know I had in me. A huge thank you for your developmental edit when this novel was in its infancy. Your suggestions brought so much to the page, including Ben.

Michael Neff of Algonkian Writers Conference, thank you for your recommendations that had me scouring a thesaurus, ultimately leading to the final title.

To my writers groups, I'm so glad I found you. Your gentle generous critiques made me a better writer, and continue to do so whether at our own Algonquin Round Table or a dining room table in Florida.

To friends whose family stories, told to me over the years, piqued my interest and ultimately found their way on to the page. Thank you for sharing the secrets.

To my brother, Jerry Liebowitz, for your genealogy help and to Roni, my sister-in-law though more a friend, for the inspiration for this novel. Who would have thought one casual conversation on a beach would result in this?

To my sons whom I adore–Michael for being my personal Google and Dan for switching from hockey writing to baseball, for just a few minutes, making my scenes at Citi Field and Dodger Stadium more realistic than I ever could have. Thank you both for your love and support throughout this adventure.

To my family–my *whole* family, the Roysensteins. Thank you for *everything*. I cherish you all.

And, most of all, to my husband, Sam, whose love grounds me; without it I wouldn't be me.

DISCUSSION POINTS
FOR BOOK CLUBS

In our first encounter with Carolyn, she's sitting on the floor in her mother's bedroom deciding which pieces of her mother's jewelry she wants to keep and which to sell? How did you initially characterize Carolyn and did your feelings remain throughout the novel?

Does the title, *The Disharmony of Silence*, give you a hint as to what the novel is about? How does the ending relate to the title?

Very early in the novel, the topic of family arises along with a hint of a secret. Ida seems to be holding back information from her eleven-year-old daughter, Lena, as to why the Roths aren't coming to Seder. Did you feel it was important information that would weave through the story as it progressed?

Discuss the structure of the narrative. How did the dual time-line affect your understanding of the characters? How would the story change if we only had Carolyn's point of view?

When Lena dies, Rebecca insists that Jack should never know the baby lived. Teckla disagrees and argues with her mother, but, ultimately, keeps the secret. In chapter 20 Teckla, again, agrees to keep her mother's secret. Why? Do you agree with her reasons and how do you think you would react in a similar circumstance?

Carolyn isn't able to trust men, other than Stan, because of her failed marriage with Alan. In chapter 35 she begins to understand why he lied to her and in chapter 36 we see Carolyn have a change of heart. Do you think this change affected her decision at the end of the novel?

Is there a difference between lying and keeping a secret? Is one worse than the other?

Why do you think Ida never told Kate about her having a sister?

Do you think Carolyn is really fooling herself when she says, in chapter 33, *"Shit, now I had to lie. But this one was considered a white lie. For Kate's benefit. That's okay to do, isn't it, when you think the truth might hurt someone?"* Is there a difference between a lie and a white lie? Is one better than the other?

In the last chapter, Kate explains her reasons for not wanting to research her genealogy. She explains what "family" means to her. Do you think Kate's definition of family rings true to Carolyn? Is that why Carolyn keeps quiet? Or, does she remain silent because of Kate's deep hurt due to her father's family?

Is Carolyn lying to Kate at the end by not revealing her discovery? Is omission a lie?

What is the true meaning of family to you?

NOTE FROM THE AUTHOR

Word-of-mouth is crucial for any author to succeed. If you enjoyed the book, please leave a review online—anywhere you are able. Even if it's just a sentence or two. It would make all the difference and would be very much appreciated.

Thanks!
Linda

ABOUT THE AUTHOR

Linda Rosen, fitness professional turned writer, lives with her husband splitting their time between New Jersey and Florida. She was a contributor to *Women in the Literary Landscape: A WNBA Centennial Publication* for the Women's National Book Association and has had stories published in *Foliate Oak* and *Crack the Spine*, both in their online magazine and print anthology. Follow her at www.linda-rosen.com.

Thank you so much for reading one of our **Women's Fiction** novels.

If you enjoyed the experience, please check out our recommended for your next great read!

The Apple of My Eye by Mary Ellen Bramwell

"A mature love story with an intense plot. This book has something important to say." –William O. Shakespeare, Professor of English, Brigham Young University

CPSIA information can be obtained
at www.ICGtesting.com
Printed in the USA
FSHW011551220920
73986FS

9 781684 334308